Cutest Little Killer

Maggie Pill

CHAPTER ONE

I was anticipating lunch, but it was only 11:42, and my hours are 9:00 to 12:00 and 1:00 to 5:00. Good business means keeping your word, so I'm careful to observe the standards I set for myself.

While I dug around in my desk for a mini Hershey bar to tide me over, the door to the outer office opened and closed. Walk-ins aren't common for private investigators, and I cringed as I looked down at my rumpled khakis and elderly t-shirt. Mom always says I should dress as if I expect clients every day, because first impressions are very important. My counterargument is that I can't stand to spend eight hours with a shirt buttoned to my Adam's apple and a tie like a noose around my neck.

As a compromise, Mom made me something called a *dickey*. Cutting the front out of a crisp, white shirt, she glued the neck onto a plastic headband from the dollar store. To that she tacked a conservative blue and gray necktie, slicing it in the back and basting the ends under the shirt collar. When I hear the door in the anteroom open, I slide the dickey around my neck, slip on a navy blazer I keep draped over the back of my chair, and change my look in seconds. Today Mom's creation covered a Hoobastank t-shirt with a stain center front, probably chocolate sauce from last night's dessert.

"I'll be right out," I called, checking a small mirror on the wall to be sure the jacket covered the edges of the dickey. Looking like a competent professional, I went out to impress my unknown visitor.

Visitors. A boy and a girl stood side by side a few feet back from the empty reception desk. Someday there will be a secretary out there, but for now I have only part-time help, a criminal justice major named Bobby who works most afternoons for real-life crime-solving experience.

The boy was husky and about sixteen, and he kept his gaze focused on the floor a little to my right. The girl was eight or nine and stunningly pretty, with lots of dark hair, dark eyes, and the facial symmetry mankind interprets as beautiful, no matter what other standards are applied. She did a head-to-toe scan, and I felt measured, like back in middle school when they chose sides for Dodgeball.

Figuring a parent had dropped them off at the entrance and then gone to park the car, I prepared to engage in a few minutes of chatter. "Hello, there. I'm Max Dunham. Who are you?"

I looked at the boy as I spoke, but it was the girl who answered. "I'm Della Street, and this is Paul Drake. It's nice to meet you, Mr. Dunham."

Playing games with the detective? "I've seen *Perry Mason,* kiddo. Della Street and Paul Drake are characters created by Erle Stanley Gardner."

Her face pinched. "We're aware that our aliases are transparent, but we prefer to operate anonymously until we decide if you can be trusted."

That was a mouthful for a person not yet four feet tall. I listened for parental footsteps in the hallway. Nothing. "Is someone else coming?"

"No." While I assimilated that, the girl went on. "We're here to offer a business proposition." Her tone suggested I'd be an idiot not to consider it. I coughed into my fist, hiding a smile. Her manner was pompous, but it was hard not to forgive someone with dimples that cute.

"I'm listening."

She seemed unsure how to proceed. Clearing her throat she said, "Your website is very professional."

"Thanks. My m—I have a woman who helps with stuff like that." Wondering what two kids wanted with a detective, I'd already come up with several possibilities I wouldn't be interested in. Cheating at school. Anonymous insults on Twitter. A stolen cell phone. I turned again to the boy, believing he'd better understand my argument. "I'm a homicide specialist. *Homicide* means—"

"We know what it means." It was the girl again. "You're an expert on murder, and that's what we want." She glanced at her companion. "Paul and I are interested in hiring a hitman."

I paused, wondering how a quiet Monday had turned into a pair of underage clients in search of a killer. I'd unlocked the door at 9:00 a.m., as usual, noting with satisfaction the lettering on the glass door.

AAA Investigations
Max Dunham, Homicide Specialist

It read backwards to me, but the message is for people coming in, not the guy looking out. Three *A*'s makes my business come up early in alphabetical listings. The specialty is included to discourage those with cheating wives or deadbeat husbands from seeking my services.

I was going on vacation at the end of the week. Wanting to leave with a clear desk and an untroubled mind, I'd spent most of the morning doing final reports for recent clients. Since I'm not yet proficient with my business software, it took a while to get the information in the right slots. Printing the financial detail pages, I called attention to the amounts owed with a yellow highlighter and addressed the envelopes. I send online bills too, but a sheet of paper in a person's hands demands action.

With that done, I was free, except for testifying in an upcoming trial. Once I'd done my bit to convict a certain creep of murdering his business partner, I could exchange Michigan's winter for a Mexican beach, where I'd sip cold beer and search for Ms. Right-for-Right-Now.

I hadn't told my parents about the trip, for reasons many sons of snowbirds will understand. If I even mention getting away from Detroit, Mom and Dad assume I'm dying to come to their condo in Florida and hang with them. That means a week in a dinky spare bedroom, playing pickle-ball with a bunch of retirees, and hearing them preach that millennials don't understand what life's all about. Better, I figured, to casually mention it when I returned, with a bewildered comment: *I'm sure I told you I was going, Mom.*

I also had a plan for lunch. An unusually bright February sun had shone through the window since ten, and the parking lot below turned from frosty gray, which meant ice, to a darker tone that indicated melting. A little Greek restaurant a few blocks from my building has good food and a friendly atmosphere. Over their chicken salad special, I'd engage in meaningless banter with people who aren't in crisis. I like my job, but sometimes a guy needs a break from ranting and/or sobbing clients.

All that to say that if these kids had arrived fifteen minutes later, I wouldn't have had to sit there and try to look un-shocked when the girl requested my help finding and hiring a hitman.

Before responding to the prospect of making someone dead, I assessed the visual clues my visitors presented. Under winter coats they wore school uniforms, navy pants with deep red sweaters over white shirts. The boy looked like he'd slept in his, but the girl could have served as an ad for whatever private school they attended. They both wore oxford shoes, but hers looked new while his appeared to have made a stroll through a landfill. Neatness and the lack of it aside, their coloring and features matched. They were almost certainly brother and sister.

The girl was in that rounded stage that precedes the growth spurts of adolescence. Her hair curled around her heart-shaped face in spirals that hinted attempts to tame it were useless. She had a confident, almost snotty, air, but in her eyes was a hint of anxiety, as if she hoped I was what she was seeking but feared I wouldn't be.

When the silence stretched for too long, I said, "You want me to connect you with a killer."

"Please." It was a command, not a request. She waited expectantly, lips tight and chin raised a little.

I turned to the brother, interested to see his reaction, but he stared at the floor, face blank. At his sides, his hands clenched and unclenched as if he wished he were somewhere else. How aware was he of their reason for coming? Was he brain-damaged? Learning disabled? Two burdens he carried hinted he was prepared for a hike, perhaps to Katmandu. A knapsack on his back bulged in odd directions. The outside mesh pockets revealed ear buds, a water bottle, a flashlight, and one of those king-size Reese's Peanut Butter Cups. Hanging from the straps were colorful decorations, some woven, some beaded. Southwestern art, maybe Navaho. If that wasn't enough to carry around, he'd slung a gym bag over one shoulder. It was plain black, with none of the tacked-on personality of the backpack, but a Bosca logo revealed it hadn't come from Target.

Sis was neat, sharp-eyed, and verbal. Brother was sloppy, unsure, and silent. I was reminded of those side-by-side pictures in magazines: *Do this. Don't do that.*

When the girl cleared her throat impatiently, I realized it was my turn to speak. "Why do you want to hire this...person?"

"We need someone eliminated." She licked her lips. "While we're not experienced in such things, we have some ideas as to methodology." A shifting of the boy's feet caused her to look down at her hands. "Not right away, of course. When we get to the planning stage."

9

My tongue felt dry, and I realized my mouth had been hanging open. "You have ideas on how to kill someone." If I sounded lost, I was.

She took my comment for encouragement. "Did you know that the first Duke of Clarence was drowned in a barrel of wine?"

"In wine."

"Malmsey, to be exact." She sniffed once. "My brother favors using traditional methods, but since we only plan to do this once, I lean toward something historically interesting." Recognizing she'd strayed from her purpose, she got back to business. "We're aware that your calling is *investigating* murders rather than *committing* them, but we suppose that crime detection brings you into contact with the type of person who might help with our project." She folded her hands at her waist. "We're asking you to serve as go-between, at a price you'll find attractive."

"Um, look." I addressed my argument to the boy, but I swear it wasn't male chauvinism. It simply didn't seem right to discuss murder for hire with a pre-adolescent who should have been home watching *Trollhunters*. Though the boy wasn't an adult, he was a lot closer to it. "I'm not sure what I can do for..." Could I call them children to their faces? "...Um, minors."

"We're offering one hundred thousand dollars for the work." The girl's volume rose a tone, hinting she wasn't pleased at being ignored. "If you provide a name that results in an arrangement, you'll receive ten thousand for your contribution." She paused, and I suspected I was supposed to take out my list of killers and start looking for a likely prospect. Instead, I stood mute, unable to decide if I was dreaming or she was joking or what. It went on like that for maybe twenty seconds, the kids waiting expectantly while I opened my mouth several times, attempting to form a reply. I even raised my index finger once to signal that communication was imminent. In the end, it wasn't.

When it became obvious I was without an appropriate response, the girl spoke again. "Ten thousand dollars for a name and a phone number, Mr. Dunham. That's easy money."

Still flummoxed, I took a tangential approach. "You have a hundred thousand to spend on this?"

With the air of one who realizes negotiations have come to a critical juncture, the girl extended a palm toward the boy. Sliding the gym bag off his shoulder, he opened the zipper enough to show me what was inside. "A stack of hundred-dollar bills a half-inch high equals ten thousand dollars," she informed me. "Five stacks five inches high makes a hundred thousand. One extra for your finder's fee. All cash. No record."

Forcing myself to ignore more money than I'd ever seen in one place before, I focused on the impossibility of their proposal. "You can't hire someone to kill someone. It's—"

"It's done all the time," Little Not-Della-Street interrupted. "While we know we could get it done for less, we require expertise and a quick turnaround." I imagined the girl bent over a thesaurus, looking up the words she'd need to convince me they were serious about murder and mature enough to cut a deal with a killer.

Serious I bought. Mature, not so much. Gesturing toward the inner doorway I said, "Will you step into my office? I think this matter requires further discussion."

A glance at her brother hinted Not-Della thought she'd won some previous argument. With what I interpreted as patient forbearance, Not-Paul gestured for her to precede him. Okay, he was aware of what was going on. I wasn't sure if that was reassuring or twice as scary.

As he passed through the doorway, an odor that was hard to describe wafted toward me. I tried to keep the revulsion from showing on my face, but the boy smelled. Bad.

My office is classy. Mom found a real walnut desk at Goodwill that she calls a "statement piece," meaning it sets a serious tone. It's kind of ornate, and a little big for a twelve-by-fifteen room, but it's in good shape, with only one gouge near the right front corner, and my Detroit Pistons paperweight hides that. Behind it are bookshelves we stained dark to match the desk and filled with impressive-looking hardbacks found at resale shops. (I don't read much, but Mom says books add atmosphere.) The only window overlooks the parking lot and a loading dock at the warehouse next door, so Mom made curtains from fabric she found on the discount table at Michael's Arts & Crafts. I wasn't thrilled with the pea green background scattered with turquoise fruit, but at the Salvation Army Store, she found a half-dozen ceramic pieces in turquoise (an apple, a pear, a bunch of grapes, and a banana). Once she set them here and there on the bookshelves, the fruity curtains didn't look so out of place. For client seating, she found wooden straight chairs at St. Vincent de Paul, stained them dark too, and recovered the seats with the same fabric as the curtains.

Stopping inside the doorway, the girl took a long look. "Did you do this?" An instant later she rephrased. "I mean, did you do your own decorating?"

"Um, no. I had a woman come in."

"But you're okay with medieval furniture and fruit? It's—" She stopped, winced as if something hurt, and ended with, "It's interesting."

A few times before I'd had the feeling my office was wrong somehow, but no one had ever said it out loud. "Please, sit down."

The guest chairs were near the front of the desk, but the boy pulled his into a corner before sitting. "My brother likes his back to a wall," the girl said. "Wild Bill Hickok was the same, as I'm sure you're aware."

"I've heard that."

The girl pulled her feet up onto her own chair and set her elbows on her knees. "One day the only empty chair at the poker table faced away from the door. Hickok sat there and was killed soon afterward by a single shot to the head."

"Interesting." I returned to the business at hand. "I'm going to be honest with you. Private investigators don't recommend killers for hire."

"We understand you can't advertise it as one of your services," Not-Della said loftily, "but you must know one who hasn't been caught yet."

"I would never be involved in something like that."

"What if a person *needs* killing? What if you looked at it as…" She paused to frame the argument. "…a public service?" When I said nothing, she added, "You'd provide us with assistance that's necessary, even vital. We could give you the money as a sort of …humanitarian award."

I shook my head. "Sweetheart, good people don't kill other—"

Before I knew it, she was out of her chair, leaning over my desktop, and shaking a finger under my nose. "I—am—not—your—sweetheart!"

Reaching out, the brother put a hand lightly on her arm. For a moment, we all froze. I breathed. She breathed. I assume the brother breathed, though I was afraid to take my eye off her in case she tried to brain me with my own paperweight.

"I'm sorry," she finally said through clenched teeth. "We're under a great deal of strain." Pushing her hair back, she sat down on the chair again and went on in an even tone. "We don't assume you're in favor of hired killers, Mr. Dunham." She put a hand on the edge of my desk. "I assure you; this is a matter of life and death."

As she spoke, the boy raised his eyes to mine for the first time, and the impression I'd formed of his intelligence changed dramatically. The kid was no Neanderthal. He was alert, aware, and every bit as convinced of the necessity of their mission as she was.

Leaning back in my chair, I struggled to decide how to proceed. While there was no way I'd agree to their proposal, I knew what would happen if I said that aloud. Detroit has scores of investigators, and these two could be making their pitch in some other P.I.'s office in less than twenty minutes. Would the next guy say no? He might take the hundred thousand and leave town. He might recommend an actual hit man. For that much money, he might even do the job himself. In any of those scenarios, the kids could end up in big trouble.

I could have sent them on their way with a stern warning, telling them how dangerous it was to go around offering large sums of money to strangers, but there was something about them, a combination of smarts and innocence. If these kids had an adult who could give them guidance, they wouldn't have come to me.

"Tell me about this person I'm supposed to kill." Seeing a joyous glint in the girl's eyes, I raised my hands, palms out. "I am not agreeing to anything, but I'd like to hear your reasons."

"I can give you a general picture," she cautioned, "but I will withhold real names until the three of us reach an agreement."

"Fine."

Clearing her throat, she began, "My brother and I had wealthy parents who are now dead. Being minors, we were assigned a guardian."

"How did your parents die?"

She glanced at Not-Paul, who gave a nod of consent. "Our mother was killed by a crocodile, specifically, a female black caiman."

"Oh, for—" I let out a disgusted breath. "Did Ernie Baker send you here to prank me?"

She turned to her brother. "I told you he wouldn't believe that part." To me she said, "No one ever does."

The boy spoke for the first time, his voice flat and deep. "'S true."

That gave me a place to start. Hiding my movements behind the desk, I took out my phone and opened Safari. "Where did this happen?" Typing and scrolling with my thumb, I looked for an article that matched what she'd said. It was surprising how much stuff there was about crocodiles, and I tried to appear to be listening to the girl's slightly long-winded explanation as I skimmed headlines.

"In the Amazon River Basin of Peru. You're probably aware that humans have a terrible effect on the Rainforest. Our parents made it their mission to document…"

As the girl caught me up on ecological concerns in South America, I found a news item that matched. A decade ago, an American woman named Amy Gage had died in a crocodile attack in Peru. A photo from happier times showed her with her husband, son, and an infant slung across her chest in a length of brightly colored cloth. The man's chin-length hair exhibited the same wildness as the girl's did. The son, without doubt the boy now seated in a corner of my office, stood in front of his dad, his expression sober, his skin as brown as the top of my desk.

"What organization did your parents work for?"

"They worked independently. Funding wasn't an issue for them."

The headline confirmed it: *Heiress and Scientist Amy Gage Dead at 38.* The text described the tragic event, a blow to the woman's family and environmentalists around the world. *Gage had become a leading voice in the fight against creeping industrialism and the destruction of natural areas*, the author claimed. *She leaves behind husband and fellow scientist Raymond and two children, Peter and Lucy. Gage's father, Wilfred Corrick, was a wealthy industrialist who left his entire fortune to his only daughter. Her life's work, Amy believed, was "reversing the damage to our planet that men like my father are responsible for."*

I suspected that Amy Gage would have resented the term *heiress* included prominently in her death announcement. She might have been especially peeved that it came before *scientist* in the headline. Judging from the girl's reaction to being called *sweetheart,* Little Apple hadn't fallen far from Mother Tree.

For the record: There's nothing wrong with feminists, but when dealing with them, a guy likes to be aware.

At the bottom of the article was a head shot of Amy Gage. Except for the fact that Amy had poker-straight hair, it was like looking at not-Della twenty years from now.

"So your names are Peter and Lucy Gage, and you grew up in the boonies." They looked shocked for a moment, but then Lucy glanced at Peter, resigned.

"What are boonies?"

"The boondocks." I got no response. "Areas outside civilization."

"Boonies." Blinking, she filed the unfamiliar term away. "We'll leave the discussion of what *civilization* means for

16

another time, but yes. Until recently, we lived with our father among Amerindians who call themselves the Yarru."

I almost blurted out, *Was your father nuts?* but caught myself. Kids love Mom and Dad, no matter how weird they are. "Why did your parents decide to raise you in the Amazon jungle?"

"Mom explains it better than I can, if you don't mind taking a few minutes to watch a video." Intrigued, I agreed. Lucy took out her phone, did some navigating, and set it on the desk before me. A plump woman appeared in an office background. The time stamp at the bottom of the screen said it was December 19, 2011. Introducing herself as an associate professor of anthropology at Tufts University, the woman explained that her guest for the day was Doctor Amy Gage, half of an environmentalist couple living with a primitive tribe in South America.

The host apologized in advance for the poor, somewhat jerky, quality of the video, explaining that Dr. Gage's location was remote. After a few seconds, the woman I'd seen in the newspaper article appeared on screen. Seated on a fallen log, she appeared blurry and slightly distorted from the camera angle. Despite the odd up-slant, her casual clothing, blunt-cut hair, and lack of cosmetic enhancements, Amy Gage was gorgeous.

The interviewer started with, "Doctor Gage, can you tell our viewers how you and your family came to live in the Amazon River Basin?"

Gage smiled. "Ray and I met at the University of Michigan, where I studied environmental science and he majored in anthropology. We're concerned about the effects of modernization on indigenous groups and how the earth is being harmed, perhaps beyond redemption, by human activity. Ray's roommate came to Ann Arbor from Peru, and he told us how the nation's uncontacted tribes, who live closer to nature than anyone else on earth, suffer when interlopers trespass on their lives. The more we learned, the more we believed that someone from the outside should provide first-hand reports about what was happening. Society has much to learn from these people, and it's outrageous that governments allow incursions into primitive areas solely for profit."

"Can you be specific?" the interviewer asked.

"Some countries allow their own laws protecting sensitive areas to be ignored in the name of business. Others refuse to enact any laws at all. Interlopers ruin land the tribes have occupied for centuries. They bring in diseases aboriginal people have no immunity to. And they treat native lives, beliefs, and practices as if they don't matter."

"You decided to document these things."

"Yes."

"How did you get an uncontacted tribe to let you join them?"

"The Peruvian I mentioned sent a message to the tribe's headman, explaining that we'd like to spend a year, possibly two, with them. The information we gather, air and water testing and observations of tribe members' health and stress levels, will be used to convince outsiders to leave the Yarru and tribes like them alone."

The interviewer frowned. "Doesn't the act of contacting a tribe mean you're not leaving them alone?"

"We understand that is a concern," Gage said, "but it's essential to show the world the value of these unique societies."

"So you and your husband now live with this tribe."

"Our children as well." Her smile revealed pride. "Lucy was born here, so she's considered a full member of the tribe."

"How are you educating them in such primitive conditions?"

"The Yarru understood that we would bring modern devices with us, to support our work. The headman, Grandfather Tama, put the question of how our equipment would be handled to his people, since all tribal decisions are made by mutual consent. They agreed to allow our 'magical things' if we keep them as private as possible." Gage grinned. "That's why I'm out in the middle of nowhere right now."

"Surely they see your computers and cell phones."

"Their reaction is to look away." Gage chuckled. "When we take photos, we mostly get silhouettes and backsides."

The interviewer's tone turned condescending. "That's common, I'm told. They fear being captured by unfamiliar gods."

Gage's expression turned cool, like the disapproving glare Lucy had already turned on me several times. "It's equally likely the Yarru sense what too much technology can do to the soul."

The interviewer chose to be diplomatic. "I'm sure you're right. Now, tell us about your lives there in the Rainforest."

"We do whatever tribe members do, from foraging for food to paying homage to their gods. The only difference is that we occupy a hut separate from the communal one the tribe members share. What we do in our living space is up to us, but outside it, we are Yarru."

"You feel you're gaining valuable information about these people?"

"Oh, yes. This society is as worthy of respect as any other."

"And how do you spread their message to the outside world?"

"I talk with people like you, who help us publicize the plight of indigenous people. We publish monthly impact statements on the effects industrial, commercial, and even public sector projects have on the tribe's environment. And we document and report incursions onto tribal lands."

"You and your husband work together on these reports?"

"We do, though he leaves the personal appearances to me." Amy's gaze flickered to the side, and I pictured the other Doctor Gage waiting somewhere off-camera.

The interviewer's chunky jewelry rattled softly as she moved in her chair. "How do you manage to communicate in the middle of the jungle?"

"With solar-powered batteries and generators, we can connect to the outside world via satellites. It isn't always easy, due to the canopy, the terrain, and of course, the rainy season."

The interviewer glanced upward, probably at a clock. "Doctor Gage, we appreciate your sharing your experiences with our audience."

Gage thanked the woman graciously, and the screen went blank.

"Amazing," I said. "Your mother was—" I almost commented on Amy's beauty but changed to "...well-spoken."

"That's all we have left of her," Lucy said. "A few months later, she was dead."

"What happened?"

"She was taking a water sample, and a child waded into the river to watch. He got too close to a caiman's nest, causing the creature to attack. Seeing the animal coming, Mom managed to toss the boy onto the bank, but that left her in its path. Before help could reach her, she was gone."

"It sounds like a dangerous place for two kids to grow up."

That got me a cold stare. "I understand there's a city near here where drinking water was sometimes fatal to children. That went on for years."

"The Flint water crisis isn't a great example of American ingenuity," I admitted. "How old were you when your mom died?"

"Almost two."

"Why did you stay in Peru?"

"We think Dad felt close to Mom there. Peter says that for a while he talked about coming back to the U.S., but after a year or so, he stopped even mentioning it." Lucy shrugged. "We were quite happy there."

That surprised me. "Did you know what life is like here?"

"Oh, yes. We could watch news, TV shows, and videos whenever we chose. Nothing we saw made us eager to leave the tribe."

"Until something happened to your dad."

"He was killed by poachers." Peter made an admonitory sound, and Lucy rephrased. "We *think* he was. When they found his…body, the animals had gotten there first, so it was hard to tell exactly how he died." Her voice took on an angry note. "But he didn't just collapse out there. We think—" She glanced at Peter. "*I* think Dad was filming a poaching operation and they caught him at it." Licking her lips, she added evidence for her claim. "Dad's phone wasn't with his body. No animal ate that."

While that wasn't proof of anything, I said, "I'm really sorry."

"Thank you." She picked at some lint on her sleeve as she went on. "It's been three months, but…we miss him a lot."

"I take it his death changed your lives?"

"Completely. We would have stayed where we were, but we had no choice in the matter."

Her resentment was obvious, and I said as gently as I could, "Surely you understand why you weren't allowed to stay in the jungle alone."

21

Her brow rose in what I already knew was a warning. "Do I?"

"Well—"

"Imagine that I force you to leave Michigan and live with the Yarru. Food is a mystery. You have no shoes, so the earth feels different under your feet. You wear nothing but a loincloth. Your skin reacts badly to the change in temperature. The language sounds like shouting in your ears, and ambient light and noise jab at your brain like jolts of electricity." She mimed stabbing at her head. "How would you react, do you think?"

"I'd be unhappy."

"As we are." She folded her arms. "Aside from those admittedly minor objections, we find this society full of people who are unabashedly ignorant and dismissive of anything outside their own experience. We doubted we'd fit in, and that's proven correct."

"How so?"

"From the start, everyone here has been determined to 'help' Peter to 'get over' his shyness." She glanced at her brother affectionately. "He's perfectly fine the way he is."

Though I didn't think the word *shyness* covered the boy's near mute condition, I was eager to move the story forward. "That would be hard to take. What else?"

Dimples appeared again as Lucy's lips twisted. "Almost everyone I meet takes offense when I make even small attempts to educate them."

Having an inkling of how Lucy might "educate" those around her, I hid a smile with my fist. "I see. Does that include your guardian?"

"Definitely. He's very resistant to logical argumentation."

"Tell me about him."

"His legal firm has managed our affairs for years."

"No relative or friend who might have become your guardian?"

"Mom and Dad were both only children, and our grandparents are dead." Lucy's tone turned judgmental. "Sedentary Western lifestyles." I chose not to comment on life expectancy in the Amazon Basin, and she went on. "Dad has friends, of course, but they're scientists who live in the...boondocks, like we do." She corrected herself. "Like we did."

"Then the law firm's responsible for your care."

"We're quite capable of looking after ourselves. Peter can make a meal out of anything, and I'm well-versed in the standards of cleanliness considered necessary here." She frowned. "I'm not obsessive about it, as homeowners in the advertisements we see here seem to be."

That apparently reminded Lucy of a possible murder method. "Toilet bowl cleaner and bleach are toxic when mixed. In a single year in India, one hundred ten people died while cleaning latrines. If we got him to—" Frowning as if in pain, she stopped. I glanced at Peter, whose expression revealed nothing.

To get back on track I said, "I understand that you're both mature for your ages, but the law says you must have an adult in your lives."

"We had a candidate in mind who was perfect for the role, but sadly, she was unavailable." Before I could ask who that was, Lucy went on. "Then I suggested we advertise the position and hold interviews, Peter and I and someone representing the firm." Her mouth quirked with disgust. "I might as well have asked for world peace and a cookie."

"I'm surprised your father didn't name someone in his will."

"He trusted the head of the firm, Carson Coburn, but unfortunately, Mr. Coburn had a stroke shortly after Dad died." Folding her hands, she set them in her lap. "The remaining attorneys assigned a guardian with neither our approval nor our input." Lucy had come to the crux of her presentation. "And that's who we need to kill."

"I understand. You've got money you should be allowed to spend however you want, but—" Lucy's gaze turned frosty, and I stopped.

"Is that how we seem to you?" she demanded. "Spoiled brats angry because we can't buy all the toys we want?"

"I never heard of you before today," I said defensively. "How am I supposed to know what you're like?"

Though her lips remained pinched, Lucy granted me the benefit of the doubt. "Fair enough. I'm nine. Peter is fifteen. Our father provided us with an excellent education, despite our remote location. Here in Michigan, we attend the Lawson Academy in Rennington Hills. We're both in accelerated learning programs, having tested far above our grade levels." She paused to specify. "I do best in languages and history. Peter excels in math and science." Mention of languages diverted her attention for a moment. "Do you know that in primitive tribes, no one misuses words or mispronounces them?"

"Interesting." I was overusing that word, but what else? "I'll grant that you're both smart." She frowned at my dismissal of their obvious intelligence, so I added, "Good grades are nice, but you know—"

Reading my mind, Lucy said, "Life in the Rainforest requires that one develop common sense. Those who tease a jaguar or handle poison dart frogs carelessly don't live long. Therefore, our theoretical learning is balanced with practical knowledge."

"Okay. You can do geometry, and you'll never get run over by a rampaging herd of capybaras."

My little joke resulted in another of Lucy's off-topic moments. "The Mongols executed the last caliph of Bagdad by rolling him up in a rug and letting a herd of horses trample him." She paused, possibly waiting for me to say I could arrange something similar. When I didn't, she said, "We're trying to integrate ourselves into your society. Peter recently joined the robotics team, and I help my teacher, Ms. Dixon, at school events—unless it's something ridiculous, like cheerleading tryouts."

"Sounds like you're adjusting."

"It's not easy." A grunt from Peter seconded that. "The smart kids hated us from the first, because we're always at the top of the grading curve. The others find it entertaining to make us the butt of their jokes."

"How's that?"

"They call me Lucy of the Apes and make grunting noises at me in the halls. I explained that South America has platyrrhines, not apes, but nobody listened. And because Peter doesn't like to talk, they do mean things to try to make him say something."

"Kids can be cruel." I regretted that the moment I said it. Peter and Lucy didn't need me to confirm what they were living through. I tried again. "It's only been a couple of months, right? Once you get used to the way things are here, the other kids will accept you."

"So we'll forget the harassment we've suffered and become lifelong friends with budding snobs and dogmatists?"

"Well, maybe not. But you'll get used to them, and to the school."

"Your education system is horrible," Lucy said. "Listening to someone drone on about Alexander Hamilton or Enrico Fermi for an hour. We always studied what interested us at a particular moment or what connected to the work we were doing. We didn't stop after precisely fifty-five minutes and move to a new subject." She pushed her hair back, adding, "And who invented those desks, Torquemada?"

"Tests," Peter commented, and Lucy nodded to indicate he'd brought up an excellent point.

"When we first got there, they gave us days and days of tests, paper and pencil stuff that measured about a quarter of our capabilities." She huffed haughtily. "Nobody at Lawson cares that Peter can make pure water out of muck with a simple distillation method he read about online and then improved on. Nobody asked if I could find my way home from anywhere in the world using the stars as a guide. They only want to know if we can choose correctly from answer *a, b, c,* or *d.*"

"Your education before was...intuitive." I was proud of myself for coming up with the word.

"Exactly. Now we learn irrelevant facts and regurgitate them on demand. Tomorrow's Tuesday, so I'll be multiplying improper fractions and reading about the French Revolution." That brought up another distraction, and off she went. "Did you know Napoleon was probably poisoned with small doses of arsenic?" She waved dismissively. "That's not a suggestion. Arsenic poisoning is slow and inhumane. We wouldn't consider it, no matter how depraved the subject is."

"Explain why you say your guardian is depraved." I tapped on the blotter with my pen. "He wasn't your choice, but that's not his fault. He chose a school you don't like, but eventually you'll make friends there."

"I doubt I will ever find friends among the USians."

"Excuse me, who?"

"*USians* is my term for people of the United States. Big *U*, big *S*, i-a-n-s." Her tone turned preachy, but I was becoming used to that. "I'm sure you know you're not the only Americans. Canadians are American. Peruvians are American. Mexicans are American."

"I get it. And you pronounce the term *You-si-ens*?"

"Yes. USians are often more ignorant than the Yarru."

"More ignorant? Give me an example."

She had one ready. "Last week we went to a craft show at the Arab-American Museum in Dearborn. A Yemeni couple had a booth stocked with beautiful baskets, and we stopped to look. While I was trying to choose one to buy, a man beside me noticed his shoelace had come untied." Lucy leaned forward to emphasize her words. "He put his *foot* up on their display shelf to retie it."

I frowned. "Why is that a problem?"

"You really need to do some reading," she chided. "Showing the bottom of the foot is an insult to Middle Easterners. Imagine taking out your penis and waving it at someone from Chicago." My mind stalled for a second at the image she'd created, but Lucy went on with her story. "When I told the man what he'd done was insulting, he said, 'You're in 'Merica, little girl. We don't worry about what foreigners think.'" Her eyes flashed as she asked, "Why wouldn't he consider their feelings?"

"He didn't know."

"But once it was pointed out to him, he should have apologized. The Yarru value the traditions of others, even when they don't share them, but among the USians, it's, 'Don't know. Don't care.'"

I sighed. "Let's get back to why you want your guardian killed."

"First, I'd like to give you a dollar."

"Why?"

"If I pay you, we become your clients, and as such, you can't repeat what we tell you."

That was wrong on several counts. I'm not a lawyer, so client privilege doesn't apply. They were proposing a felony, which even a lawyer would be bound to disclose. And on a personal level, I wasn't the kind of guy who'd agree to keep quiet about a murder plot. Intrigued by the situation, I let Lucy give me a dollar, which I put in my desk drawer before repeating my question. "Why do you want to kill this...?"

"Oscar Coburn." Lucy rolled her eyes, hinting that I should have guessed the answer by now. "Because he's planning to kill us."

CHAPTER TWO

Before drawing any conclusions about a case, an investigator should check out his prospective clients. Liars spout outlandish stuff without batting an eye, and the earnest certainty of conspiracy theorists makes it tempting to believe their claims. While an inexperienced guy might think, *Those poor kids. Their guardian's trying to steal their money,* my ex-cop persona warned, *Max, keep your dickey on.*

"Will you excuse me for a moment? I have to use the rest room."

Peter glanced up for a second. Lucy gave me a long, assessing look. "Of course," she finally said.

Leaving them in my office, I crossed the anteroom and went through the door marked "Men," where I took out my phone and called a friend at the Wayne County courthouse. "Polly, are you busy?"

"Hey, Max. You caught me at lunch, but we're about to go back into the courtroom." My buddy's wife is a court reporter, which I hoped meant she could help me out.

"I won't keep you long, but I'd like your impression of an attorney named Oscar Coburn."

"Oscar? He's okay, I suppose. I don't often sympathize with his clients, but he's competent, and he takes the job seriously."

"Have you ever talked with him about his personal life?"

Polly laughed. "Us little people don't chat much with the attorneys, Max. But we sit around waiting for judges or juries or whoever sometimes, so I hear them talk. I know Oscar took on a responsibility recently that's more than he bargained for."

"What was that?"

"Well, there were these rich kids whose parents died, and he agreed to become their guardian. He was probably thinking of the fat paychecks that come with that kind of thing, but it sounds like he's beginning to understand the pitfalls of being a stand-in dad."

"Like what kind of pitfalls?"

"I only hear bits and pieces, but it sounds like the kids are barely civilized. The girl tells wild stories and then throws a fit if people don't believe her. The boy doesn't talk much; in fact, I hear he can't even look at people directly. They've decided they don't like Oscar, so they play pranks on him all the time. The other day he came to court with a big smear of peanut butter on the rear of his pants."

"How does he take these pranks?"

She made a *pfft!* of disgust. "Too well, if you ask me. I'd have some strong words for kids like that, but Oscar says he's teaching them acclimation and they're teaching him patience." I heard a voice call, and Polly said, "Sorry, Max. I have to go."

"Thanks, Polly. Say hi to Baker for me."

"Will do. Bye."

Polly had provided what I'd hoped for, an unbiased view of Oscar Coburn. Immature clients who were "barely civilized" didn't sound ideal, no matter how tragic their story. Besides, I was practically on my way to Mexico. Less than five days. Only five nights. Flushing the toilet and running water in the sink, I returned to my office, practicing in my head how I'd convince the Gage kids to give up their quest for a hitman.

The body has concerns beyond what occupies the mind. As I sat down in my chair, my stomach gave one of those long, loud, feral growls you can't even pretend to ignore. "Um, sorry," I apologized. Taking it as an opportunity to gain a little more time with them, I asked, "If I got a pizza, could you eat a slice?"

Lucy glanced at Peter, who responded with a twitch of his lips that I read as an enthusiastic yes. "We'll be happy to pay," she said graciously, "since we've kept you from your usual lunch break."

Being the host, I probably should have treated, but the online article had mentioned their mother's estate was almost a billion dollars—that's with a *b*. If Dear Old Dad had been even minimally careful with the money, they could easily afford the price of a pizza. "Thank you. Does anyone know where you are?"

Lucy smiled. "Peter got fitted with braces last week, so the school secretary knows he'll miss class sometimes for dental appointments." Grimacing, Peter showed me wire-encased teeth. "I told her I had to go along as his… interpreter."

"No one checks?"

"They got a text from our nanny's phone confirming my story." She grinned. "Ilsa mouths her passcode numbers as she punches them in."

"Then you're free for a while longer."

"Yes. We need to be outside the school at three fifteen when Adam, our driver, comes for us."

I hesitated. "You do like pizza, right? You mentioned that the food here is—"

"It was an adjustment, but we've become accustomed to most USian foods. We're okay with everything except your tendency to pile sugary toppings over sugary bases."

No DQ for dessert then. "I'll order a Detroit-style and we'll talk some more."

Behind his blank expression Peter's aspect lightened, as if he liked where things were going. I wasn't sure if it was my interest in their case or the prospect of pizza that had turned his mood positive.

Neither kid objected to a pie with all the toppings, which earned them a few points in my book. I get irritated when people pick off the onions or insist on no mushrooms. When a bunch of ingredients are baked together on a nice crust with lots of sauce, a person shouldn't quibble about the details. It occurred to me that in the Amazon Basin they'd probably eaten things I couldn't imagine, like fried grubs or chicken feet, so it stood to reason they wouldn't mind chomping down a few black olives. I called Pizza Forever, pausing to ask what they wanted to drink. In answer, Peter took from his backpack a pouch much like a wineskin Baker takes snowmobiling. "We don't approve of plastic or wasted paper." Lucy sounded smug, but that might have been guilt on my part. As a bachelor who survived on microwave meals and take-out food, I couldn't recall the last time I'd acted to save the planet.

While we waited, another rumble felt imminent in my abdominal area. Shifting in my chair I asked, a little too loudly, "Why do you believe your guardian is planning to kill you?"

"Peter heard him say it." I glanced at Peter, who nodded but let Lucy tell the story. "When my brother has serious studying to do, he likes to find a small space and close himself in. It helps him tune out distractions, like traffic noise and power tools." Lucy's eyes searched mine, looking for signs of disapproval or derision. "He functions most efficiently when there's no one looking over his shoulder."

"He's got a little social anxiety."

"*Scopophobia* is the correct term. The condition runs in families, though no one can say why one member has it and another doesn't."

That explained Peter's shyness, though the tragic loss of first one parent, and more recently the other, probably hadn't helped. "Our father was scopophobic too, which is why Mom did the public stuff, like interviews. After her death, Dad switched to written reports, but they were much less effective."

"People like hearing things from a source better than reading things from a screen."

"True. I was learning to take on Mom's role." Lucy paused. "Peter and I didn't plan to pursue the university education the world expects scientists to have. We felt our unique situation qualifies us as experts in our field." She raised a finger. "You've probably heard of Richard Leaky, who became an eminent palaeoanthropologist mostly by working with and learning from his parents."

"I'll bet your dad was proud of you both."

"He was." Her voice wobbled a little as the shadow of how life should have been darkened her mood. "Peter has a natural talent for botany. He took plants the Yarru use for medicine and made them better, either more potent or easier to use. For example, there's a stalk the Yarru chew to a paste to put on wounds. Peter figured out how to extract the sap, which is the healing part, and store it, so when someone gets hurt, they don't have to go out into the jungle and find the plant."

We'd strayed off topic again, but I was getting used to it. "About this murder you heard the guy plotting..."

There was no hurrying Lucy. "We suspected from the first that Oscar took us on for financial benefit. He has no interest in us as people, and in fact seldom speaks to us unless he's trying to impress some outsider."

"He's not warm and fuzzy."

A grimace said I didn't know the half of it. "The first thing he did was buy a house in Rennington Hills that's much too large and spread out to be even mildly efficient." Her mouth turned down. "He moved in with us, claiming we need a role model."

Peter's contemptuous snort revealed his opinion of Oscar as an example. Still, Polly had said Coburn was all right, so I tried to remain objective. With their odd background, the kids probably resented being forced to wear underwear and eat with forks. Even with no wrong on either side, an adjustment period was inevitable.

"Oscar enrolled us at the academy and then hired a nanny, Ilsa Dausman, who's responsible for our schedule and our meals." Lucy snickered. "She orders in most of the time, and we hate the amount of waste it generates." Her tone turned derisive. "Ilsa particularly likes shopping, which Oscar encourages as a pastime. He keeps telling us to buy whatever we like."

I sent up a trial balloon. "At least he's generous."

"With our money," Lucy said sardonically. "He keeps trying to seduce us with some new device or app or fad, completely ignoring our distaste for your consumer society's lack of regard for the planet."

"You mentioned someone named Adam?"

"Adam Saracco drives us where we need to go. A woman named May comes in a few days a week to clean and do laundry. We seldom see her, and she speaks only a few words of English."

While I didn't relish the prospect of arguing with a precocious nine-year-old, it sounded to me like Coburn was conscientious. "Look, Oscar got you a house. He's arranged a good education and hired staff to see that you're okay. He's willing to let you shop till you drop if you want to. He doesn't sound like a bad guy."

"I'm getting to that." Lucy took a second to recall where she'd left off. "I mentioned that Peter likes small, quiet spaces. One day last week, he went into a closet off the library to do some homework. A few minutes later Oscar came in, closed the door, and made a phone call. He had no idea Peter was listening."

"He heard something he wasn't supposed to?"

Lucy cleared her throat before answering. "I misspoke earlier."

Ah, here we go, I thought. She'd come to a point where she had to admit Oscar's depravity wasn't quite as deep as she'd first suggested.

That wasn't it. "I said Oscar wants *us* dead, but what Peter heard him say was that he wants *one* of us that way. 'Better if there were only one,' he told whoever he was speaking to. 'I could deal with a single kid.'"

"Which one of you does Oscar want gone?"

"We don't think he's decided yet, but Peter's more likely." When my brows met in a question, she explained, "With Peter alive and well, Oscar has three years as our guardian."

"When he reaches his majority, he'll take control of the estate."

"And do a much better job," Lucy said firmly. "Right now, we have two gas-guzzling cars that leave a horrible carbon footprint. We told Oscar to be more environmentally responsible, but he said money should be enjoyed, and we should stop 'fussing' about the poor, the climate, and the planet."

"Have you told anyone that he's not following your wishes?"

Her voice rose. "Who would that 'anyone' be? Oscar's brother? His cousin? The peppy woman who's dying to get ahead at the firm?" Her voice went high and breathy. "'Yes, Oscar.' 'Of course, Oscar.' 'You're so smart, Oscar.' Would she help us kick him out, do you think?"

My phone buzzed, and I checked the display. "Pizza's here."

"Peter, will you go downstairs and get it?" Lucy asked.

I started to say that the guy would bring it up—He definitely knows the way—but she caught my eye and shook her head. As soon as her brother was gone, Lucy's tone turned serious. "Mr. Dunham, it took every bit of persuasion I could muster to get Peter to come here today."

A glow of relief shone in my mind. "Your brother doesn't want to murder this Oscar guy."

Her eyes rolled in irritation. "That isn't it. Peter and I agree on everything but the method."

"Was it your idea to hire a hitman?"

"Yes. Peter argued it would be difficult to locate one, since we can't find them online like you do plumbers and home decorators. I suggested we ask a private investigator for a recommendation, figuring someone in your field would know the local criminal element well." Lucy's gaze took in my office. "I want you to know that if we choose someone else, it won't be because we object to your lifestyle."

"My…lifestyle?"

"We know about homosexuality, though it doesn't seem to exist among the Yarru. Dad believed that was because of the strong cultural focus on sex as a reproductive tool in tribal societies." Seeing the look on my face, Lucy's confidence deserted her. "Am I wrong? The…décor, the fake shirt…I assumed…" Apparently aware she was making things worse, she let her words trail off. After a moment she said, "Whatever the case, we're equal opportunity employers."

I glanced around the office, trying to see it as an outsider might. I love my mom, but if her influence was leading in that direction…I decided the fruit had to go, maybe the curtains too. Definitely the dickey.

As I made mental renovations, Lucy dropped another bombshell. "While Peter and I agree on the solution to our problem, he believes we should, um, remove Oscar ourselves." As she went on, I leaned my chin on a fist to keep my mouth closed. "Last night as I went into the dining room, I spotted Peter's elbow sticking out from behind the door. I peered around it, and there he stood, holding a baseball bat."

"He planned to kill Oscar when he came down to dinner?"

She shook her head. "He was rehearsing. Still, you can see why I suggested we need professional help."

No argument there.

Lucy went on as if discussing a possible visit to the Detroit Zoo. "*I* don't think we should proceed on our own, but Peter says a professional isn't necessary. We turned to the Yarru method of decision-making."

"The consensus your mother mentioned."

"Yes. Respect for all opinions." Lucy's upper lip pressed against her lower one. "We've seen how disrespectfully people here speak to each other, even in the halls of government. We can hardly believe it."

"Sometimes I can't believe it either."

"When there's disagreement among the Yarru, the parties involved explain their views, one at a time, without interruption. Once a person finishes, the next speaker must summarize what he said before presenting his own argument. Points of agreement are made clear that way, so areas of dispute can be examined and discussed."

It sounded good, but working with a dozen opinions wasn't the same as dealing with millions. Glancing at the doorway, where Peter might reappear at any moment, I gestured for her to go on.

"We arrived at a compromise. If we can find a suitable candidate within a week, we'll hire that person. If not, we'll execute our own plan."

"Only one week? That's pushing the timetable."

"It's difficult to face each day wondering whether we'll both be alive at the end of it, Mr. Dunham. We need to get Oscar out of our lives."

Playing on Lucy's obvious care for her brother, I tried a new argument. "If you're caught, Peter would take the blame, being older."

"Agreed," she replied. "And despite its inability to lock up robber barons and corrupt politicians, your USian justice system has excellent forensics."

"Yes." We were moving in the right direction. "DNA. Fingerprints. I doubt you'd get away with it."

She rewarded my blatant attempt at dissuading her with a look of irritation. "Precisely my argument for hiring a professional and paying him or her top dollar. I want us both to be safe from prosecution."

The image of Peter lying in wait for the guardian had disquieted my mind. "Your brother's best idea is to go after Oscar with a baseball bat?"

"That would be a last resort." Lucy's creative side emerged again. "It would be best if it appeared to be an accident. The Frankish king Louis III was chasing a girl on horseback when he hit his head on her doorway lintel and fractured his skull. A soccer player from Cameroon was killed when an angry fan threw a bottle that did the same." Reading my disbelief, Lucy toned it down a notch. "It could look like an attack by an unhappy former client."

I fell back on my earlier comment. "Interesting." Inside my head I was screaming, *You're discussing felony murder with a nine-year-old!* I'll admit, it was fascinating, hearing this self-possessed child blithely combine historical anecdotes with current considerations for murder.

"I gather Peter doesn't approve of your colorful scenarios."

"No. He favors the sort of run-of-the-mill incidents one can find in any action novel, such as cutting the brake lines on Oscar's BMW." Her expression revealed fond forbearance. "I had a time convincing him that method is unsuited to the flatlands of southern Michigan."

"I see." For the record, I did not see. I didn't want to see. It was becoming clear these kids had talked about this a lot.

Lucy's gaze focused on the bookshelf over my shoulder. "In 1919, several people in Boston died in a flood of molasses. I'm not sure how one manages that, but a flowing substance would obscure the evidence nicely, don't you think?"

Leaning across my desk, I looked Lucy directly in the eye. "If I were to agree to help with this, you'd have to promise not to act on your own. Nothing unique. Nothing generic. Nothing."

"That sounds fair," she responded, "but as I said, time is a factor."

"For me too. I'm leaving town on Saturday for a week's vacation."

Her chin jutted, and the goodwill I'd accrued dissipated. "I see. We'd hate to disturb your plans merely because one of us might be murdered."

"Look, I'm not sure—"

Lucy stood. "It was a mistake to come here."

With the image of Peter crouched behind a door holding a ball bat still in mind, I made a desperate proposal. "I didn't say I wouldn't help. Five days should be enough time to…investigate your claim—"

"You're hoping to disprove it." Her tone was flat, her eyes hard.

I raised a hand as if swearing a vow. "I'll give your claims a fair chance, I promise."

She hesitated. "It would be good to have someone at work on this. Peter thinks Oscar's getting ready to take action."

I considered saying Peter might not be the coolest cube in the tray, but their obvious closeness called for a more diplomatic approach. "He seems to follow your lead. If you told him to wait—"

Lucy waved that away with a sharp gesture. "I appear to be dominant only because I'm comfortable in social situations. Peter isn't mentally deficient. Nor is he likely to be dissuaded when he knows he's right." She laid a hand on her chest. "We'll do what we must to stay safe, and we'll do it together."

I heard the outer door, and Peter appeared, holding a square, fragrant box and wearing the eager expression common to teenaged males about to be fed. It was hard to reconcile his boyish delight with the image of him taking a bat to his guardian's head. Polly had said Lucy was known for wild stories. Had she invented that one to get me on her side?

When I stepped forward to take the box, I got another whiff of Peter and hid a grimace of disgust. Had years of living in a primitive spot made the kid averse to bathing? No, his stench was far worse than regular B.O. Did he have some sort of health condition? Or was there a Limburger cheese sandwich in his backpack?

When I offered to go get paper plates and plastic forks, Lucy looked horrified. "Why add to this nation's unconscionable waste of resources?"

Tacitly admitting that dining implements are the natural enemies of pizza, I opened the box, let them choose a slice, and took one for myself. After a bite I asked, "Have you considered that what you're proposing is morally wrong?"

Lucy had a smear of sauce on her chin, which she wiped away with the back of her hand. "While they generally avoid conflict, the Yarru believe that if someone intends to harm you, it's permissible, even wise, to take action to prevent it." Her tone turned hard. "If we'd been more proactive, Dad might still be with us."

"Why do you say that?"

"He was alone in the forest that day because of an earlier incident." Lucy set her half-eaten slice down as she told the story. "Mahogany, some call it 'red gold,' is valuable wood. One day when Peter and I had wandered away from where Dad was working, a band of predatory loggers came looking for trees to steal. We stepped into a clearing to find that we faced a half-dozen men armed with machetes. We tried to back away, but one of them saw us and shouted, '*Allá! Allá!*'" Lucy's voice rose as the memory returned. "We turned and ran full tilt back the way we'd come. They followed, determined to shut us up."

Caught up in the drama, I forgot Lucy's reputation for storytelling and imagined the scene as if it were a movie: the kids stumbling through dense vegetation, their pursuers shouting, and their father looking up in surprise at their approach.

"What happened?"

"Dad always carried a sidearm when we left the village. He fired a couple of shots into the air, and the poachers turned and ran." Lucy's expression turned grave. "Peter and I were told to stay in the village until we were sure the poachers had moved on. Dad went out alone, since he couldn't abide a gap in his data." She picked up her pizza again. "If he'd killed one or two of them, they might not have come back."

Raymond Gage had obviously been a swashbuckling hero in Lucy's mind, but what little girl doesn't see her dad that way? I had the impression that most scientists live monotonous lives, observing, measuring, analyzing, and recording. I glanced at

Peter, but there was no help there. He was wholly absorbed in working on his second slice.

A rattle in the outer office stopped us all. "I'm here," a voice called. "Do I smell pizza?"

"That's my intern," I told the kids. Raising my voice, I said, "Come in, Bobby."

He appeared in the doorway, his thin face lit with joy at the sight of company. "Sorry I'm late," he said. "There's a pileup on I-90, three cars in the ditch and traffic backed up while we maneuvered around tow trucks and cop cars. Nobody was hurt, so that's good."

Bobby's a type who might have been created by Charles Dickens. At first meeting, you think, *No one's that happy all the time,* but Bobby is. I have no idea why he chose a profession as depressing as criminal justice, but the local community college paired us up, and we do okay together. Still, a conversation with Bobby is mostly waiting for him to take a breath and then squeezing a word in. Whatever's beyond hyper, that's him.

"Help yourself to a slice." Food is one way to slow down Bobby's constant flow of words, and I didn't have to ask twice. The guy would probably work for free if I bought lunch every day. "Bobby, meet Lucy and Peter. They're here to discuss some work I might do for them." I purposefully left off last names, and Lucy shot me a look of gratitude.

"Great to meet you." Bobby shook hands with each of them. I cringed when he said, "Lucy, did anyone ever tell you you're gorgeous?"

Her smile faded. "No one I'd care to become further acquainted with."

Bobby took her outrage in stride. "I completely agree. Beauty's an artificial construct that's now outmoded and unnecessary. It's much more helpful to speak of an individual's usefulness or personal values."

"Or intelligence."

"Right," he agreed, "but as a society, we notice a person's looks."

"Your society," she said imperiously. "Not mine."

Again he deflected her anger by ignoring it. "Then you're not from here? How kewl. We should talk."

His comment presented an opportunity, and I said, "I'd like you to do the intake paperwork with Lucy and Peter while I finish up some things I need to get done before two." To the kids I said, "If you become my clients, I'll need Form 13 in place."

Bobby's expression changed slightly. Form 13, much like File 13, is garbage, useless information we write down to make a client think I'm seriously considering their case. After a day or so, I send Form 13 clients a polite note saying I have to refuse their business, citing reasons like time constraints and other obligations.

Lucy glanced at Bobby, who covered his initial response with an expression that revealed nothing. "Okay."

"If you'll go with Bobby here, I'll get back with you in about twenty minutes."

Lucy's look was probing. Peter blinked a few times as if trying to decide how he felt about the shift to Bobby's care. In the end they did as I asked. As they exited, I made a stretching gesture, signaling Bobby should drag the process out. He nodded understanding, and I heard him arranging chairs for them in the anteroom and commenting on the current weather while he searched the desk for the form and a decent ink pen. I got up and quietly closed my office door. I wanted to do some further checking on the Gage kids, and I also needed to make a list of questions to ask when they came back. When something as weird as a request for a hitman lands on your desktop, it's tough to cover all the bases without a little time to reconnoiter.

It was possible to look into the kids' claim if I chose to. Except for giving testimony late in the week, I was free until Saturday. I figured I could spend a day or so researching the guardian. If he seemed wrong, I'd drop a word into the right ears. If Peter and Lucy were full of hot air, I'd leave Michigan with a clear conscience.

There was one further consideration. If I found the kids capable of doing or even attempting what they claimed, I'd have to warn Oscar Coburn. While that would feel like tattling, I couldn't sit by and let two decidedly weird orphans plot a man's death. I was all too aware that the next P.I. on their list might find it hard to refuse the bag of cash Peter carried over his shoulder like it was nothing.

I'd taken notes as Lucy talked, and I read through them, letting what she'd told me organize itself in my mind. With a second slice of pizza in one hand, I typed *Oscar Coburn, Detroit attorney* into the search bar with the other. Scanning the pages of coburnlaw.com, I got the disquieting sense that Peter's solemn dignity and Lucy's precocious cuteness had led me into a web of lies. The law firm seemed legitimate. Oscar Coburn had worked there since graduating from the U of M's law school in 2007. Each attorney had a specialty, and Oscar's was criminal cases. I shifted to lawyers.com and found that in his thirteen years of practice, he had a decent track record and no public reprimands from the Bar Association.

Next, I looked at reports of Raymond Gage's death. The media's tone was much the same as it had been when his wife died: a wealthy, eccentric person was no longer with us—Oh, and he was also a scientist. Some of the articles had a hint of "See? Bad things happen to rich people too." All of them summarized the event in much the same way: Gage's death was a great loss to environmentalism and to his two children. One blogger hinted their wealth would serve as a cushion for their grief. I wondered how in the world that was supposed to work.

There'd been local coverage of the kids coming to the U.S. as virtual strangers to their own culture. Once the court made its decision as to their placement, Oscar Coburn was interviewed by a local TV reporter. That was what I wanted, a chance to see the man for myself.

Oscar's conservative black suit probably cost more than my car, and his discreet red-and-gray tie said he had excellent taste. A Teutonic type with wide shoulders, light hair, and striking blue eyes, he'd have looked equally at home in a metal breastplate and conical helmet. His demeanor was relaxed. Lowering the volume so the kids wouldn't hear, I listened to the interview.

"This isn't what I expected to be doing at this point in my life," he said when the reporter asked how he felt about taking on two half-grown kids. "We all have things to learn, but they're smart and adaptable, and I'm willing to listen. We'll be fine."

"The children were raised in a primitive environment. Do you think the parents were wise to subject them to that sort of lifestyle?"

Oscar's shoulders shifted. "Not a decision I'd have made, but Lucy claims scientists often do unusual things to advance learning. She told me that in the 1980s an Australian scientist drank a broth of some very nasty stuff to prove that stomach ulcers are caused by bacteria, not stress. And Isaac Newton poked himself in the eye with a needle, just to see what would happen." Cocking his head, Oscar smiled. "I guess we each decide what our contribution to the world will be. Now, me? I'll practice law and leave jungle life to courageous people like the Gages."

"But now the children have to acclimate to Western society. How do you plan to help them with that?"

"We've chosen an excellent school, and I met with the teachers and principal, so they understand the situation. Since I work long hours, I plan to hire caregivers who will keep the kids safe and see to their needs." His expression turned sober. "While I realize I can't replace their father, I'm determined to be available when Peter and Lucy have concerns."

"You've thought this through," the interviewer said approvingly.

"The most important thing is for the kids to feel they have someone who cares about them. Wealth without limits is often a curse, and they're at a further disadvantage, being new to what American life offers."

The woman nodded understanding. "I'm sure they're dazzled by everything they can do and see here."

"In a little over a week, they went from eating guinea pigs and roots to being able to have a feast delivered to their door." Oscar's handsome face reflected concern. "Some will try to take advantage of their naiveté."

"You see your job as preparing them to face the world by the time they're old enough to be on their own."

Oscar put a hand to his chest in a gesture that suggested modesty. "I hope I can help with that, for my old friend Ray's sake."

The interview contained no specifics as to where the kids would live or which school they'd attend, and I approved of Oscar's discretion. As he'd said, his job was giving Lucy and Peter time to adjust to a new way of life while fending off con artists after their money.

Hearing Bobby's printer warming up, I realized my research time was slipping away. I had to give the kids some sort of answer, and I had no idea what it should be.

Oscar seemed genuinely concerned for Peter and Lucy's welfare. He was no shyster. His firm was respected and respectable. How could I convey that to a couple of kids with little understanding of how things work in the modern world?

The word *snake* caught my attention, and I tuned in to a story Lucy was telling Bobby. "...was huge, but Peter had seen Grandfather Tama handle big snakes, and he copied his method. You move slowly toward it and pick up its body from underneath. That's the tricky part, because you can't let a boa wrap itself around your neck. Once he had control of it, Peter carried the creature outside and let it go." After a dramatic pause she finished, "I didn't even know I'd been in danger until I woke up the next morning."

A boa in the bedroom? Another story that might be true, might be Lucy performing for an audience.

I went back to my computer screen. An article on civil rights that Oscar Coburn, Esquire, had done for a legal advice website a few years earlier was well-written but full of jargon that blurred its clarity, in my opinion. A posed shot with hands gripping his lapels made him look like William Jennings Bryan, but a glint of self-deprecating humor showed in Coburn's eyes. I could almost hear him mutter, "Corny, but it's what people expect." Skilled with words, the guy also had the sense of theater many good attorneys exhibit.

As far as his personal life went, I made a few deductions based on reports of local social events. At forty-five, Oscar was considered a catch, but so far no woman had managed to get him to the altar. I found photos of him at galas over the past few years with different women, each one slender, gorgeous, and expensively turned out. A society blogger termed Oscar "a local professional who's often chased but never caught."

There was a tap on the door, and Bobby opened it to allow Lucy and Peter in. His look was a question: *Was that long enough?* My response was a nod, though I could have used more time. Like a week.

When they were again seated, I started the questions I'd prepared.

"Where did the money you've got in that bag come from?"

As expected, it was Lucy who answered. "The Amazon River Basin is a scary place these days. We never knew when we'd run into trouble, so Dad got some USian cash to use for bribes or ransom payments."

"Who knew about it?"

"Just us. We kept it in a garment bag under Dad's cot."

"Weren't you afraid someone would sneak in and steal it while you were collecting samples or whatever?"

They both chuckled at that. "The Yarru have no use for money," Lucy said. "Once a developer tried to buy his way onto their land. When he explained how rich the tribe would be, Grandfather Tama asked him, 'What need has the earth for shapes made from paper?'"

"If cash is no good there—"

"Poachers are different. They understand money and want it. Dad says—said—they were desperate men, willing to destroy their nation's greatest treasures for financial gain."

"There's desperation and there's greed."

She shrugged, granting me the point. "Either way, USian money encourages negotiation."

"So you had emergency cash. How did you get it into the U.S.?"

"Dad's friend at the Peruvian embassy, Alberto Diaz, was eager to help us in any way he could."

An odd sound made me turn to Peter, whose chin bent to his chest as his shoulders shook. After a moment I realized he was laughing.

"Stop it," Lucy ordered.

"What's so funny?

She sniffed before answering. "Sr. Diaz has suggested, more than once, that when I reach sixteen, his son and I might marry."

"What?"

Lucy's cheeks turned bright pink. Peter made the sound again, big brother laughing at little sister's embarrassment. "Sr. Diaz liked and admired Dad. In his mind, a…blending of our families is desirable."

"*Niñita linda*." Peter spit the words out in a gust of humor.

Lucy's glare indicated his contribution didn't amuse her. She offered no translation, but I knew that much: "Beautiful girl."

"When Dad was killed, Sr. Diaz sent a guide and bearers to bring us to his home. After several days of walking, a long bus ride, and a train, we stayed with his family in Lima until a passport was arranged for me and we could leave for Detroit." Her voice took on an odd tone as she recalled those days. "The trip was…scary. So many things I'd only seen on a screen before. So many strangers with unusual behaviors. The Diaz family was kind, but no one, nothing, was what we were used to."

"It must have been tough, facing that alone."

"Well, we had Denice."

"Who's that?"

"In the past, I suppose she'd have been called our governess, but *tutor* is probably a more current term."

It was the first I'd heard of a tutor, but I didn't want to go off in yet another direction. "You brought the money out with you."

"Yes. When it was time to leave Lima, Sr. Diaz asked if he could help with anything else. Peter had been thinking about the money, and he asked if the señor could get a package to Detroit for us. He sent it to his embassy in Washington, D.C. in a diplomatic pouch, which, I'm sure you know, can't be searched. From there it was sent to Detroit's Mexican embassy, since Peru has no Michigan office. The staff there was told to keep it for us until we came for it."

"Didn't your guardian ask why you went to the Mexican embassy?"

"Oscar probably never heard about it. On the way home from school one day, we told Adam that a friend had sent a hand-woven tapestry as a condolence gift, and we needed to stop and pick it up." Lucy made a huff of disgust. "He was about as interested in it as he is in quantum theory."

"Okay, so you've got emergency cash. It's really not wise to carry a hundred thousand dollars around with you."

Lucy's dimples appeared again. "Would you have believed we had it if we hadn't shown you?"

"No, but shoved in a gym bag like dirty laundry?"

"Usually we keep it in a place no one would suspect."

That was something, but again, the next guy on their list came to mind. If he grabbed Lucy by the neck and ordered Peter to hand the money over, what could the boy do except comply?

Checking my list, I saw *Cops?* "Have you considered going to the police with your concerns? It's how we do things in a civilized society."

Lucy's dark eyes snapped. "Oh, we tried your *civilized* method. They might as well have patted my head and sent me home to take a nap."

"Why do you think that was?" I hoped she'd at least entertain the idea that her story wasn't believable.

"The officer wanted Peter to tell it," Lucy replied. "When I explained about his scopophobia, I got that blank look people put on when they're waiting for you to stop talking so they can tell you no."

That brought me to the final question, which I needed them both to agree to. "If I look into Oscar's activities, are you willing to delay any action you have in mind until I finish?"

Lucy glanced at Peter, who nodded agreement. "We've developed some strategies to keep him distracted and unable to implement his plan."

"Strategies?"

"Guerilla tactics. They'll make it difficult for him to concentrate."

"Guerilla—?"

She counted off examples on her fingers. "Jeb Stuart in the Civil War. The Lusitanians against the Romans. The Seljuk Turks against the Byzantines. The Viet Cong against U.S. troops. You keep the enemy on edge with unexpected interruptions and small inconveniences. It's often as simple as lobbing dried peas at him with a slingshot." She giggled. "You should see Oscar slap at his neck and look around for bugs."

"That sounds like the bratty kids you assured me you weren't."

Shivering, Lucy crossed her arms. "We're underdogs, Mr. Dunham, with no support and no way to defeat a powerful enemy. To even the field, we use harassment. It might seem silly to you, but it helps our morale to feel like we're fighting back."

I recalled Polly's comment about peanut butter on the seat of Oscar's pants. "Tell me about your guerilla tactics."

Lucy grinned, and Peter made the odd noise I now recognized as his version of laughter. "This morning Peter cut a bar of soap into flakes and stirred it into Oscar's trail mix."

"That's—" What could I say? ...*beneath you*? ...*mean*? Kids often pester authority figures they don't like. Ask any substitute teacher. I settled for "—counterproductive."

"Why?" Lucy demanded. "He's planning to murder one of us. How much worse will things get if he's mad at us?"

If the kids pranked Oscar regularly, he knew they had issues with him. I shivered a little myself, thinking it might become my responsibility to tell the man that the situation was worse than soap flakes in his granola.

The next few minutes were frustrating. The best I was able to achieve was three days in which to study the problem. Lucy made it clear that if at the end of that time I didn't agree to help, I was honor-bound to keep my mouth shut. "If you break your word," she warned, "we'll claim you tried to extort money from us." Sounding almost sad, she added, "Being rich means we can afford really good lawyers, and they'll make you look like the worst kind of con man."

With that warning, they took up their coats and prepared to leave. "Remember," I said as Lucy zipped her jacket all the way, so her neck was completely covered, "don't try to...don't attempt...anything on your own till we talk again. If you feel like you have to continue the guerilla stuff, keep it mild, okay?"

She stopped at the door, her expression patient. "We don't *want* to kill Oscar, Mr. Dunham. We've promised three days, and unlike most of the people we've met in this world of yours, we don't give our word lightly. When that time is up, we'll launch a preemptive strike to protect ourselves, with your help or without."

Bobby saw the Gages out with a line of bright chatter and a wish for them to have a great rest of their day. I watched from my window until they emerged from the entry below and turned toward the street. Lucy's steps on the wet pavement were as light as a filly's, while Peter's were as plodding as a plow horse. Opposites, dedicated to each other by blood and bonded by circumstance.

I bagged up the trash (I maintain a constant battle with mice in my rented piece of heaven), and then removed the dickey and stuck it at the back of a filing cabinet, under some old papers. After some hesitation, I put the ceramic fruit in there too. I'd get new stuff, something in brass, maybe. Bold. Masculine. Caught up in the mood, I took down the green and turquoise curtains and stood back. The window looked okay with only the dark-toned wooden blind. Rugged.

When Mom got back from Florida, I'd tell her…something.

Bobby leaned against the doorframe, watching. "Who were they? I filled out File 13, but I'm pretty sure every answer Lucy gave was a lie."

I summarized the story, leaving out the hiring-a-hitman part. I ended with, "They think this guy Oscar is a villain straight out of Lemony Snicket. Once I prove they're mistaken, I can hop a plane to Cabo San Lucas with a clear conscience."

"You don't think there's something to it? The girl seems smart."

"Smart doesn't mean mentally competent," I warned. "How likely is it that a judge handed two kids over to a murderer?"

"He wouldn't be the first lawyer who helps himself to the funds of a client too old or too young to check up on him."

"But isn't it more likely the kids are reacting to stress? They recently lost their remaining parent. They have more money than they'll ever be able to spend and no idea how to handle it. They're living in a culture they only observed up to now." I leaned back in my chair. "I think they're inventing conspiracy theories for their own strange reasons."

"And they picked you to dump their paranoid fantasies on."

"Yup. Lucy claims Peter overheard this plot in a phone call, but Oscar could have been blowing off steam. Or Peter's issues might have colored his interpretation of what he heard. The topic of conversation could have switched, and he blended two threads in his mind. Or he might just be angry at the man who controls his future."

"Yeah, kids his age think they don't need somebody telling them what to do." Bobby burped before asking, "Should we contact the cops?"

"They tried that. Lucy says they were ignored."

"Maybe the police looked into it and decided they're wrong."

"If the cops told Oscar, they probably got an earful. Lucy says he loves telling others how odd she and Peter are. Still, she admits he isn't malicious about it, just insensitive."

"You are so kewl, Max." Bobby tapped his own forehead. "I love seeing your thought process. Lots of guys would have blown those kids off in five minutes. You fed them pizza, listened to them, and now you're trying to figure out how to help, though you doubt there's any real threat."

I chuckled. "That's how I make the big bucks." I hadn't mentioned the money amount, but I'm not sure if that was me being careful or if I was embarrassed to admit I'd been offered a ten-thousand-dollar bribe and hadn't turned it down cold.

Bobby went off to deal with the daily emails, and I went back to my research. Oscar Coburn's standard of living had taken a big step up since Raymond Gage died. He'd had an apartment in Shelby Township, but now he lived with Peter and Lucy in a beautiful home north of the city. He had access to two expensive cars owned by the estate. In January he'd spent a four-day weekend at a resort in Aruba, no doubt on the kids' dime.

Adam Saracco did general work around the house and drove the kids to school and back each day. Lucy had mentioned that he also took Oscar to work most days, which made me envious. Detroit's maze of freeways, always under construction, is often snow-covered and slippery in winter. Having a driver would be heavenly.

The nanny, Ilsa Dausman, was originally from Austria, so I looked her up on the INS website. Her papers were in order and good until 2028. The cleaning woman's paperwork was good too.

Next, I checked social media, a lazy but quick way to get to know people. The kids weren't there, nor was Oscar, but Ilsa appeared to be working as a nanny only until she got her big break in show business. In every photo posted, she leaned toward the camera, showing bright blue eyes and lots of cleavage. That brought into question her qualifications as a nanny, but I avoided drawing conclusions. Hedy Lamarr had a brilliant mind behind all that sex and sizzle.

Though he had a presence on three sites, Adam Saracco seemed largely uninterested in sharing. He'd posted only a few times, mostly pictures: the American flag, a back view of him holding what looked like an automatic weapon, and a poster from the original *Rambo* movie.

At the Register of Wills site, I was able to read documents pertaining to the kids' situation, since guardianships are a matter of public record in Michigan. As the firm's representative, Oscar was required to submit an annual accounting to the court. That was good, though any decent lawyer could probably have his way with the kids' funds and still make it look okay. As Lucy had put it, to whom could they complain?

Oscar needed to have at least one Gage child alive to continue his present lifestyle. Raymond's will stipulated that if both Peter and Lucy died before reaching eighteen, the money went to charity, a large chunk to an organization called Crocodiles of the World. Some comedian's tagline summarized my thought: "You can't make this stuff up."

Going back to the Coburn Law site, I read up on the other associates. Sara Dailey, the niece Lucy mentioned, had taken over leadership of the firm late in 2019, when it became clear Carson Coburn would not be returning to work. She specialized in contracts, and her page described her as "dedicated to the protection of clients' assets and peace of mind." An array of photos showed Sara attending benefits and ribbon-cuttings.

Oscar's younger brother Kevin's page was spare, a short bio and a headshot of a self-conscious, round-faced forty-something. *Nerd* is the descriptor that came to mind, though I know better than to judge a person from a single photo. Kevin graduated law school in 2018, which seemed late, considering his age. He was described as the firm's "Litigation Initiator," and reading on, I deduced that meant Old Kev actually did the firm's ambulance chasing. A disclaimer in fine print at the bottom of his page stated, "In some instances, your case may be referred to one of our outstanding collaborating firms." I took that to mean that after he snagged clients, the firm farmed out the less lucrative cases to other lawyers for a share of the profits.

The last attorney featured on the Coburn Law website was recent law school graduate Marla Johnson, a capable handler of wills, deeds, and trusts, according to her bio. Her page was more complete and up to date than the others, with tidbits of interest, client reviews, and examples of cases she'd worked in her short tenure at the firm. Ms. Johnson obviously subscribed to the belief that in today's legal world, attorneys either toot their own horns or get ignored.

Returning to social media, I found that Cousin Sara participated only at LinkedIn. Kevin posted here and there on Facebook and Instagram, mostly about fantasy sports leagues he was part of. Marla Johnson was active on a half-dozen sites, sharing photos of herself all over the city, busy with her career and loving it.

I sat back for a moment, letting questions come to mind. Married with a teenaged son, Kevin seemed the obvious choice for guardian of two orphans. While Sara had no children, she'd released the official statement of Raymond Gage's death, calling herself a friend of the Gage family. If they'd been close, why hadn't Sara stepped up to care for the kids?

Whatever the reason, Oscar had the job. The question I had to answer was simple: Was he abusing his role and scarfing up benefits like a bear in a berry patch? I intended to find out before it was time to head for the airport on Saturday.

Checking the grandmother clock Mom bought at St. Vincent's, I saw it was closing time. Bobby had gone a half hour earlier, calling a breezy farewell. I tidied my desk and headed home, which wasn't much of a trip, since my office and my apartment are less than twenty feet apart. The owners of my building, Lifesaver Insurance, allow me to work and live rent-free for several reasons. First, I do leg work for them, identifying cheaters and proving that's what they are. Second, having a licensed investigator on the premises discourages break-ins. Finally, the suite I occupy is removed from the other offices in the building, and that's putting it mildly. While most are on the ground floor, I'm two stories up and at the back of the building. My clients could enter through the front doors, but they'd have to ride the world's slowest elevator up to the third floor and then follow a long hallway to the back. They'd pass between the HVAC plant and the computer tech's work room, and then past two large storage areas that smell of machine oil and dust. Most visitors use the back stairs, which require a little effort but lead directly to my suite. An added advantage to that entrance is privacy, with fewer people seeing and speculating as to what a client's business is with a private eye.

While the spot might have been punishment for some long-ago executive who didn't work well with others, I like having no neighbors. My suite consists of a twelve by ten anteroom with larger rooms on either side. I made the twelve by fifteen one on the left my office. The other space, twelve by twenty-four, is home, with a microwave, fridge, bed, TV, my weights, and a love seat. The anteroom has half-baths along one wall marked "Men" and "Women." Being somewhat traditional, I use the men's when I have the urge, day or night.

The lack of a full bath meant that for a while I had to shower at the local gym. Then I met the firm's tech guy, Benny. Since insurance companies know OSHA's rules on hazardous materials better than most, there's an industrial shower in one corner of Benny's work room. Being a good guy, he gave me an extra key. Before any of the staff arrives on a given morning, I've already used the Emergency Shower and Eyewash Station, mopped up the wet spots, and returned to my own space.

I set the chicken pot pie I'd chosen for dinner in the toaster oven and waited, humming tunelessly. With thoughts of the Gage kids, Oscar Coburn, and Cabo swirling in my head, one might think I ate without enjoyment, paced the floor until bedtime, and then tossed and turned all night. I'm not that kind of guy. I watched some TV, checked Instagram for funny memes, and played a few games of *Clocktower*. At ten-thirty I went to bed and slept like the proverbial baby. It's mind over matter. You set the day aside and let your subconscious mind catalog input. That way, Mom always says, your mind and your body will be ready to solve problems when you wake up.

CHAPTER THREE

Tuesday morning, I was in the office early. Though I believed Peter and Lucy had misjudged their guardian, two things kept me from cutting them loose. One was that they—well, one of them—might be in danger. The other was that even if they weren't, they thought they were, and I didn't want them trying to rectify the situation on their own.

I texted Lucy at the number she'd given me. *Will observe O today.* In a few seconds I got an answer. *O in court this a.m. Delaying tactics ongoing.* Not sure I wanted to know about that, I checked the court schedule to see where Oscar Coburn would argue a case today.

Next, I contacted my research assistant, Mom. My parents winter in Florida, where Dad plays golf four days a week, more often if the weather's good. Mom attends pool exercise sessions, "does" lunch with this girl or those girls, and futzes around their condo, making sure the throw pillows exactly match the drapes. She also spends a lot of time on the computer. While that's not unusual, Mom's intense, almost creepy, interest in crime is. Over the last few years, she's developed a talent for ferreting out bits of information that she puts together, forming conclusions that are amazingly accurate. Mom refers to her online sleuthing as a guilty pleasure, "like a reality show without commercials and an irritating host." My maternal parent, a retired second-grade teacher, has in retirement become a top-notch hacker, with skills that both amuse and scare me.

It started when I was a Detroit police officer. I lived at home then, and at night when we sat down to dinner, Mom would ask about my day. As I told stories of drug trafficking and fraud, Mom listened with both ears. Dad watched TV over her shoulder, shoveling lasagna or Swiss steak into his mouth in large forkfuls and disposing of it with minimal chewing. If he tuned in from time to time, he was likely to offer advice like, "Son, you need to get out of that job before you get popped by some gang-banger."

Mom never worried about stuff like that. She trusts God will look after her youngest child, since she sends Him reminders daily. With such concerns left to the Lord, Mom probed for details on how certain cases were handled after the police made an arrest. Being a lowly officer, I didn't always know what happened to arrestees, so Mom started digging into online records and news reports to find out. Days, sometimes weeks later, she'd fill us in at dinner about who'd been bound over for trial and who was released for lack of evidence. As time went on, her bulletins began revealing more than the average citizen should know about how the city and my department worked— or didn't, in some cases. She was aware of deals made behind closed doors and that some charges were dismissed due to police or prosecutorial misconduct. One night as she cleaned the kitchen and I loaded the dishwasher, I asked, "Mom, you're not going into places on the internet you shouldn't, are you?"

Her answer was a funny little smile and a comment. "Two words, Max: *plausible deniability*."

I worried about Mom's snooping, but she seemed to be good at it, and the info she found was sometimes helpful. A detective in our precinct, Tom Disney, treated us street officers like we were human beings, hanging out at the front desk to chat or texting us to say thanks when we contributed to his cases. When Mom's revelations seemed pertinent, I'd take Disney aside and say something like, "You might look for a connection between the murder victim's pastor and his girlfriend." When a few of my suggestions panned out, Disney decided I was the new Sherlock Holmes. Though pleased to help, I never revealed my source. Who starts a hot tip with, "My mom says—"?

In my six years as a Detroit cop, I learned that it requires courage every single day to deal with the worst of our society's people. It also takes emotional strength to keep from starting to see everyone you meet as the enemy. I could handle those things, but the job also requires doing what the brass orders each shift instead of a dozen other things we could do to help people. One day, standing between a group of protestors and a city councilman who was a loud-mouthed bigot with the IQ of a millipede, I decided I was done with being a cog in a wheel. I wanted to become a P.I. and choose my own jobs. Screw the guaranteed medical.

Dad saw the move as dumb. Mom saw it as my destiny. On my birthday and at Christmas, she bought me new tools for agency business, some useful, some a little weird. I've never used the phone jammer she bought me, or the SpyGuy thing that would allow me to eavesdrop on phone calls within fifty feet. I'm no James Bond, though it's clear Mom thinks I'm close.

What I have found helpful is her talent with computers. She ferrets out information I'd never learn by asking, and no one knows how I got it. Yes, it's hacking, but Mom insists she's no Black Hat. "No malicious intent, Max." She'd never fix a parking ticket or erase a DUI charge for a client. When I express guilt that she spends so much time in front of a computer for my benefit, Mom waves it off, saying it's the most useful she's felt since she left the classroom.

Mom was 1500 miles away in Fort Myers, but that's no problem in the age of technology. I waited until 7:00 a.m., when Dad would be on his way to the Oaks Golf Course. Mom would be drinking coffee on the patio (in the afternoon it's sangria with lots of ice), which overlooks a canal where alligators come onto the lawn to sun themselves. That brought Amy Gage to mind and I winced, hoping she'd died quickly.

"Hi, Sweetie," Mom said. "It's good to hear from you."

"Is everything okay in sunny Florida?"

"Hunky dory. How about you?"

"I need your help." I told her about the Gage kids, and she listened carefully. When I finished, she asked, "What can I do to help?"

"Get me everything you can about Oscar Coburn. I've already seen the easy-to-find stuff on the law firm's website and mentions in the news. He seems legit, at least for a lawyer, but he's also not shy about milking the Gage estate for perks. I need to decide if there's even a remote possibility the kids are right about him plotting to kill one of them."

"If this guy's spending two orphan's money like it's his, you *know* he's a crook."

"It's rotten," I cautioned, "but it's not necessarily illegal, and it isn't like he's taking bread out of their mouths or anything."

"All right," Mom said. "Maybe things are copacetic, but I intend to look long and hard at the guy."

"If we decide Oscar is okay, I'm going to have to warn him to watch his back." I mentioned the amount Lucy had offered and heard Mom gasp. "These kids might need counselling or some form of intervention. Plotting to murder your guardian isn't normal."

I heard her fingernails click, as if she were anticipating keystrokes she'd soon be making. "We'll see what's what."

Leaving her to tackle the internet, I got ready to head to the courthouse. I don't exert much effort dreaming up disguises, but a guy can change his appearance in minor ways. The day was sunny but crisp, so I chose a puffy coat Mom bought me that I didn't like much, covered my hair with a toque, and put on a pair of black-rimmed glasses with non-prescription lenses. Checking the full-length mirror attached to the door, I decided I looked more like Austin Powers on the ski slopes than Max Dunham on a case.

It wasn't far from the Lifesaver building to the 36th District Court on Madison Avenue, so I walked, eliminating the need to find a parking spot for my Mustang. My breath made little puffs of steam as I walked, and the sidewalk was icy in places, but overall, the trip was invigorating.

The trial Oscar Coburn was involved in was on the 4th floor. Once I passed the security screening, I took the stairs, unwilling to wait for the elevator. I confess, I was eager to see the "depraved" guardian in action, and a trial is free entertainment (if you can stand the snail-like pace), a little drama with crime, legal pomp, pathos, and often, glints of humor.

There were a few frowns when I opened the door, but the prosecutor was speaking, and attention quickly returned to her. Oscar's back was to me, and he was busily taking notes. Choosing a seat where he was unlikely to look directly at me, I slid silently into place.

The prosecutor finished her summary, and the judge asked if defense counsel was ready to proceed. I got my first good look at Oscar in the flesh as he rose to state in rolling tones that the defense was indeed ready.

I'd come in too late to get the particulars, but I recognized the defendant. Melvin Cruse had been arrested multiple times over thirty years for a range of offenses. He'd even been charged with murder during my cop days, but he was later released due to some procedural foul-up. While every accused criminal is entitled to the best representation possible, I would never have agreed to be Cruse's lawyer. Being in the same room with him made me want to go home and take a second shower.

Today's question was whether Cruse had extorted money from a downtown pizza parlor for "protection" from harassment and property damage. The Assistant District Attorney claimed the case was proven, but it was Oscar's turn. He called Harlan Sweeney as his first witness.

A beat-down looking man with a weak chin and a need for a decent haircut, Sweeney hurried to the witness box as if he were running a gauntlet. When he reached the chair he sat down, relief evident, but had to be asked to stand again for the swearing in. His face flushed as he obeyed, but his voice was firm as he agreed that he would tell the truth in the proceedings.

Oscar waited at the defense table until the witness was seated again. Then he approached and said in a friendly tone, "Mr. Sweeney, you're the father of David Sweeney, who testified earlier in this trial, correct?"

"Yes." After a moment he added, "Sir."

"And you're aware that your son told the court that he overheard my client and his employer talking on the twelfth of July last year."

"I am." Sweeney's expression was earnest but slightly confused, and I guessed he wasn't sure why he'd been called for the defense.

"Could you tell the court if your boy ever lies, Mr. Sweeney?"

The ADA was on her feet in an instant. "Objection."

Oscar was unruffled. "Setting the stage, Your Honor."

The judge, a dour-looking older woman, said, "Overruled. Tread carefully, Mr. Coburn."

"Yes, Your Honor."

Sweeney followed the conversation with interest, turning his head to look at each speaker as if seeking direction. Oscar stepped a little closer to the witness stand. "Mr. Sweeney, has your son ever told stories that turned out to be untrue?" When Sweeney hesitated, he went on in a friendly manner, "I recently took responsibility for a boy the same age as your David and a girl a little younger, and I've learned to question some of the things they tell me. Do you know what I mean?"

Sweeney nodded, probably unaware he was doing so. "I guess kids fib sometimes."

"My two often invent tales that make them look like heroes." Oscar made a wide gesture. "The boy saw something no one else did and saved his family from mortal danger. The girl helped to avert a catastrophe." Lucy's snake story came to mind, but I focused on Oscar, who leaned toward Sweeney and lowered his voice a little. "Does your son ever exaggerate to make himself feel important?"

Seeing where it was headed, Sweeney shook his head, causing the hair he'd stuck behind his ears to fall along the sides of his face. "David wouldn't lie to the police or in court. He's not like that."

"What if he didn't intend for it to go that far?" Oscar asked mildly. "What if he didn't hear what was said or thought he recognized my client but later realized he was mistaken?" Turning toward the jury, he said, "It's hard to step back from something once you've said it, right?"

"Objection," the other lawyer said. "Calls for speculation."

The witness answered anyway. "My son wouldn't lie to the police."

Oscar backed away, both figuratively and literally, but he faced Sweeney directly. "David told you he overheard his boss talking to another man, and the stranger threatened Mr. Polaski."

"That's right."

"This stranger said, 'Pay up, or we'll burn your place to the ground.'"

"Yeah. That's what Davey told me."

After a few seconds, Oscar said thoughtfully, "Sounds like a line from a movie, doesn't it?"

Sweeney's chin jutted. "He heard what he heard."

"As you say. I merely pointed out that it's very…dramatic." Sweeney opened his mouth, but Oscar went on. "Your boy testified that when he got home from work that night, he told you what he thought he'd seen and heard. You said he had to go to the police with the information. Was he willing to do that?"

Sweeney squirmed in the chair. "Well, he was nervous about it, like anybody would be. But it was the right thing to do."

"I commend your dedication to public good, Mr. Sweeney, but why do you think David wasn't eager to repeat the story?"

"He didn't say he *wouldn't*. He was…concerned. Your client is—"

Oscar spoke before he could finish. "David's boss, Mr. Polaski, hasn't confirmed your son's story, has he?"

Sweeney shifted in his chair. "Well, no. I figure he's scared to."

Now Oscar's tone turned gently chiding. "You can't possibly know what's in Mr. Polaski's mind, Mr. Sweeney. Let's stick to the facts." The man's chin lifted as if he'd like to argue the point, but a glance at the judge's stern countenance made him bow his head and remain silent. Oscar turned to the jury again, though he spoke to Sweeney. "What we have are two conflicting stories. Your son says his boss was threatened. His boss says he wasn't. Your son says the man he saw talking to Mr. Polaski was Melvin Cruse. Polaski says it was a passer-by asking for directions." Silence fell as Oscar went to the defense table, picked up a sheet of paper, and consulted it as if seeing it for the first time.

"Do you remember an incident in which you found you were missing a bottle of Gray Goose vodka? I believe you'd won it in a raffle and were saving it for a special occasion."

Sweeney swallowed before answering. "I guess."

"What did your son say when you asked about the missing liquor?"

The answer was a mutter, and the judge growled, "Speak up, Mr. Sweeney."

The man's face reddened as he said, "He told me his mom stopped by, and she took it."

"And was that true?"

His head drooped, and his voice dropped again to a whisper. "No."

"Isn't it true your neighbor found the empty bottle in her trash bin? Didn't you learn your wife was in Lansing that day, visiting her sister?"

Sweeney's head fell even lower. "Yes."

"David's mother doesn't live with you and David?"

"No. She…found herself a new man."

"And left her son behind."

Sweeney's voice dropped. "Yes."

"Did David take his mother's abandonment badly?"

"Something like that's bound to be hard on a boy."

Oscar nodded sympathetically. "The kids I mentioned earlier, the ones I care for now, lost both their parents. I believe the reason they make up stories is because they'd like things to be different." He paused before asking, "Does your son wish things were different at home?"

"Maybe, but that's—"

"David lied about the liquor, didn't he? He and some of his buddies drank it, and he blamed his mother because he's angry. Isn't that right?"

Sweeney shook his head. "It ain't the same thing. Kids want to try liquor, and they don't want to get in trouble when they get caught, so they lie. Davey telling what he heard at the store that night, that's the truth."

"A story that makes an unhappy boy feel important." Oscar turned his back on the witness. "No further questions."

The DDA asked some questions that allowed Sweeney to repeat that he trusted his son, rebuilding what she could of the boy's credibility. When she finished, the man was excused, and the trial went on. I watched as three different witnesses touted the many good qualities of Melvin Cruse. One of them, his current girlfriend, might even have meant what she said. She claimed he was with her on the day in question, and though the prosecutor tried to make her admit she was lying, she was the type that avoids being proven a liar by simply refusing to let herself believe she's lying. She got the indignant tone of voice right and everything.

The judge seemed to be napping while the prosecution attempted to disprove the glowing opinions given. I couldn't predict the result, but given the victim's unwillingness to admit to being threatened and the doubt Oscar Coburn had cast on the only witness to the threats, things weren't going well for the state of Michigan.

The clincher came at the end, when Coburn called Steven Balough to the stand. Balough had a just-missed-dreamy face, handsome enough but lacking something somewhere. He wore deep-blue jeans and a shirt more suited to the local cowboy bar than a courtroom. "Mr. Balough, you were once a member of the Detroit Police Department, correct?"

"Yes."

"You worked your way up to detective?"

"Yes."

"And then you were fired."

A second of hesitation. "Yes."

I studied Balough's face, trying to decide if I knew him from my days on the force. I didn't, but I detected a trace of arrogance I'd never liked in a cop, a hint he saw himself as above the law, not a servant of it.

"Why were you fired?"

"They said I fabricated evidence."

"'They said?' You don't accept that?"

"No."

"Tell us what happened."

"We had this case, a guy that was supposedly strong-arming business owners in the downtown area. The more I looked into it, the more I thought we were barking up the wrong tree." He glanced around the courtroom as if searching for a friendly face. "I said that out loud, and all of a sudden I'm in trouble."

"What kind of trouble?"

"This drug deal goes down, and some money comes up missing. They found it in my locker."

"Who decided to search your locker, and why?"

"I don't know."

"Did you put that money in your locker?"

"No way."

"You didn't skim a little off the night's take for yourself?"

"No, sir, I did not."

Oscar approached the jury and put a hand on the railing that separated them from him. "Who'd do something like that, Detective Balough, and why?"

"I don't know who," the witness said resentfully, "but I know why. The other guys in the squad wanted Mel Cruse real bad. They didn't like that I wouldn't go along."

"The detectives in your squad wanted my client, Mr. Cruse, 'real bad.'" Oscar came back toward the witness, running his hand along the railing. "Do you mean bad enough to lie to get him convicted?"

Balough sniffed. "They lied about me, and I was one of them. I doubt they'd have a problem lying about a guy they think belongs in prison."

A stir went through the courtroom, anger from some and shock from others. The defendant put a fist over his mouth and coughed, and I sensed he was hiding a smile. "No further questions." Oscar returned to his seat, his gaze sweeping the jurors to let them know he'd scored big.

The prosecutor countered Balough's testimony, forcing him to admit he had no idea who'd set him up and didn't have proof that anyone did. His enemies were a vague "they," and their reasons were unclear. She asked why the police would conspire to take down one man when they dealt with dozens of criminals daily. She got Balough to admit his testimony was nothing but assertions. Still, he came across as aggrieved and wronged. I wondered how many on the jury would believe his story.

All it would take was one juror with a lying teenager or a grudge against cops, and Cruse would be back on the streets. Again.

When the defense rested, the judge informed the jury she would give instructions when they reconvened after lunch. As people shuffled out of the room, I hung back, ostensibly reading some plaques hung along the back wall. Oscar and the prosecutor appeared to be on good terms. I guess all's fair in the courtroom. As they each filed papers in various slots in their briefcases she asked, "How are you doing with those kids you mentioned?"

"Good, good. Peter tears through everything the academy can teach him." After a pause he added, "I only hope he gets over his fascination with practical jokes soon."

The woman chuckled. "My nephew went through a phase like that."

"The nanny had a screaming fit yesterday because she found a tarantula on her bedspread. It turned out to be plastic, but it was apparently very realistic from a distance."

"Ugh! How about the girl—Linda, is it?"

"Lucy. I believe we've managed to convince her that taking two showers a week won't wreck the planet. God knows, she can certainly afford the water bill."

"You said they tell lies?"

He chuckled. "Sometimes. As I said, I've learned to—"

Oscar made a sound of disgust. "Ugh."

"What is it?"

I looked over my shoulder to see him pull a plastic zipper bag from a file slot in his briefcase. When he'd jammed a folder into place, the bag's seal had failed. Something dark and viscous ran onto his hand, his notes, and the table.

"What's that?" the ADA asked.

He sniffed at it. "Smells like molasses." Taking a clean handkerchief out of his pocket, he tried unsuccessfully to wipe up the mess.

"You're going to need soap and water," his companion said.

He sighed. "Yeah."

"They did that?"

Oscar dabbed at a sticky spot on his sleeve. "They're mad at me."

"And that's how they get back at you?"

He put up a hand. "Honestly, they're great most of the time, but they've been upset the last few days. I've tried to get one or the other to tell me what's wrong, but...I suppose I'll have to act like a lawyer and give them the third degree." Tossing the bag and the damaged papers into the briefcase, he closed it, giving the DDA a rueful smile. "We'll be okay once they learn to trust me."

"You're a good guy, Oscar."

"Taking responsibility for two young lives is new to me." He made a rueful grimace. "I make mistakes, do and say the wrong things."

Half turned toward them, I saw the woman put a hand on Oscar's arm. "They'll come around."

They started for the door, so I turned away, leaning close as if reading the inscriptions. "Most days are okay," Oscar said as he opened the door for his companion, "but some days I don't know what to do."

When they were gone, I left the courtroom, adding up what I now knew about Oscar Coburn. As a lawyer, he pulled out all the stops. Since I wasn't born yesterday, I acknowledged that the practice of law requires such tactics. As a replacement parent, Oscar seemed understanding and a little overwhelmed.

Were Peter and Lucy Gage pranking me? If so, why? Why now? Why the outlandish story? Why the dire threat? Was it a joke for a couple of rich kids prone to acting out?

I tried to imagine which of my friends would think it was funny to set two nutty kids on me while I was trying to get my ducks in a row to head south. Nobody I knew was that sadistic, or that weird.

A disturbing thought arose. What if the kids planned to murder Oscar and blame it on me? If Peter bashed in his guardian's head with his trusty ball bat tonight, would I be implicated somehow?

CHAPTER FOUR

To better understand Peter and Lucy Gage, I needed to hear what people who interacted with them daily had to say about them. Hired help usually knows exactly how honest their employers are, so Ilsa Dausman and Adam Saracco were first on my list.

Asking direct questions at the outset of an investigation, at a point where you have no idea which way things are going to go, limits your options in a big way. To get around that, I called Bobby, whose classes were just getting done for the day. "Are you up for some undercover detective work this afternoon?"

"Undercover?" It was like tossing a steak to a Rottweiler. Bobby believes the essence of a P.I.'s job is disguise and dissembling. I explain that the keys to success are astute observation and careful sifting of information, but Bobby still pictures himself as the Man of a Thousand Faces. When I think about it, being Bobby is so exhausting that playing a role might seem like a mini vacation.

"So you really think I can do this?" Before I could answer he asked, "What's my character?"

Ignoring the first question, I replied to the second. "A neighbor? A jogger, maybe."

"So you think they'd believe I'm a jogger? It's not like I look athletic." Again, he went right on. "So why did I stop today? Why not yesterday or the day before?"

"We can talk about that on the way out there."

"You're sure I can do this?" A breath, then, "Am I gay or straight?"

"Does that matter?"

"Gay might be easier. The stereotype, you know? Gays love to chat?" I shook my head, but then he hit on a better idea. "What if I'm a potential home buyer?"

"Good idea. You can mention you have kids and get them talking."

"That helps with what to wear. How will I get in? It's gated, right?"

"I've got a plan. I'll pick you up in twenty."

As Bobby hung up to fuss over his disguise, I searched the residents' guide for Deer Creek Estates, the gated community where Lucy and Peter lived. Details about those places aren't public knowledge, but I subscribe to a range of apps and websites that provide deeper knowledge than the average surfer finds. All it usually takes is money and a promise that I won't use the information to harass or harm anyone.

Like apartment buildings where visitors must be buzzed in, gated communities are only as secure as the people living there allow them to be. In the listing I found two elderly residents who lived alone within a few blocks of the Gage place. The first one was so deaf I couldn't make myself understood, but the second was better. When I claimed to be a distant relative researching the history of "our" family, she agreed to let me interview her. I'd have to listen to an old woman's reminiscences for an hour or so, but she agreed to call security and have them let my car through the gate. While I chatted with the old lady, Bobby could pump the hired help for information about the Gages.

Deer Creek Estates was an exclusive, expensive development about twelve miles north of the Coburn Law Firm's offices in Southfield. I gave my name at the guard station, said I was visiting Dinah Ellerson, and was allowed in. The lots were big, at least an acre each. Some were half hidden behind enclosing walls and metal fences. Those without enclosures were impressive too, and in my humble opinion, looked more like homes and less like high-end mental hospitals.

Driving past the Gage house, which was mostly invisible due to garrison fencing with twelve-foot metal spikes, I pulled over at the next corner. Bobby threw off the blanket he'd been hiding under in the back seat and climbed out. He wore normal clothes, but he'd added a wig and glasses that had to be leftovers from a Bring Back the '70s party. With a wave, he headed off toward #815 while I went on to #1103.

Dinah Ellerson was likeable, despite dentures that no longer fit well and a pronounced stoop. She invited me into her lovely home with the enthusiasm of one who doesn't get much company, and we sat down on opposite ends of her couch with a box of mementos and photos between. Passing pictures to me one by one, she talked about the family, admitting without shame that her father had become wealthy running booze to Detroit from Windsor, Ontario, during Prohibition. I took notes and even found myself laughing at stories of Grandpa Harrier braving the waters of Lake Saint Clair in the dark of night to escape the cops. "The law is an odd thing," she observed as she ended his saga. "It carries the might of policy but can't operate effectively if hosts of average citizens dislike it."

I enjoyed the hour with Mrs. Ellerson, though I almost choked on the amaretto-flavored coffee she served. I often ask myself what happened to coffee with no vanilla, no cinnamon, no latte, no nothing except ground-up beans, but I never come up with a good answer. Unwilling to complain aloud, I said I was watching my caffeine intake and couldn't have a second cup.

After thanking my host for her help and for a plateful of homemade cookies she insisted I take away with me, I drove back to where I'd dropped Bobby off and parked on the roadside. Cars went by that were three, eight, maybe even twelve times more valuable than my 2004 Mustang, but I spoke lovingly to it.

"Don't hang your grill, Baby. Those are toys of the moment. You're a classic."

Bobby didn't show for what seemed like a long time, so I messaged Mom, adding the Gages' nanny, Ilsa Dausman, and their driver, Adam Saracco, to her list of people to research. Lucy claimed they were both "too dumb to plan a crime, much less carry it out." Still, if Oscar planned to harm the kids, he'd hire employees unlikely to question what he said and did.

I got back two words from Mom: *On it.* I played one game of *Sniper* before my message app dinged. *Saracco served four years for burglary,* Mom had written. *Details emailed.*

At that moment Bobby finally appeared, exiting a drive across the street and several properties down.

"What were you doing?" I asked when he got into the car.

"Extending the cover," he replied. "How would it look if people at the Gage house heard that no one else met a prospective buyer today?"

"I bet everyone here compares notes daily on stuff like that," I said sarcastically. "What did you find out?"

"Well, I had to hang around a while, but it helped that the sun is out." He veered into Bobby-speak, and I repressed an urge to bop him on the forehead. Bobby's stories have asides attached to the asides. "I don't know about you, but for me, the three months from the winter solstice to the spring equinox in Michigan seems like three years. By February, everyone is dying for a little sunlight. So even though the temperature is only forty degrees, I figured someone would come outside eventually."

"And someone did?" It was a pitiful attempt, and Bobby ignored it.

"So the house is gorgeous, did you get a good look at it? I mean, it's like a modern-day castle, with mixed roof pitches, windows of different shapes and sizes, and cobblestoned walkways. That fencing goes all the way around, which kinda gives it a prison feel, but I'd say they paid at least a million for it."

"They can afford it." Forcing a patient tone, I prodded, "Did you get to talk to anyone?"

"So this honking big BMW sat outside the front entrance, and this man came out with a bucket and a rag and started washing the road salt off the rocker panels. Can you believe that?"

"Adam Saracco. Tell me about him."

"Muscular build, average height, not the chatty type. A face like a peasant in a Brueghel painting."

I didn't get the art reference, but I got the idea. "You spoke to him?"

"I said I was looking to buy at Deer Creek and wanted input from property owners." Bobby turned in the seat to face me directly. "An appeal to his vanity, yeah? Pretending I thought he owned the place."

"And did he fall for that?"

His smile disappeared. "Well, no. He gave me this up-and-down look and said, 'You couldn't afford to rent a room over somebody's garage.'" Fingering the untidy wig, Bobby added, "If I'd had more time to get a disguise together, I'd have done better. I mean, if you look at second-hand stores, you find really nice scarves and stuff." He scratched at his scalp, and the wig wiggled. "The right clothes give you a better attitude too. If you look the part, people don't question that you're wealthy enough to own a house out here."

Picturing the ex-con zeroing in on Bobby like a hound sniffing a new dog in the kennel, I knew if I'd gone myself, Adam would have smelled cop for sure. "Did he talk about the Gages?"

"No. In fact, he planted his feet kind of wide and started cracking his knuckles. I've done a bunch of reading on body language, so I know that's a precursor to a threat of some kind. But this voice behind me says, 'Here is the package, Adam.' It was the nanny."

"Ilsa Dausman."

"You didn't tell me she was hot."

"I didn't notice," I lied. "What's she like?"

"So she's got this accent, and it's really cute. I always wanted to be able to do accents. They say you gotta have an ear for it, but—"

"You talked to her?"

"Um, yeah. I gave her my spiel about asking homeowners for advice, and she giggles real high and says, 'Oh, sir. Ve don't own this place. Ve only vork here.'" Bobby tried to do the accent, and no, he didn't have the ear for it. "She's flirty. Kept batting her eyes at me and at the driver too."

"How did he react?"

"No interest. She did tell him she'd seen a mouse in the kitchen this morning, which seemed to please him. He said he'd pick up some traps on his way back from the post office." Bobby chuckled. "He seemed happy to have something to hunt down and kill, and I never saw a woman do the whole 'Eek, a mouse!' thing any better than Ilsa. Hours later, she was still having the vapors about it."

"She's the delicate type."

"Yeah. Anyway, I told her I was recently divorced and looking for a home where I could bring my kids every other weekend." Bobby grinned. "She liked the idea that I was single and rich enough to afford a place at Deer Creek, so we had a nice chat."

"What did Adam do?"

"He seemed disgusted that she was being so friendly, but he didn't say anything. He took the package and drove off." Another factoid struck. "Did you know that the U.S. Postal Service delivered 143 billion pieces of mail last year?" I raised a fist, and Bobby reeled himself in. "Anyway, I asked the woman—Ilsa—what her job is. When she said she watches two children, I acted real interested. She said her employer doesn't like her talking to anyone about them, and I said that was smart, but it would be nice if the kids were close to mine in age, in case I decide to buy out here. Then I asked if they're nice, and she said, 'They're eenteresting.'"

"Interesting?"

Bobby frowned. "I didn't get the sense she was that fond of them."

"Do you think she *dis*likes them?"

He considered. "It was more like she didn't have an opinion."

"Like the kids are a job but no more than that."

"Right."

"Did you ask if they had trouble telling the truth?" That had been my one specific request.

"I did. I mentioned a nephew who tells big stories at school and said I wondered what someone does with a kid like that."

"And she said what?"

"She repeated a story Lucy tells. Quite often, poachers came into the territory where they lived, so one day she and Peter decided to teach them a lesson. Peter sneaked up and stole a rifle they'd left leaning against a tree. While the men chased him through the jungle to get it back, Lucy drove their truck into a swamp and got it stuck good and deep."

"She drove a truck?"

80

"Ilsa says Lucy insists it's true. Do you think that's possible?"

I made a noncommittal hum, but the image of a nine-year-old who'd seldom even seen a truck hopping in and driving one away put more strain on my already weak faith in the girl's veracity. While I tried to find reasons to believe her, Lucy kept giving me reasons not to.

"What did Ilsa say about the story?"

"That children who've been through traumatic situations often make things up, but they usually stop lying with time. It sounded like she was repeating what someone had told her." Bobby drummed his fingers on the dashboard. "Is that what you were hoping for?"

"It will do for now. I'll drop you at the office."

"Are you still thinking you'll be gone next week?"

"No reason not to. This will sort itself out in a few days."

"What if the kids are right?"

"We tell the law firm."

"What if they mean what they said about killing their guardian?"

"We warn him. After that it's his look-out, not ours."

Bobby chewed on that for a while. "I guess you're right. It's not like we can make appointments for them with a local shrink."

Once I left Bobby in charge of client communications, I followed my phone's directions to the Lawson Academy, where Peter and Lucy were presumably seated at desks, learning about fractions and the French Revolution. Pressing the intercom button at the door, I stated my business, was buzzed in, and proceeded to the office, as the voice directed. The secretary listened to my story, spoke on the phone, and then said the principal could see me in about ten minutes if my business wouldn't take long. I assured her it wouldn't, and she went back to whatever she'd been typing when I came in.

It was instructive to watch the woman operate. Kids came into the office non-stop, bringing various concerns for her consideration. Someone had vomited in the north hallway. Mr. Danes had run out of dry erase markers. Emily Peters needed someone to contact her mother, who wasn't answering her phone. The woman handled each request calmly, often without pausing her typing. Most impressive was hearing her include something personal to each kid. "How's your mother doing, Allyson?" or "Did you ever find your tennis shoes, Jack?" I marveled at her ability to keep several hundred kids' worries and triumphs in mind, but I hear that's part of the job description for school secretaries.

When Frederick Oaks ushered me into his office, he apologized for making me wait and cautioned that he had a meeting in fifteen minutes. "I'm afraid you'll have to talk fast."

I slid my P.I. license across the desk for him to see. "I'm an investigator working under the auspices of the state of Michigan." That was true, sort of, since the state issues my license. "As you probably know, a *guardian ad litem* is charged by the court with monitoring situations involving orphaned minors." Notice I didn't say *I* was that person. There are people who do that, and I guessed as a school principal, he'd dealt with them before.

Oaks seemed neither impressed nor unimpressed. "Specifically?"

"Lucy and Peter Gage."

"Ah." I'd been hoping for something like, *The little darlings,* or *What weirdos,* but he only waited, his thin face politely blank.

"Do you feel the children's current situation is healthy for them physically, mentally, and emotionally?"

After a moment, he replied, "I have no reason to think otherwise."

"Then they're doing well here?"

"Since you're from the state, I'm sure you have access to their grades and the teachers' comments."

While I gave Oaks points for doing his job well, his discretion wasn't a good thing for me. "Sometimes it helps to speak to those who see the day-to-day interactions between guardians and their wards."

"Mr. Coburn seems concerned. He attended an initial parent-teacher conference to meet the staff and get a sense of how the children will be assisted as they adjust to their new situation."

"We wonder if Mr. Coburn might be having trouble adjusting," I said. "As a lifelong bachelor, it has to be a shock to suddenly have two children to deal with."

"He took them on willingly, as I understand it." Oaks allowed me a nugget of information. "Mr. Coburn and Dr. Gage were friends, at least as far as Gages' lifestyle allowed them to be."

"Then the money had nothing to do with it?"

Oaks chuckled. "I suppose the financial rewards were welcome. Still, Mr. Coburn's experience hasn't always been positive."

"Why do you say that?"

He took a moment, probably to put his thoughts into discreet terms. "The children had an unusual upbringing. Their integration into what we consider normal life presents problems that we here at Lawson deal with as compassionately as possible.

Mr. Coburn is supportive of both the children and our requirements as an educational institution."

"Do you think he likes them?"

Oaks looked uncomfortable. "That's not something I would feel qualified to speak to."

I stood and retrieved my hat from the chair beside me. "I don't want to keep you from your meeting. I appreciate your time."

When I left the principal's office, the secretary was on the phone, reading off a list of numbers. Since I was already in the building, I decided to do some further snooping. Leaning toward her and mouthing "Thank you," I palmed one of the visitor's passes stacked on the desk. In the hall, I turned and went the opposite way from the exit, stopping briefly to write *Mike* on the line where the name goes. There were almost certainly surveillance cameras around the building, but if you have a name tag, act like you belong, and aren't wearing an extra-long trench coat, people ignore you.

It didn't take me long to find the staff lounge. As any student knows, that's where you learn what the teachers have to say about who's a pain and who's a brain, who got in trouble today and who never will. The place was empty, but I took off my jacket and hung it over a chair, bought a pop from the machine in the back corner, and sat down with a six-month-old magazine.

When a buzzer sounded, the halls filled with noise, and I glanced out to see students going by in both directions. In about thirty seconds, a woman appeared in the doorway, carrying a thermal jug in one hand and an apple in the other. She glanced at me. I smiled and went back to my reading. She pulled out a chair at a different table and sat. I ignored her.

Soon another woman entered, carrying one of those pre-made snack-packs sealed in plastic. Once again, I looked up and smiled. She said, "Hi. I'm Stella. Who are you subbing for?"

"No one," I admitted. "I came to put in an application and thought I'd hang around for a while and get a feel for the place."

"It's a madhouse," she said, "but no worse than any other."

"I met a really cute little girl in the principal's office—Lucy, I think the secretary called her. Kid has the vocabulary of an Oxford don."

"*That* one." The nameless woman's tone indicated disapproval. Stella's gaze moved to meet her companion's, and the woman's chin shifted, possibly indicating defiance.

"If all the kids are like her," I said, "I bet teaching here is a blast."

"Lucy is definitely one of our more precocious students." Stella's tone was carefully devoid of emotion.

"Strange," the other woman muttered. I didn't think the comment was supposed to reach my ears, but I have excellent hearing.

"Why do you say that?"

She blushed faintly but having said it, held her ground. "She and her brother were raised like hyenas." She shivered theatrically. "You should see how they eat."

"When they first came," Stella corrected. "They're better now." To me, she explained, "They should probably have had some basic etiquette lessons before starting school. The impression they made that first day was...unfortunate."

"Someone here helped them with it?"

Stella glanced at her companion. "They figured it out by themselves, but kids don't forget."

"I have caught Lucy coming out of the boys' restroom. Twice." The dour one held up two fingers. "She said the girls' was full of 'squawking females,' and what difference does it make what it says on the door?"

I could see how Lucy wouldn't consider the American custom of separate bathrooms important. This woman obviously did.

"I tried to talk to the brother about it," she went on. "I thought being older, he could explain things to Lucy." Her tone hardened. "The pervert stared at my chest the whole time."

"That could be cultural," Stella said. "In some places it's rude for kids to look an adult in the eye."

"Well, it's creepy. And when I got done talking, he just turned and walked away."

"He's pretty shy." Stella went in a different direction. "Lucy's a pretty girl, though. She'll be a real heart-breaker someday."

"I tried commenting on that," her coworker claimed. "The second day, I kept her after class and said really nicely, 'Honey, you're quite pretty, but we need to tame that hair.' Lucy informed me that she likes her hair the way it is, and it's stupid to judge people based on physical beauty. She suggested I compliment mental achievements, since students can work to improve their minds. She said she can't help that she was born beautiful." The teacher sniffed. "You can't be nice to some people."

Twisting in my chair, I turned to look at her directly. "You seem pretty down on the girl."

Though she looked away, she couldn't leave it alone. "I got sick of making adjustments for her." Her tone turned falsely sweet. "'Lucy isn't used to sitting at a desk, so she may keep a study rug in the corner.' Or 'Lucy's already read *Where the Mountain Meets the Moon*, so she may visit the school library while the class reads it aloud.'" In her own voice she went on,

"I've heard the same things about the brother. If 'poor Peter' starts feeling stressed in the classroom, his teachers have to let him walk the hallways until he feels calm again. He could be out there vandalizing lockers and plugging toilets, but they're required to let him go because he 'needs space.'" She put finger quotes around the words. "If their guardian hadn't given the school a big, fat donation along with tuition, those two would have to follow the rules like everyone else."

Blushing at her coworker's vehemence, Stella said, "They learned behaviors that seem odd to us. Adjusting has got to be hard for them."

"But coddling them makes it worse," the other woman opined. "You'd think they'd be eager to learn how they're supposed to act, but the boy doesn't participate half the time, and Lucy is downright defiant. How are they going to learn if they won't let decent people—"

Anger had warmed my face as she ranted, and suddenly, words came out of my mouth unbidden. "You mean decent people like you who bad-mouth children because they don't fit your bigoted definition of normal?"

She didn't back down. "We're *try*ing to *help* them."

"You're *try*ing to *change* them." Rising, I took my jacket off the chair. "I think I'd rather work in a place where the teachers have a little compassion for the students."

With Stella wide-eyed and her coworker glaring, I left the lounge, closing the door behind me. In the silence of the hallway, I took a deep breath and tried to relax. This was what Peter and Lucy faced every day. Who'd want to attend a school with teachers like Ms. Self-Righteous?

On the way to the parking lot, I passed a basement stairwell that probably led to the heating plant. Three teen boys and a girl huddled there, none of them wearing a coat. The girl rested her back against the door, letting the boys serve as windbreaks. They were smoking, though that wasn't obvious at first glance. I passed without comment but thought better of it and turned back. "'Sup?"

Three of them kept their cigarettes at their sides, as if I might not notice smoke wafting up from their hips. The fourth, a boy of about sixteen with eyes that said no threat I made would scare him, took a drag on his and then said sarcastically, "Not much, *sir*. What is up with you?"

"I'm wondering if you know Peter Gage."

The girl tittered nervously. Two boys looked down at their feet. Mr. Tough asked, "What's it to you, *sir*?"

"I want to know how truthful he is."

"That would be hard to judge," one boy said. "Pete don't say much."

The others snickered, and the girl said, "All that kid's got is stink."

For a second time I was getting a bad impression of people at Lawson, but I tried again. "I need to know if he'd make up a story to get attention or damage someone's reputation. It's important."

Mr. Tough eyed me for a few seconds. "The question is this, *sir*. What is this information worth to you?"

These kids probably had more cash in their pants pockets than I had in my bank account, so offering money was pointless. Remembering the parting gift Dinah Ellerson had given me, I gambled on the fact that it was getting late in the afternoon and they might have the munchies. "I have a dozen homemade cookies in my car."

"What kind?" It was the boy who hadn't spoken before.

"Peanut butter."

A glance decided them. "Get 'em."

I was back in thirty seconds, the foil-covered plate of cookies in hand. They looked them over, apparently approved, and each took one. "What exactly do you want to know about Pete?" Mr. Tough asked once he'd taken a bite and nodded approval.

"Whatever you've got."

The girl wrinkled her nose. "Like I said, he stinks."

"And he beat on Calvin," Boy #2 supplied.

"Why was that?"

"Not sure. We were in gym class, and Calvin went up to Pete and said something. Next thing we know, Pete's giving him a beat-down."

Boy #3 was more fair-minded than his companions. "I was there," he said. "Calvin was giving the new kid a hard time, like he always does. He said a couple of things, and the kid didn't answer back. Then Calvin shoved him and said something about him being a freak. It was so quick I almost missed it, but Pete decked him with one punch." He scrunched his face, pushing his glasses back where they belonged. "Calvin's nose was bleeding. Pete gave him his t-shirt to soak up the blood."

"Did he say anything?"

"He said, 'Sorry,' which is the only word I've ever heard Pete say. Coach came running over and asked what happened, but Pete just looked at his feet. Cal made a big deal of it, said Pete attacked him for no reason. Coach knows Calvin pretty well, so he didn't fall for that, but we all got this big lecture about not resorting to violence. Then he made them shake hands." The kid smiled. "I thought old Pete was gonna pass out with the whole class staring at him."

"Do you know what Calvin said to Peter?"

"He was calling him names and stuff." He had the grace to look embarrassed as he added, "Some people call him Native

Boy and the Gay Peruvian, because he's got that yarn-y stuff tied to his backpack."

"The sister's gay, for sure," the girl opined. "On her first day here, the teacher asked Jeanie Sparks to show her around, and on the way to lunch, Lucy grabbed hold of Jeanie's hand." She huffed a laugh. "Jeanie let her know right away *that* wasn't gonna fly."

I frowned. "In some countries, friends do that."

She flipped her hair back with her non-cookie hand. "Well, around here we know gay when we see it."

Once again, anger overcame my discretion. "I haven't met a snarky mean girl since high school. Nice to know you're all still the same."

She pushed her hair out of her eyes, using her middle finger, and I got the message. Nothing I could say would give these entitled, spoiled teens a sense of compassion for newcomers lost in their tiny, haughty world. Disgusted, I turned and started away.

"What about the rest of those cookies?" Mr. Tough called out.

Without looking back, I said, "I'm keeping them in case I meet some people with class."

As I set the plate of cookies on the floor in the back seat of my car, a tap sounded from somewhere above, and I looked up to see Lucy at a window on the second floor. She held up a finger, signaling I should wait, and disappeared. A few seconds later she emerged from double doors, set a book in place as a doorstop, and hurried over to me. "It's good for five minutes. Then the alarm starts beeping."

"Why aren't you in class?"

"The others are at gym. Ms. Dixon let me stay behind and help her straighten the classroom." There was a wealth of unspoken information in her statement, and I pictured a compassionate teacher allowing her oddest student to avoid the worst class of the day for outcasts: gym.

"She went to the office for something." Lucy glanced up at the window. "I can't stay long."

"Don't they have cameras that will show you leaving the building?"

"Yes, but no one actually monitors them. They're more for looking back to see who's responsible when there's trouble." Pulling her blazer tight to keep out the cold, she asked, "Are you checking up on us?"

"I told you I'd be fair. That means I ask questions about you two as well as about Oscar."

"And what have you learned?"

"Peter was in a fight in gym class."

Lucy kicked at a chunk of snow with her foot. "True."

"It's not good to go around punching people who make you mad."

Her lips set in a firm line. "In this culture, you have to prove you're strong before people will leave you alone. The boy tested Peter, and he proved he can and will defend himself."

"You said the Yarru believe in cooperation and peace."

Lucy chuckled. "That's not the same as being a pushover. Now what about Oscar?"

I took a breath. "To be honest, I haven't found anything that makes me think he's a killer."

"Then keep looking, because he is." She regarded me for a second as if trying to decide whether to tell something. "Peter loosened the bolts on his chair last night before dinner. He took quite a tumble."

"Lucy, you promised—"

"We promised not to kill him," she said primly. "I've never read of anyone dying from falling off a chair." Pausing, she corrected herself. "It can happen with office chairs, but that's usually when people stand on them to reach for things. Oscar would never do something that dumb."

"Did you put molasses in his briefcase this morning?"

She looked away. "It's childish, we know, but we need to keep him nervous about what we'll do next."

"You're more liable to make him want to kill both of you."

"But he won't. It's all about the money." She lowered her voice. "We think Oscar changed Dad's will."

"How would he do that?"

"He's a lawyer. Who'd know how to do it better?"

"What did he change?"

"Dad had talked about naming Denice as our guardian."

"You mentioned her before. Where did she come from?"

"Dad came home to Detroit in 2017, when his father was diagnosed with end-stage kidney failure. During his visit, he decided Peter and me needed what he called 'rounding out.' He said someday we might want to know more about the outside world than what we saw on the internet."

"Probably a good idea."

Lucy gave me a look. "Anyway, this is Denice." She'd taken out her phone, and she showed me a photo of herself and Peter standing beside a woman as plain as a loaf of store-bought bread.

"She came to Peru to teach you about life in the U.S.?"

"About everything, really." Lucy's eyes filled with tears she didn't acknowledge. "We miss her."

"And your dad trusted her."

"We all did, after a short…adjustment period. When Dad died and we came to Michigan, Denice helped with everything.

We assumed she'd stay on until Peter reached eighteen, but then we found out that Dad's will named the Coburn Firm our legal guardian. Then Denice's mom got sick, and she had to take care of her."

"But you think your dad intended to change his will and name her."

"We do, but things like that are hard to accomplish in the jungle. Peter remembers Dad wondering how he was supposed to get the signatures of two witnesses on the document." Lucy sighed. "He couldn't have predicted how soon we'd need a guardian."

"You trust Denice?"

Lucy's reply was firm. "Completely. Dad used to say she was worth her weight in *cucharas*." When I looked confused, she said, "Spoons. I don't get it either, but he found it funny."

"Okay. I'll try to find out if there's any record of a proposed change to your dad's will."

She glanced at the window. "I should get back inside."

"I'll be in touch."

Before leaving my parking spot, I phoned the Rennington Hills Police Department to make an appointment with the officer Lucy had talked to about Oscar Coburn. In a clipped voice, the woman told me she'd be at the local sub-station until six.

When I arrived, Officer Laura Banks glanced at the clock and made a note of the time. About thirty, Banks had blond hair pulled back in a no-nonsense bun and a no-nonsense expression. I saw right away that Peter Gage would have found talking to her intimidating.

Banks explained that deployment analysis had determined the area could be served by a single officer on duty daily from ten in the morning till six at night. Deer Creek Development, the largest entity in the area, had private security, and other than that, the Oakland County Sheriff's Department provided law enforcement through a shared-funding deal. More clerk than cop, Banks represented a police presence, answering the phone, and relaying information between agencies.

I'd presented myself as a reporter for a local magazine looking for human interest stories. After some preliminary talk, I said, "Two kids came to you with a concern last week. Since they were recently in the news, we think they'd make a great feature article. What can you tell me about the Gage children's request for police assistance?"

Banks remained still except for the hand with which she was eating the hot-hot-hot taco chips she'd shaken onto her desk blotter. After chewing for several seconds, she asked, "Where did you hear about that?"

"A neighbor tells me the kids are afraid for their lives."

The muscles in her jaw hardened. "We looked into their concerns. I can't comment further."

"If they presented you with evidence—"

"They didn't," she interrupted. "They told me a story."

"Did you follow up on the story?"

"I did."

"You spoke to their guardian?"

"I spoke to an employee who shared that the children have issues."

"Issues?"

"They recently lost their only remaining parent. They feel like aliens in Michigan. They're unhappy."

"You don't believe they're under any sort of threat?"

Banks shifted in her chair, her body betraying irritation even if her expression did not. "I believe they wanted their concerns to be heard by someone in authority."

"Then you feel you did your job adequately?"

Her gaze turned ice cold. "People who complain to the police don't understand that they expose their own behavior to scrutiny right along with the person they accuse."

"You don't believe them."

"Evidence suggests those children lie to get attention. Their guardian is caring and considerate, but he has a busy law practice and is often absent from home."

"What evidence do you have that they make things up?"

Her eyes rolled. "Have you met them? The boy obviously has brain damage, probably from some accident in Africa or wherever. And the girl? With her big words and big eyes, that one should be on the stage."

While I wasn't sure myself that Lucy and Peter were truthful, Banks' dismissal bothered me. "It sounds to me like you were pretty quick to ignore a couple of orphans who need your help."

I saw her struggle with whether to confide in me, but Banks was miffed at my suggestion she'd been derelict in her duties. "In the last two months, the nanny has called 9-1-1 four times because Lucy reported a prowler outside. Sheriff's deputies responded each time, but they found no evidence to support her claim."

"There was no prowler?"

"Like I said, dramatics." She relented a little. "I get it. The kid grew up in the bush. Now she's in a city with unfamiliar noises and TV shows where people get shot dead in every episode. It must scare her silly."

"If there's one thing Lucy Gage isn't, Officer Banks, it's silly."

Frowning, she pulled a pad of paper toward her and picked up a pen with orange-tipped fingers. "What's the name of your paper again?"

I'd programmed my phone for such a possibility, and sliding a hand into my pocket, I hit the button. As the phone burbled, I grimaced apologetically. "Sorry, I have to take this call. Thanks for your time."

Outside, I ended my call to myself and stood in light snow that had begun falling, trying to decide how much of Lucy's story I believed. The cop had investigated. Finding logical explanations for the kids' odd ways, she'd concluded, as others had, that Peter and Lucy were having trouble adjusting to recent tragedies in their lives. The fact that Lucy hadn't mentioned the late-night 9-1-1 calls suggested she knew they put her in a poor light, detracting from her credibility and lending credence to the idea that she wanted attention.

What did I know for sure?

Oscar Coburn was probably milking the Gage estate for his own benefit. That was distasteful, but it didn't make him a potential murderer. Acting in loco parentis, he was allowed a generous paycheck and the right to share the kids' comfortable lifestyle.

The Gages were traumatized kids whose lives had been completely upended. Their behavior shocked, even disgusted, people who dealt with them daily. As a result, they were confused and unhappy. Who knew what conspiracies they'd cooked up to ease their discontent?

CHAPTER FIVE

I worked in the office Tuesday evening, skimming documents Mom had sent and printing out any I thought required closer reading. Adam Saracco's criminal record was for breaking and entering, possessing stolen goods, and unlawful entry. In early 2015, two police officers had observed Adam walking down the street in broad daylight, pulling a kid's wagon containing a big-screen TV wrapped in a comforter. When they asked him where the TV came from, Adam claimed a stranger had given it to him because he didn't want it anymore. A brief investigation had revealed a door yawning open a few houses down, a TV missing from its stand, and a bed with only sheets. At his hearing, the judge asked why Adam had dragged his swag down a busy street, practically advertising the crime. He'd replied he had to walk, since his car was in the shop.

In other words, Adam went to prison because he was dumb. Most criminals are, despite legions of evil geniuses the entertainment industry creates for our amusement.

Once Adam had paid his debt to society, his lawyer, Oscar Coburn, offered him a job and a second chance at life. Mom had learned this from a blog called "Help Them Rise," which listed and applauded efforts of prominent Detroit citizens to aid the less fortunate. The blogger reported that Oscar had several times assisted men he'd defended unsuccessfully, finding them jobs and apartments upon their release from prison and even providing small loans until they got back on their feet. "You get to know a person over the course of a trial," he was quoted as saying, "and you realize that better circumstances might have led them to better choices. I can't always keep my clients out of jail, but I can help them start over once they're free again."

It was getting close to Mom's bedtime, but knowing she was dying to talk over what she'd found, I gave her a call. After the "How are you?" stuff and the weather report—temps had hit 90 degrees that afternoon—I told her what I'd learned. "What's your impression of the guardian?" she asked when I finished.

"He seems okay. He's patient with the kids, though their behavior is pretty bizarre. What are you seeing?"

"Little things. The guy doesn't seem to have friends, just business associates. When Oscar travels, for example, he goes alone. He uses the firm's staff for grunt work and keeps the important stuff to himself. He's had plenty of women up to now, but when the kids arrived, he removed himself from the dating game. Says he has a responsibility to see that the children get a good start on their new lives."

"That speaks well of him, I'd say."

"Agreed." Mom shifted gears. "I don't much care for his sleazy legal tactics. His client could not possibly have foreseen the detrimental effects of his actions. It's the fault of the landlord, business owner, or hospital—unless the client is a landlord, business owner, or hospital."

"Mom, that's what lawyers do for a living."

"I don't care. It's not right."

"Well, I feel a little sorry for the guy. Lucy and Peter have tried his patience in every possible way."

"Kids do that."

"Not like this pair." I told her about the molasses in Oscar's briefcase and Lucy's admission they'd sabotaged his chair. "He's trying to be nice. They're trying to drive him out of their lives."

In a tone that hinted at smugness, Mom said, "Did you see my note about his search history? He's been reading up on mental incompetence."

"He might think the kids need professional help, and he might be right. Peter is socially dysfunctional. Lucy is emotionally volatile. I'm told they distort the truth when it suits them, so I don't even know how much to believe of what they tell me."

"Spend time with them. Then you'll be able to trust your instincts."

"I hope so." Paging through the information she'd sent, I said, "The law firm seems to be in a state of flux."

"Yeah. The old man, Carson Coburn, didn't recover from his stroke like they hoped, so the by-laws kicked in." Hearing clicking, I guessed Mom was searching for a name. "Oscar was in line to take control, but the rules were rewritten, and the niece, Sara Dailey, heads the firm now."

"Do you think Oscar refused the job?"

"The other two might have joined forces and squeezed him out."

"He hasn't got much incentive to fight for it," I said, thinking out loud. "Controlling the Gage estate is less work and more lucrative too."

"Huh." Mom was obviously reading. "The original by-laws said if Oscar didn't take the job, they should hire outside the firm."

"Does that mean the old man trusted Oscar more than the other two?"

"Trust is relative," Mom replied. "The younger son, Kevin, is a putz, and I bet Papa Coburn knew that."

"What's wrong with the niece?"

"She lacks outdoor plumbing." Mom's tone was tinged with disgust. "In an email to Oscar, Carson once said that while having a female attorney helped their image, he never wanted a 'girl' running the place."

"Everybody knows that boys are born to rule the world," I teased.

Mom made a rude noise. "That's all changed. Sara will head the firm, but I doubt Carson will ever know."

"She'll be busy," I observed. "Oversight of Oscar's guardianship won't be high on her to-do list."

Mom got it. "And like I said, Kevin isn't the sharpest chisel in the toolbox. His grades were dismal, and his professors were skeptical of his abilities. One wonders how he passed the bar exam."

"Okay then. Ray Gage died and days afterward, Carson Coburn had a stroke. Seeing an opportunity, Oscar got himself named guardian, though the kids think their former nanny was supposed to."

"What happened to her?"

"She left the state due to family illness."

Mom made a hum of understanding. "Oscar got control of all that money. Sara got to be boss. Kevin gets...what?"

"If he's as dumb as you say, maybe Oscar promised they'll never push him out, even though Daddy's no longer around to protect him."

"That's plausible." Mom went on to her next item. "You said the school principal thinks Oscar and Ray Gage were friends, but I watched Oscar being interviewed shortly after Gage's death, and he referred to him as 'Doctor *Robert* Gage.' That doesn't speak of close acquaintance."

"I agree." Still perusing papers, I'd come to a list of expenditures from the Gage estate over the last few months. (I try not to ask myself how Mom gets stuff like that.) "Oscar's recent purchases are interesting. Not sure how they relate to the kids' welfare."

Mom snickered. ""I wondered about that. Which one asked for a 5-iron that runs over twenty thousand dollars?"

"Their house is huge. Lucy and Peter hate the waste it represents."

"I'm telling you, this guy is no sweetheart. Some of Carson Coburn's emails remind Oscar that the law isn't there for him to manipulate."

"After seeing Oscar in action today, I don't think Dad's advice made much of an impression." I set the stack of printouts aside. "But nothing we've got proves Oscar is breaking the law."

"He can justify expenditures as benefits for the kids. Like he'd say he plans to teach them golf, so he bought the best club available."

"As guardian, he's entitled to a hefty fee, so he's living large and pocketing an income too."

Mom made a *tsk* of disgust. "The only time I've found when Oscar extends himself without the prospect of a financial reward is with the ex-clients I mentioned. I find that suspicious."

"Guys on parole know to keep their mouths shut and obey orders."

"Right," Mom said. "And small-time crooks follow the lead of people they perceive as smart. Adam Saracco might be going straight with his former lawyer's assistance, but he'd also be a useful tool."

"But I haven't found anyone who seems to think Oscar is a bad person. He's likeable. He's socially gifted, though a little aloof. His self-assured but easy-going manner impresses those around him."

Mom snorted. "Max, you know the average Joe can't see past an expensive suit and a confident smile."

I stood, causing my chair to bump into the wall with a thud. "We can't stop Oscar from bending the law. My concern has to be if he'd kill a child, and from what we know at this point, that's unlikely."

Unwilling to let go of her dislike of a man she'd never met, Mom said, "I'm going to keep digging."

"Send whatever you find that's interesting. I read every word."

"Love you, Honey. Go to bed now, so you stay sharp."

When my phone rang at three a.m. Wednesday morning, I was halfway into my eight hours.

"'Lo?"

"Mr. Dunham, it's Lucy Gage. You said to let you know if anything unusual happened."

After a beat, my brain shifted into gear. *Lucy. Unusual.* "What is it?"

"Someone tried to get into my room. Ilsa has called the police."

That brought me to full attention. "You're sure it wasn't a dream?"

"No!" Her voice rose, more angry than scared. "A noise woke me. I went to the window and there he was, looking in. He wore a mask. I shouted, and he went away."

"The police are on the way?"

"Yes."

"Is Oscar at home?"

"No. He stayed the night in Grand Rapids."

"I'll be there as soon as I can."

"Shall I call the gate and have them let you in?"

"No. The fewer people who know I'm at Deer Creek, the better." Ending the call, I took some black sweats out of my pants drawer and started getting dressed.

On my first visit, I'd noted ways to get onto the property unseen, because that's what I do. Parking outside the development, I scaled the enclosure, which wasn't as forbidding as it appeared. While the wall's surface was smooth concrete, pillars spaced every fifteen feet or so were made of cultured stone, an esthetically pleasing touch that also provided convenient footholds. There were security cameras at the gates, but in typical fashion, the company had skimped a little to save on hardware and maintenance costs. There were lots of places where a guy could climb the wall without getting his picture taken. I was over in no time, and I dropped to earth in a small playground. I hurried to the Gage house, sliding into the cedar shrubs that lined the sidewalk whenever a car came along. There were only two, a truck with the security company's logo and a battered car with an amber roof light. Every so often a newspaper flew out the passenger side window.

At the Gage home the gate stood open, and in the driveway was a sheriff's car, its bar lights flashing. I wandered up the drive, doing my best to look like a gawker. "What's going on, Officer?"

The deputy gave me one of those "Wish you weren't here" looks. "You need to move along, sir."

He was joined then by a second deputy, who said tersely, "Nothing." In a lower tone, he added, "Again."

Ilsa Dausman came outside, wrapped in a fuzzy shawl that didn't do much to hide the lacy negligee underneath. "Did you find him?"

"No, ma'am. We're still looking."

"It is upsetting, zese disturbances in ze night."

"Yes. It is."

Ilsa's gaze swept the area. "I'm sure I will not be able to go back to sleep." Speaking to the younger of the two officers, she let the shawl dip to reveal a creamy shoulder and a plunging neckline. "I've got goose bumps everywhere, see?"

The guy gave her chest an appreciative look. The other one looked away and noticed I was still there. "Sir, I asked you to move along."

"Oh, right. Sorry." I backed away as Ilsa smiled up at the deputy who smiled down at her cleavage. Turning, I started for the street. Once they were gone, I'd find a way onto the property and do my own investigating.

As I neared the gatepost, a beam of light appeared on the concrete in front of me. As soon as I noticed it, the light rotated upward, showing Peter Gage standing under a large maple tree. A tilt of his head indicated I should join him. Then the light went out.

"Is Lucy okay?" I asked when I got close enough to speak quietly. I sensed more than saw the boy's nod. "She said a man tried to break in."

"They don't believe her." Wow. Four whole words. Go Pete!

"When you go back in, tell her I'm here. I'll see what I can find out."

"'K." As my eyes adjusted to the dark, I saw that Peter wore his coat over a t-shirt and jogging pants that probably served as pajamas. Despite the hour, the backpack he was so attached to was in place. Carrying his favorite things around must have provided reassurance.

Ever since Lucy had told me Peter believed they could take Oscar out themselves, I'd been trying to think of a way to discourage him from taking that option. This was my perfect, maybe only, opportunity. "Peter, um, don't try…anything without talking with me first, all right?"

It sounded vague, but how do you tell a teenager he shouldn't kill someone without permission? Isn't doing things without adult input exactly what being a teen is all about?

104

"Whatever we do, we need to plan it together." A head bob signaled understanding and acquiescence, I hoped. "Great." I considered giving his shoulder a manly squeeze, but we weren't that close yet. Besides, he stank again, or still, so I was more comfortable standing back. "I'll contact you tomorrow so we can talk."

Without further communication, Peter turned and began circling through the trees toward the house. When he'd had time to get back inside, I went on to the gate. Stepping through, I almost bumped into a guy with a flashlight, bent low as he apparently searched for footprints in the snow. When he stood, I saw that he wore the uniform of the association's security service.

"Hey!" he said irritably. "What are you doing in there?"

"I was out walking—and I saw the cop car go in, so I went to see what it was about." I gave him an innocent smile. "The deputy asked me to leave, so that's what I'm doing."

"I've never seen you before. Do you live here?"

"Temporarily, yeah."

"And where are you staying...temporarily?"

Since I only knew two addresses in the development, I gave him Mrs. Ellerson's. The guy gave me a Barney Fife gaze, one eye squinted with distrust. "I know the owner of that house. Considering her age and your looks, I think we should go ask her if she's got a guest."

I nodded, intending to appear compliant and bolt when I got an opportunity. That changed when the man drew a Taser from his belt and brandished it like a saber. "If you take off, I'll use this and let the deputies arrest your spazzed out carcass."

Single file, we walked the three blocks to the Ellerson home. Though a light burned somewhere deep inside, the place was silent. My companion rang the bell. In a while the door opened, revealing the woman I'd conned earlier with a story about being her relative. She wore a full-length nightgown with a long, cable-knit sweater atop it and fleece-lined slippers. She'd closed a novel around one finger to hold her place. Her expression revealed curiosity rather than alarm. "What is it, Frank?"

"Sorry to bother you in the middle of the night, Mrs. Ellerson."

"I was up. Old people sleep funny." She glanced at me. "But I wasn't expecting company."

"They had a prowler call down at #815, and I found this guy on the property. He says he's staying with you, so I'm here to see if that's true."

The old woman looked at me speculatively. If eyes can plead, like novelists say they can, mine were on their knees begging. After a moment she said, "This is my second cousin, twice removed."

"And he's staying with you?"

"He came all the way from Maine to interview me about our family history," she replied. "Offering a place to stay was the least I could do."

Frank was disappointed, but he didn't waste any more time on the matter. "Thank you, ma'am. Sir, I hope you enjoy your stay in Michigan, but I recommend you stay out of police business."

He left. I stood on the porch, not sure what to say to the woman who'd saved me from arrest. As I tried to come up with something, Mrs. Ellerson made a proposal. "Why don't you come inside and tell me what's really going on?" Raising her right hand, which had until that moment remained in the pocket of her sweater, she showed me a small pistol. "If I don't like what you say, I'll call Frank back and let him take you into custody, as he was clearly dying to do."

Inside, we sat down in the same places we'd taken earlier, when I lied my face off. "I'm a private investigator," I said, taking out my license and handing it to her. "I'm trying to help two orphaned children who live here at Deer Creek." Feeling my face warm I said, "I'm sorry I was dishonest before."

She examined the license and handed it back. "My family's history has been done to death by some cousin in Canada. Every story, place of residence, and birth is entered in detail on the internet and updated annually. There's no reason for anyone to go looking for information."

"Then why did you agree to see me?"

"I wasn't busy." After a pause she added, "I had the pistol in my pocket the whole time."

That made me wince. "You'd have shot me?"

"Not unless I had to." She examined the gun fondly, though she took care not to point it at me. "My late husband bought me this little gem."

"Is that a SIG Sauer?"

"P238 Compact," she affirmed. "A .380 works well for me."

"When I carry, which isn't often, I like the Smith & Wesson. I got used to it as a cop, so I stuck with it."

She regarded me as if shifting her opinion. "We should visit a shooting range. I'd like to see how I stack up against a trained officer."

"There's a good place in Shelby."

"I've been there a few times." I must have looked surprised, because she explained, "I practice at least once a month. It's what responsible gun owners do." Shifting gears, she said, "Tell me about these children."

I didn't want to lie to her again, but a guy can't blab his clients' business all over either. "They claim they're in danger, but no one believes them. I'm looking into it quietly, since I'm not sure where the threat is coming from."

"But you believe there is one?"

I sighed. "Let's say I feel compelled to investigate the possibility."

She considered that. "It would be good if you were close by."

"That would be tough now that Rent-a-cop Frank knows my face."

"What if you were innocuous rather than anonymous?" I frowned in confusion, and she pointed toward a hallway off the kitchen. "Down there are housekeeper's quarters no one is using. You could stay there, and I'll add you to the guest list so you can come and go as necessary."

"Why would you trust me in your home, Mrs. Ellerson?"

She smiled, though her eyes were sad. "My late husband, a judge in family court, was often appalled at how little power children have over their lives. Besides, I consider myself a good judge of character." With a twinkle, she added, "I intend to confirm what you've told me, so I suggest you don't return a third time if you haven't been honest with me now."

"Deal."

A half-hour later, when the county car exited the main gate, I left Deer Creek the way I'd entered, walked to the used car lot where I'd parked my car, and headed for home. Visions of Mexico had begun to dim, but I brought them back with force of will. I still had time to find out who was truthful and who was not, though Lucy's reports of a prowler made things murkier. Still, Dinah Ellerson had given me the opportunity to observe the situation closely, which should help. Once I was sure what was happening, I'd turn the whole mess over to child services, Coburn Law, or someone else with the authority to deal with it. While I warmed my skin on the beach and cooled my insides with a Mai Tai, the kids' future would be decided by people wiser than a humble P.I.

After a two-hour nap, I packed a bag for a stay at Dinah's. Then I went into the office, put the printouts I'd made for later perusal into a folder, and laid it atop my clothes and shaving kit. Hearing the entry door open, I went to the doorway. When I recognized my visitor, I wished I'd hidden under my desk until he went away. "Dodger."

He turned on his hundred-watt smile, all teeth and no sincerity. "Maxie, how they hanging?"

I shrugged. "What can I do for you?"

"Not a thing, Maxie, not a thing. I was in the neighborhood, and we haven't talked in a long time, so I stopped by to see my old friend."

Dodger, whose real name is Roger Ainsley, is a fellow ex-cop and not someone I consider a friend. Knowing he never does anything without a reason, I was always cautious with him. "How you been?"

"Good, good. You?"

"Good."

Dodger is about my age but looks older, with saggy eyes and jowls like a church elder in a '70s movie. His ancient coat was missing a button, and his shoes were too thin for winter. Though he'd been good-looking when we met, now Dodger looked as worn as his clothing.

He shuffled his feet for a second, and then spoke with his old brightness. "Ever see any of the guys, Maxie?"

"Baker and Marzac meet me for a beer every month or so." The topic was touchy. I'd left the force by choice after planning my second career and preparing for it for months. Dodger had left to avoid being fired. Suspected of dirty deeds (done dirt cheap, no doubt), he'd been given the choice of quitting or being called to account for his crimes.

Two months after I opened my P.I. office, I'd been horrified when Dodger called to suggest I take him on as a partner. When I refused, as politely as I could manage, he hadn't argued. Instead, a few months later, he'd opened his own agency. Considering his reputation on the force, that had taken guts, but if there's one thing Roger the Dodger's got, it's nerve.

He seemed determined to keep the conversation going. "Is Marzac the one that talks like a fairy?"

"I wouldn't know. I've never met any fairies."

Vaguely aware he'd offended me, Dodger said, "I wasn't criticizing the guy. He sounds weird, that's all."

"Dodger, I was about to head out."

He glanced to where my overnight bag sat on my desk. His eyes lit, and I caught a hint of what he was after. "Got a big case?"

I shrugged. "The usual stuff."

"No murders for the murder specialist?" He tried to make the question inoffensive, but everything Dodger says offends me.

"Not right now."

"How about a murder somebody's planning on doing?"

With a sinking feeling, I realized I wasn't the first P.I. the Gage kids had consulted. I could have swatted Lucy for not telling me, and I added another black mark to my mental tally of her faults.

Not sure what he knew, I played dumb. "I can't investigate a crime that hasn't happened yet."

"No." His torso leaned sideways, an unconscious pantomime of crookedness. "But if you needed help with something that's too...weird for you, you know you can call on me."

Was he offering to kill Oscar, or to provide the name of someone who would? "What kind of help are we talking about, Dodger?"

"We'd have to discuss that." He stepped forward to nudge me playfully with an elbow, and I fought the urge to back away. "I wouldn't want you to miss an opportunity if I can step in and make it work."

I tried to end what was becoming an uncomfortable exchange. "I haven't got anything going right now, Roger. I have a court appearance Friday. After that I plan to take some time off."

He sniffed. "You must be doing all right in the money department."

"Guys like you and me don't get rich. Not honestly," I added meaningfully.

His eyes revealed longing. "But if a chance came along, if you got offered a big score, you'd remember your old buddy from the academy, right?" He raised a hand for me to slap. "The bros in blue."

I didn't slap, and he lowered his hand, pretending he hadn't meant for me to.

"I couldn't forget you, Dodger." I didn't add that I would if I could.

After a wet rumble, he coughed, wheezed, and then coughed again. Soon he was in a fit of hacking that made me step back, trying to hide my distress. The guy was a non-stop smoker, and the nasty sounds coming from his lungs were disgusting. It went on for some time, to the point where I wasn't sure if I should slap him on the back or call 9-1-1.

"Could—I have—water?" he finally panted.

Relieved at a remedy that simple, I hurried to my apartment, got a disposable foam cup, and filled it from a bottle in the fridge. When I got back, Dodger seemed to have recovered. "Thanks, bud." He drank the water and tossed the cup into the trash can. "Doc says I should cut back on the cigs, but it's hard, you know?"

"Sorry to rush you, Dodge, but I have an appointment downtown in twenty minutes." Taking my coat off its hook, I shrugged it on and opened the door, indicating he should precede me.

We took the back stairs, and Dodger puffed like a city bus by the time we reached the ground floor. At the exit he said, "My car's out front. It was good to see you, Maxie." He shuffled away, leaving me with a disquieting sense I'd been had. I just didn't know how yet.

Outside, I pulled my coat collar up around my ears. The appointment I'd mentioned to Dodger was fictional. What I had in mind was an apparently serendipitous meeting that might give me further insights into Oscar Coburn's character. For over a year, he'd dated Pamela Jutzi, an attractive member of Detroit's elite social set. She'd abruptly disappeared from his life a few months back, and a comment she'd made on Instagram suggested the breakup hadn't been completely friendly. I hoped to get Pamela to dish some dirt on her ex.

Any good investigator knows you can't simply knock on a person's door and ask for such things. Reading Jutzi's social media pages, I saw no way to get her to trust me at first, aside from posing as a pedicurist, which could only end in disaster. However, Pamela shared a lot online, and a picture of her with two dogs had a caption that said, "Me 'n The Girls on our ten o'clock walk." That would be my opportunity.

Reading on, I learned that Pamela loved the occult and in fact considered herself to be a white witch. Skimming a few of the articles she'd posted, I prepared myself for a brief conversation on the topic. The only other thing I needed was a reason for the two of us to meet.

Stopping at my buddy Baker's house, I borrowed his Newfoundland, Dude. Baker and Polly were at work, so I texted them in case a neighbor called to report a dognapping. Dude and I are long-time friends, and he's always, always up for a road trip. I located his leash and managed to get it attached, though Dude danced in circles the whole time and ended up wiping his paws on my pants. Luckily they were navy, so the dirt didn't show much. A few minutes later we were on our way, Dude leaning over the seat of my car and drooling on my shoulder. Dodger's unexpected visit had slowed me a little, but I could still get into place by the time Pamela came down for her daily walk.

At 10:17, Oscar's former girlfriend exited High Street Apartments with a dog under each arm. Though she wasn't beautiful, Pamela was attractive in that "I've got people" way, toned muscles, carefully styled blond hair, and a jogging suit straight from Valentino. Setting the critters carefully on the pavement, she praised them for being "almost quiet" in the elevator. They were teacup poodles, one white, the other "luscious apricot," according to Pamela's online description. Each wore a coat and booties. The white one kept trying to free his feet, but due to doggie sartorial magic, the boots remained in place. Dogs and owner turned left and headed east. I gave them a bit of space and then tugged Dude away from an empty plastic bottle he was gnawing on.

Their destination was a park a few blocks down, which was perfect for my purposes. Once inside the gate, I let go of Dude's leash and, when he caught up with the smaller dogs, went into my act.

"Here, buddy! Come back here!" When I reached Pamela, I was already apologizing. "I'm so sorry. My dog loves other dogs. He won't hurt yours, I promise."

Dude demonstrated that as I spoke, sniffing at the poodles in a friendly manner. They'd gone into defensive mode when he appeared, but they soon concluded he wasn't a threat and began sniffing back.

"He's a big one," she said. "What's his name?"

"Duke." I hoped that was close enough to his real name for Dude to respond to it. "And these cuties?"

"Kim and Khloe."

She hadn't really named her dogs after Kardashians, had she? Pushing past that, I gave Pamela a searching look. "Excuse me for asking, but is everything okay with you?" When she frowned, as I'd expected her to, I hurried to explain. "You'll think I'm crazy, but I—um—I sense things sometimes, like I can tell if a person is sad or mad or scared." I faked an embarrassed shrug. "I can't explain it, but I feel like I should at least ask if there's anything I can do to help."

I waited for her response, holding my breath. If she told me to shove off, I'd have to obey or face charges of harassment. But we were two dog-lovers, and I'd confessed to having the "sense" about people she'd mentioned online as one of her "personal strengths."

Laying a well-manicured hand on her chest, Pamela replied exactly as I'd hoped. "I get those same vibes sometimes."

"Really? What do you do when it happens?"

Her lips twisted. "It's hard when it's a stranger, right? You want to help, and you feel like they need you, but you don't want to come off like some weirdo."

I grinned. "Like I did just now?"

"I don't think you're weird. You have a gift, and it's great that you use it to help others."

"My sister says it's all in my imagination."

She touched my arm lightly, and I knew I was golden. "Those who don't have the power try to dismiss it, but if you feel people's pain, I think you're morally bound to try to ease it."

"Well, then. Is there any way I can help you?" Fearing she was about to say no, I added, "Let me tell you what I'm sensing. You had something going, a relationship, I think, but it fell apart. You haven't decided yet how you feel about it."

Pamela pushed long bangs away from her eyes, but they fell back immediately. I wondered what it was like to peer through hunks of hair all day. "I was with this guy. He turned out...different than I thought."

"Did he hurt you?"

"Nothing like that. It was more like he acted like one kind of person, but then suddenly I realized he was a fake."

"In what way?"

She bit her lip. "He had to take in these kids because a friend of his died. He agreed to do it, but I sensed he didn't really want anything to do with them on a personal level. When he talked about them, he sounded mean, like they were going to be a pain to have around. I said, 'Listen, you don't have to do this,' but he said I should mind my own business."

"He doesn't like the kids? Why agree to take them in?"

"Money." She made a moue of distaste. He called them his 'speed bumps,' and said he intended to see as little of them as possible." She blinked rapidly. "Knowing how he was, my interest sort of died."

The interview was going great, but Dude grasped neither the parameters of our mission nor his part in it. At that moment he smacked the white poodle with a paw, purely in play. The weight differential between them made it more painful than he'd intended, and the smaller dog let out a yip of dismay and dived behind Pamela, wrapping her legs in the leash. Her concern focused first on her baby's distress and then on disentangling herself. By the time she was free and I'd pulled Dude away, she'd lost the desire to share her inner struggles. "I should keep walking," she said. "The girls need their exercise."

As her party of three went on, I took my dishonest persona and not-really-mine dog and headed for my car. Back at his home, Dude went willingly into his pen, and I used a towel I found in the shed to clean the mud and drool off my clothes as best I could. My next step was to observe Oscar Coburn in a relaxed setting. For that, I needed to look presentable.

The trial I'd observed was over (Oscar's client was found not guilty). Mom reported that on non-court days, Oscar ate lunch at one of several restaurants near his building. Posting myself in the lobby at 11:45, I waited until he came by, accompanied by a man who looked like a softer, paler, and less confident version of Oscar. The brother, Kevin. Following them outside, I noticed that Oscar's beautifully tailored coat had what looked like a sticky note on the back near the left sleeve. Stepping up close, I read its block letters: "I NEED A HUG."

At a classy little restaurant a block away, I waited on the sidewalk until the two men joined two others at a booth along the back wall. Once they started talking, I went inside and asked for a table for one. The host, a snooty type, glanced at my still-muddy pants and led me to a spot near the kitchen doors.

The place had a hushed atmosphere and dim lighting, perfect for weary lawyers looking to have a two-martini lunch and assure each other they aren't the bottom-feeders portrayed on TV. Oscar joked with the waitress as she took their orders, and she almost purred at the attention.

When my waiter came along with a menu and a glass of water, I told him I'd prefer a booth and indicated the one next to where the Coburns sat. The kid had no objection, and he carried my place setting to the new location as if it were beyond my ability to manage it.

Deep in conversation, the men paid no attention, but from my new seat I heard most of what was said. A complaint was in progress, and though the voice was similar to Oscar's, the speech was slower and...the term that came to mind was *lazier*. It had to be Kevin, and he was apparently looking at the menu. "Everything I like causes indigestion, blocked arteries, constipation, or gas," he was saying. "My doctor says if food tastes good, I should spit it out."

"I'm supposed to be careful too," one of the other men said, "I take three different drugs for hypertension." Having glanced at them while my waiter did the place setting, I guessed he was the one whose stomach pushed against the table edge. The fourth had shaved his balding head, going for the Mr. Clean look.

The waitress returned, and three of them ordered the special, a Reuben with home fries. Oscar asked for a bowl of tomato bisque. Once she was gone Bald Man asked, "How's it going with the kids, Oscar?"

"They're coming along." His tone hinted at uncertainty.

Belly Man had a voice to go with his profile, low and round. "I understand the boy has...issues."

"Peter suffers from social anxiety." Oscar sounded defensive. "He's intelligent, so he'll adjust. I find Lucy more

117

worrisome. She was only two when her mother died, and she was raised like one of the tribe."

"I heard she refused to wear clothes for a while." There was bemused humor in Bald Man's tone.

"Not *all* clothes, but she saw no appeal in some of the layers we consider normal, particularly underpants." Oscar chuckled, adding, "Now that she's experiencing a Michigan winter, she's more accepting."

"It has to be strange, having to talk a kid into putting on pants and combing her hair."

"Lucy is a strong personality," Oscar admitted. "If I want her to change a behavior, I have to present reasons she finds acceptable."

"So it's like you're arguing in court," Bald Man joked.

"Lucy's harder to deal with than any judge I ever faced." As the others laughed, Oscar's tone turned serious. "The worst thing is how…emotional she gets. Dealing with her can be exhausting."

The waitress arrived with their food. Looking over my shoulder, I saw her stoop to pull the note off Oscar's coat, which hung on a hook outside the booth. "Is this a hint, love?"

Oscar made it a joke. "I always need affection, Melissa, but if you hugged one customer, you'd have to hug them all." The waitress walked away smiling, and Oscar said to his tablemates, "I've done something to make Lucy angry. I'll have to come up with a way to appease her."

"Let her buy new shoes," Belly Man suggested. "Never met a woman that didn't work on."

Not Lucy, I thought. *Not even if they have those expensive red soles.*

When lunch was over, the two strangers left to attend a meeting. Oscar and Kevin stayed on, mostly because Kevin wanted a piece of the apple pie he'd seen in the dessert case.

"With your cholesterol levels?" Oscar groused. Kevin said nothing, and soon a large slice with ice cream on the side arrived at their table.

"Is your doctor recommending you have that procedure, or will he wait to see if the medications work?"

"We're waiting," Kevin said between bites. "I'm going to do better with my diet."

I frowned into my glass of water. Kevin Coburn wasn't that much older than I, but he looked fifty and was probably headed for a stroke, like Dear Old Dad. Reflecting Lucy might be right about Americans' sedentary, calorie-laden lifestyle, I made a mental vow to skip my bedtime bowl of ice cream and get out from behind my desk more often.

My attention was caught by a question from Kevin. "Do you suppose I could get a little advance on my share of the fees from the Gage Trust?"

"You got one two weeks ago, Kevin."

"Well, it's gone. I had some bills to catch up on, and now Sheila wants to do some renovating."

"You get a generous cut for doing nothing. Learn to live with it."

Kevin's tone turned resentful. "Ten percent split four ways. I'd be doing a lot better if I were the guardian."

"Kev, believe me, I earn my keep with those two."

I heard a nasty chuckle. "Are you saying you're sorry you pushed me out of the way?"

"I didn't—" It was apparently an old argument, and Oscar shifted gears. "You've been to the house. You know how they disrupt my life."

119

"They prank you. Big deal. They'll settle down in time."

Oscar's answering huff signaled that his brother was clueless. After that, there was only the sound of Kevin's spoon scraping the pie plate.

When they left the restaurant, I followed the Coburns back to their office building. In the lobby, I dawdled near a rack of sunglasses while Kevin stopped to buy an energy drink from a kiosk. They stepped into the elevator a few minutes later, presumably headed for the sixth floor. I considered what I'd seen over the last hour. Did it matter that Oscar fluttered the pulse of a busy waitress with his smile? Not really. Did it help to know that Kevin would have taken the guardianship? I couldn't see how. Had the lawyers' small talk told me anything new? No again. Oscar did seem to enjoy describing his wards' idiosyncrasies, but I discerned no dark intent behind it. He came across as what he was, a bachelor doing his best to cope with two unusual kids. His brother found it funny, though he clearly envied the wealth Oscar controlled.

In a way, the morning put my mind at rest. While Oscar was greedy and not as pleasant as he appeared, he didn't disgust his coworkers or slap his girlfriends around. It was hard to see him as a murderous villain, which meant I might jet off to Cabo on Saturday with a clear conscience.

I hadn't explained the prowler yet, but the simplest explanation was that there wasn't one. Knowing the kids' ultimate goal, I'd checked the dates of the police reports and learned that on the nights Lucy claimed to see a man at her window, Oscar had been away on business. Ilsa was apparently an excitable type, so she called the police every time.

Though I hated to think she was capable of such skullduggery, I was afraid Lucy had been establishing a record of attempted break-ins. Now, some night when Oscar was at home, she'd call for help. He'd hurry to her room, where Peter would smack him with his ball bat, later claiming he'd mistaken him for the mysterious intruder.

It wasn't a bad plan for removing an unwanted guardian, if not for the cold-blooded murder part.

I lingered in the building, wondering if I should go upstairs right then and warn Oscar of the danger he was in. While I didn't believe he was completely honest, the guy didn't deserve to die for his greed.

As I pondered, a woman left one of those pack and ship places and crossed the lobby. She was attractive in a wholesome way, her stride purposeful and her expression cheerful. A second later, I recognized her from her photo on the Coburn Law website. Marla Johnson, the newest lawyer at the firm, stopped at the kiosk Kevin Coburn had recently visited and placed an order for a smoothie. Stepping forward, I slid behind her in line, irritating a square-built man who would have been next.

"What's a good kind to get here?" I asked, and she turned to see who'd spoken.

Johnson was girl-next-door wholesome, with bouncy hair, lively eyes, and lips that appeared ready to break into a grin at any moment. Perhaps to make a more serious impression at work, she wore a dark suit: a black skirt and tailored jacket over a pale-yellow blouse. Looking into her round, blue eyes, I found myself wondering what Miss Johnson wore when she could dress as she chose. That kind of imagining warms a guy up on a cold winter day.

"I like the mango-maca," she said, "but everything here is good."

"I'll have one of those," I told the clerk. I paid, and then we moved aside to wait while our orders were filled. It was the perfect opportunity, if I could take advantage of it. "Do you work in the building?"

"I do." She didn't elaborate, which was wise. Cute shouldn't mean careless with strangers.

"I'm here to talk to..." I pulled out my phone and pretended to consult. "Oscar Coburn. I understand he's on the sixth floor."

Her eyes widened. "I work at the Coburn firm. Oscar is one of the senior partners, and I'm the new kid on the block."

"If it's okay, I'll go up there with you." In a teasing tone I added, "As long as you don't think I'm stalking you or anything."

"Follow if you want, but Oscar has an appointment in Ypsilanti this afternoon. He's probably already put on a fresh shirt and flossed whatever he had for lunch out of his teeth." She frowned. "You didn't call ahead, silly man?"

"It's not a legal matter. I'm an old friend of Peter and Lucy Gage."

A smile lit her face. "Oscar's wards. Aren't they great?"

"They are." I spun a story I hoped would work. "A few years back I worked for an anthropologist who knew Ray from college. We met him and the kids a few miles from the Yarru village so the two could compare notes. When I returned to the States last week, I heard Ray had died."

She tilted her head. "Yes, the whole thing has been really sad."

"I had stuff to do in Windsor, but now that it's taken care of I zipped through the tunnel, hoping to find Peter and Lucy. The court records give Coburn's name, so I think I go through him to see them."

Her manner turned a shade more formal. "Oscar keeps the kids' lives private to stop scammers from coming after their money." She softened again. "Not that I'm saying you're a scammer."

I raised both hands. "Nope. I'm just Morrie, the guy Peter taught to make empanadas over a campfire."

"And how long are you going to be in Detroit?"

"I'm between jobs, so that's up to me."

Our smoothies were ready, and we accepted them and turned away from the counter. "Have you got a minute to sit down?" I asked.

She glanced at the lobby clock. "I should get back upstairs."

"Five minutes? I'd really like to hear how Lucy and Peter are doing. It's got to be tough on them."

Marla sipped at her drink. "I can't give you specifics."

"Oh, I wouldn't ask." I gave her my best self-deprecating grin. "Lucy was seven when we met. She might not even remember me."

"Lucy remembers a lot."

"And even as a little squirt, she had the vocabulary of a Supreme Court justice."

Marla chuckled. "I know. Sometimes I have to remind myself that she's nine, not forty-nine."

"Peter's smart too."

"He is, but he has more trouble interacting with people." I suppressed a smile. Marla was already forgetting I was a stranger. "He does well academically, but he hasn't made any friends at school."

"I'm sorry to hear that."

"Oscar says he joined the robotics team. He'll make friends there."

"That's good."

A slurp indicated I'd reached the bottom of my smoothie, which, by the way, was disgusting. I'd swallowed it in large gulps, trying not to taste whatever nasty ingredient ruined the mango flavor and overpowered the almond milk.

"If I come back tomorrow, do you think I could see Mr. Coburn?"

Marla checked her phone. "It looks like he'll have a few minutes around 11:15. Stop in then."

"Great. Will you ask him to see me at that time if I keep it short?"

She put up a hand. "I make no guarantees."

"Maybe you and I could have lunch afterward."

She shook her head as if she meant to say no, but in the end, it was, "I'll see how my schedule looks."

My heart did a little flippity-flop at the possibility she couldn't say no to me. *Max, you charming dog.* Marla disappeared into the elevator, giving me one of those finger waves that attractive women get away with while the rest of us can't.

CHAPTER SIX

When I got back to my car, I texted Lucy Gage. Yeah, I texted a nine-year-old kid: *Call me when you can.* I needed to know what she'd told my old non-pal Dodger.

The call came about ten minutes later. Putting her on speaker, I said, "Lucy, I had a visit from Roger Ainsley."

"Oh."

"Did you go to him before you came to me?"

"Yes." She cleared her throat, and I realized the kid had sinus problems, probably from her recent, drastic change in location. "Having no accurate way to judge available candidates, we went alphabetically."

Dodger had named his agency AAAA Investigations, one more *A* than I had. The guy is pure cheese.

"You made the same pitch? One hundred thousand to kill your guardian and ten thousand to him as a finder's fee?"

"Yes."

"He turned you down."

"Not exactly." There was an odd sound, something rubber hitting something metal, followed by a bunch of girlish screams. "I'm in gym class," she explained. "They're playing volleyball."

"Couldn't get out of it today, huh?"

"I'm hiding behind the tumbling mats. Ms. Bartleson doesn't notice who participates as long as you're there and dressed at roll call." As a whistle sounded in the background, Lucy said, "Mr. Ainsley was our first prospect, but when I made our proposal, he ordered us to get our 'baby asses' out of his office. We were disappointed in his reaction, but once we were outside, I realized we should have proven we had the funds. I wanted to go back in, but Peter said Ainsley is a man of poor character."

My unspoken comment was *Go Pete.* Despite his social struggles, the kid had a good sense of people. "You did as he said."

"Yes. We went on to the second name on our list, which was you." There was a cheer in the background, and then Lucy asked, "How did you find out about Mr. Ainsley?"

"I think he started wondering if you really have that much money. He followed you to my office, guessed you hired me, and now he wants to stick his nose in."

"Is he dangerous?"

"I doubt it, but he isn't exactly honest either. If he could con you into handing over the money, he would."

"We'll definitely call you if we see him again."

"Is the money in that safe place you told me about?"

"Oh, yes."

"Not still in the black gym bag?"

"Of course not. It's somewhere no one will ever find it."

"One more thing. Do you think you can get Ilsa to come with Adam when he picks you up after school?"

Lucy considered. "If I say I'd like to stop at the mall and get a few things, she'll be there in a heartbeat." Her tone turned sardonic. "Ilsa can be bought for any number of designer goods."

"Do that. While everyone's gone, I'll do some reconnaissance."

"Be careful. There are alarms on every window and door, and cameras all around the house."

"Okay. I won't touch anything, and I'll cover my face. They'll know someone was there, but they won't know who."

"Let me talk to Peter. He's got the app for the security system on his phone, so he can turn everything off."

"Is Oscar okay with that?"

"Peter comes and goes at odd times and from different exits, like his bedroom window at midnight. The alarm company was going nuts, so Oscar let him put the code to disable the system on his phone."

"Then Peter can disable everything?"

"Oscar had a whole list of rules he had to agree to, but yes."

"That would be great," I said, though I'd wear my ski mask, just in case. "Let me know what he says."

"Mr. Dunham, I'm glad Peter insisted we reject Mr. Ainsley, because I believe we found a man of integrity in you. Gotta go now. See you." The screen said *Call Ended*, but the day felt a little warmer. Lucy had decided she approved of me.

Back at Deer Creek, I went to Dinah's and hung out with her until time for the nanny and chauffeur to leave to pick up the kids. Lucy had texted a *K,* which I took as an indication she'd made the arrangements I requested. The shopping trip would give me time to figure out how the prowler—if there really was one—came and went without leaving signs of his presence.

When I told Dinah my intention, she suggested, "Why don't I drive you? I can hang out near the entrance, and if someone shows up, play the confused old person to give you time to get away." When I hesitated, she added a reminder. "If Frank sees you near the Gage place, he's sure to give you grief."

"How do you know their name?"

She gave me a wicked little grin. "Frank mentioned the house number, so I looked them up in the resident guide." Dinah reached for her purse, bigger than the proverbial breadbox. "Now, shall we go?"

I agreed, with the caveat that she was not to leave her car for any reason. Dinah drove the short distance to #815 and pulled into the driveway of an unoccupied house across the street. "I'll sit here and play with my phone," she told me. "If anyone asks, I'll explain that I never drive and text, which is completely true."

Peter had texted me a diagram of the house and grounds, neatly drawn and labeled. The main floor contained the expected rooms, though sometimes there were multiple versions: dining rooms (2 full and a breakfast nook); kitchen (with a full pantry at the back); living rooms (one formal, one less so); recreation room (with a home theater and a golf simulator); and study. All were dramatically more spacious than any home I'd ever been in.

The second floor was reached by a large, wide staircase. There, the east wing was all guest rooms while the west belonged to Lucy and Peter. Lucy's rooms were situated at the front, in the northwest corner, and her bedroom window overlooked a breezeway connecting the garage to the house. Peter's rooms faced the back yard, which, due to his dislike of disturbance, probably pleased him no end.

The third and final level was also divided neatly in two, its halves reached by stairs that split on the second floor. To the right was Oscar's apartment. On the left was a large open space that Peter had labeled, "Presently Empty: Site of Future Conservatory."

Windows at the Gage home were marked with the logo of a state-of-the-art security firm. Since the prowler hadn't set them off, I assumed he hadn't actually attempted to get in. According to Mom, the sheriff's report suggested they were dealing with a possible window peeper. They also mentioned an "overly imaginative child," which indicated to me they might not have made a thorough investigation.

Waiting until there were no cars coming and, as far as I could tell, no one watching, I climbed the gate, dropped to the pavement on the other side, and hurried up the driveway. I had to agree with Bobby's assessment; the place was impressive. I walked all the way around the house, stepping into old footprints in the snow to leave no sign of my snooping. I didn't touch the windows, fearful that Lucy might be wrong about the app controlling the whole system. Through the sheer curtains, I got glimpses of the décor and elegant furnishings inside.

I examined the trampled snow along the perimeter of the house. The police had made plenty of tracks, but according to what I heard, there'd been no unexplained footprints when they arrived. Had the intruder flown to the second story via jetpack?

An answer suggested itself as I came around the west end of the house and passed under a breezeway. The garage had a loft apartment, which my map said was occupied by Adam Saracco. A side window on that level overlooked the breezeway, making it possible for a person to reach Lucy's window entirely above ground. The sun had melted the snow on the roof, so an intruder using that route would leave no sign.

Saracco was a convicted thief. Did he plan to rob his employers' home? Or worse, plan to kidnap Lucy and hold her for ransom? Adam knew the kids' routines. He knew when Oscar was away. Though it was unsettling to think a member of the household was a threat, I liked that scenario better than the one where Lucy and Peter made up a night-time visitor to pave the way for murdering Oscar.

Why would Adam Saracco appear at Lucy's window multiple times, apparently unconcerned about her seeing him, and then leave?

Thoughts of kidnapping and burglary fled as the real answer came to me. The prowler wasn't there to break in, but to scare Lucy into calling the police. Someone wanted her to seem like a girl who cried wolf.

I returned to the front of the house, deep in thought. When the object of my musings pulled up to the mailbox at the end of the driveway, I stepped quickly into the breezeway. Though I'd avoided being seen for the moment, I was in trouble. With Adam at the gate, I couldn't exit that way. The rest of the property was enclosed by ten-foot metal stakes topped with spear-like caps. Though I might be able to scale it, the process wouldn't be quick. Added to that, I had no idea what I'd find on the other side. An unfriendly guard dog? An indignant neighbor? In broad daylight, it was unlikely my presence would escape notice.

As I hesitated, unsure what to do, a familiar voice called, "Yoo-hoo!"

I peeped out. As Adam scooped letters out of the mailbox, Dinah approached, her funny knitted cap pulled low around her ears. "You *promised* you'd stay in the car," I muttered.

Adam hesitated, and I imagined what he was thinking. He could ignore the old lady and continue up the drive, but she might report his rudeness to his employer. In the end, he chose to be polite. Rolling down the window on the passenger side, he waited to see what she wanted.

I leaned out a little farther, considering the possibilities. The car sat at the left side of the gate. Adam was turned away from me, his wide face and pug nose in silhouette. Taking advantage of the opportunity, I hurried toward the gate, using trees and shrubs as cover. Dinah stood a little back from his window, forcing Adam to turn even farther away as they spoke. Dinah played the role of neighborhood snoop to perfection. "I understand the police were here last night. Not the first time either, was it?"

I couldn't hear him clearly, but Adam said something that ended with, "...no big deal."

"A false alarm?" Dinah put a ton of doubt into her voice.

I'd made it to the gatepost, a large concrete pillar that screened me from view. In gruff tones, Adam explained that the little girl who lived there was a bit of a scaredy-cat who often imagined someone trying to break in. "There was nobody out there," he assured her. "You shouldn't worry."

"Did the police confirm there was no intruder?"

"That's what the nanny says. I wasn't here last night."

"You don't live on the premises?" Another nosy question, but old people get away with stuff like that.

"I do, but last night I stayed over with a friend."

Ah, the old "I was with my girlfriend" defense.

"Well," Dinah said in an irritated tone. "I'm pleased to hear we haven't got a crime wave going on, but still, it's upsetting when a child stirs things up this way. I hope you've punished the girl for fibbing."

I peered around the gate post. Adam was focused on Dinah, who now leaned into the car like she was planning to be there for a while. Taking the best chance I was going to get, I slid out the gateway and around the pillar. Though Dinah was facing me, she gave no sign she'd seen.

Shifting the car back into gear, Adam added a final comment. "The girl's a flake, but she ain't mine. All I got to do with her is drive her where she needs to go."

The BMW went up the drive, its black-tinted windows giving it a slightly sinister look. Dinah returned to her car, backed out, and stopped in a spot where I could get in without Adam seeing. On the way to her house, I explained the two possibilities: either Adam using the over-the-roof route to scare Lucy, or the kids making up the intruder for their own purposes. "I'd say it's the former," she said with conviction. "Even on the briefest acquaintance, one can tell that man hasn't got a kind bone in his body."

131

I wondered if anybody has kind bones, but it's a figure of speech. I get that.

"Either way, I don't think the intruder is a threat. I can turn my attention somewhere else."

Dinah had made this upside-down brownie thing. Once the batter's spread out in the pan, she pours a mixture of hot water, cocoa, and brown sugar on top. As the brownies bake, chocolate pudding magically appears on the bottom. It was amazing, and even better with ice cream and a dollop of whipped cream. While I was enjoying my stay, Dinah was worse than my mom for making irresistible baked goods. I'd have to watch my waistline.

When we finished our before-dinner dessert, Dinah sat down to do some crossword puzzles. She'd already loaded her crockpot with ingredients for beef stew, and it smelled wonderful. I started for my room, but as I passed a window, I noticed a hulk-ish figure lurking near the garage. Stepping out the kitchen door, I called softly, "What are you doing back there?"

A head appeared, disappeared, and then appeared again. Finally, all of Peter Gage came into sight. He wore flip-flops, jogging pants, a jacket too light for the temperature, and no hat or gloves. On his back was the ever-present knapsack. When he was close enough that we could speak without shouting, he answered my question. "I'm waiting to talk to you."

"Okay, here I am."

He had trouble getting started, but Peter had a story to tell, and after a few "ums" and "uhs," he said, "Lucy told me you…planned to scout the property, so when Adam…went back to the house, I said I didn't feel like shopping and came with him. I saw what the old lady did to help. It was pretty cool."

"She's clever." Peter speaking in complete sentences still surprised me, but I tried to focus on information.

He glanced behind me. "What are you doing at her house?"

"Mrs. Ellerson invited me to stay so I can be close to you and Lucy in case of trouble."

"Then you believe what we told you about Oscar?"

"I can't honestly say that yet, but I'm working on it."

There was a long silence while he pondered. "That's cool."

Though I was pleased to hear Peter communicating, the odor wafting toward me was nothing less than stomach-curdling. Did I know the kid well enough to give him advice on hygiene?

I decided that was a no. "Anything new I should know about?"

"The sheriff asked Ilsa to bring Lucy in tomorrow so he can talk to her in person. I think he intends to warn her about calling in false reports." He made a disgusted huff. "It's Ilsa who insists on dialing 9-1-1 every time."

"Tell me why you pretend to be so...messed up."

"It's not pretending, really." He chewed at his bottom lip. "When Dad died and Lucy and I had to come here, I got...upset."

"Perfectly understandable with the trauma you experienced."

"Right." He licked his lips. "When I get like that, I sort of shut down. The Yarru never had a problem with it, but here people expect me to act like they do." Sticking a finger in his ear, he jiggled it around. "If I don't talk and smile and say, 'Hey, dude,' they make assumptions. That means most of them leave me alone."

"I see."

Though he spoke more freely than before, Peter still looked mostly over my shoulder. "It took Oscar about ten seconds to decide I was a freak, and it took me about that long to decide I didn't trust him."

"Why do you trust me?"

"Lucy likes you, and besides, you never once called me Buddy."

"Why did you come outside when you saw me there last night?"

"I was afraid you'd think Lucy's faking it." He shifted his feet. "I wanted to talk with you man to man."

He shivered, and I glanced at his practically bare feet. "Why the sandals? It's February."

Peter grinned. "I got used to wearing sweaters and pants, but I still hate shoes."

I considered inviting him inside but decided Dinah's presence might fluster him. "Let's go sit in my car. It's got a good heater."

As I led the way, Peter said, "This is your Mustang? Cool."

"You like cars?"

"Yeah. About the only thing I used to see online that I felt bad missing out on was muscle cars. I read everything I could find about them and spent hours imagining what it felt like to drive one."

"In South America, in the middle of the Rainforest, you dreamed about the Mustang GT?"

He walked all the way around the car, noting its lines and touching a fender. "No different than watching *Star Wars* and picturing yourself piloting the Millennium Falcon."

"Good point."

"How old are you?"

"Fifteen and a half."

"Great. When this is over and you have your permit, we'll take this baby out and see what you can do."

The look he gave me was pure joy. "Awesome, Mr. Dunham."

"Max. If you're going to drive my car, let's be on a first-name basis."

Getting into the Mustang, I started the engine and turned the heater on high. Peter couldn't get in with his backpack on, so he slid it off and set it on the garage floor. Once we were in, I noticed the nasty smell was gone. "Do you know there's something rank in that backpack of yours?"

He shrugged. "Guess I don't clean it out as often as I should."

"That might be a good project for tonight."

Peter met my gaze for a moment. "You know some animals use scent to protect themselves, right?"

"Sure. Skunks, stinkbugs."

"Maybe it works for people too."

Unsure how to respond to that, I said, "Tell me exactly what you heard Oscar say on the phone that day."

His brow furrowed as he called up the memory. "He said it would be better if there were only one of us." The next part amped up my concern, at least if Peter had heard correctly. "The other person must have asked a question, and Oscar said, 'The girl is more irritating to have around, but the boy's issues would make it easier to explain to people.'"

"That's cold."

Again, Peter looked directly at me for a moment. "I'd kill him before I let him hurt Lucy, Mr. Dunham—Max." His shoulders slumped. "The thing is, I don't think I'm a competent killer. If Oscar attacked us I could fight back, but I don't think that's how it will happen."

"No."

"I plan it out. I imagine how I'd do it. I practice." He rubbed his chin, where a few sparse whiskers sprouted. "But then I start worrying. What if I wound him and he suffers? What if someone else gets hurt? Once I considered putting ant poison in his coffee creamer, but what if that one time, Ilsa decided to try it? She drinks coffee all day long, so she might."

"You're a decent human being," I said gently, "which means you'll never be good at premeditated murder. It isn't like in the movies, where the good guy shoots the bad guy, sticks his gun back in its holster, and strides into the sunset." It was the best opportunity I'd had to make my case, and I finished, "You need to stand back and let me investigate. I'll find out the truth, and then we'll decide what has to be done."

Looking somewhat relieved, Peter shouldered his backpack and left for home. Using the key she'd provided, I let myself in Dinah's back door. As I kicked off my shoes, she came down the hallway, putting on her coat. "I'm invited to play dominoes with friends. You're welcome to come along."

"Thanks, but I intend to re-read the information I have on Coburn."

"Re-read?"

"If Oscar is plotting something, he has an accomplice. I need to decide who that's likely to be."

"What about that chauffeur?"

"Adam's a flunky, not a guy you'd trust to be your partner in murder. From what I've heard of Ilsa, she isn't either. I think Oscar hired them as pawns, to do what he wants and believe what he says. It's a plus for him that neither of them is the type who might befriend the kids."

Dinah fiddled with her zipper, finally got it connected, and zipped. "It could be someone he works with."

"The brother, Kevin, is upset that Oscar got the position, and he also needs money. On the negative side, Kevin is no genius. I doubt Oscar would trust him."

"And the other lawyer?"

"There are two. I've met the newest one, and I'm working on getting to know her. The cousin, Sara Dailey, looks to be politically ambitious. Money might appeal to her as a way to advance her career."

Dinah raised a finger. "I meant to mention that earlier today I stepped outside and found a man peering into the garage at your car."

"He came up your driveway and snooped in your garage?"

"Apparently he's been looking to buy a Mustang like yours for some time. He asked if it might be for sale, and I said I didn't think so. He thanked me and went on his way."

"What did this guy look like?"

She smiled. "A bit like an Iditarod participant. He'd tied the hood of his coat tightly around his face, like it was thirty degrees below zero instead of thirty above. And he wore sunglasses the size of saucers."

"He didn't want you to be able to identify him."

A nod said she'd caught on. "He wasn't really interested in the car."

"No. He was interested in what I'm doing at your house. I think I know who it was."

Dinah picked up her handbag. "I wonder how he got past security."

I grinned. "Hey, I did."

When she left, I padded down to the kitchen in sock feet and helped myself to the stew she'd made. Buttering a piece of bread, I set it atop the bowl and retreated to my corner of the house. Putting my food on the end table, I went to my overnight bag and opened it to get the material on Oscar Coburn. It wasn't there. I took everything out of the bag, as you do when you're sure you packed something, but in the end, I had to admit I'd come away without it.

It wasn't the end of the world. I had a comfortable, tastefully decorated room with a big-screen TV, and I could swing by the office tomorrow and pick up the folder. I'd spend the evening watching cop-show reruns and dreaming of Mexico. The problem was that dream was fading, and I didn't know if I could get it back.

CHAPTER SEVEN

Feeling like a pedophile, I hung around outside the Lawson Academy, waiting to catch Lucy and Peter before they went inside. When Adam dropped them off, I sent the message I'd already written to Lucy's phone: *Look toward Carroll Street.*

She read the text, turned to see me waiting, and said something to Peter. They exited the school gate, but an adult wearing an orange plastic vest stopped them. Lucy gave an animated explanation, her smile as genuine as her excuse was not. The woman nodded, and the kids crossed the street to where I waited.

The day was cold, and they were bundled up like snowmen, with hats, mittens, and scarves. I wondered what winter was like for someone who's never experienced it before, but their shivers hinted it wasn't pleasant. I led them into an alley, out of the wind and a bit more private.

"Have you found the evidence we need?" Lucy demanded.

I admitted I had not. "I need more time."

Her brown eyes flashed. "You said three days."

"I did. Now I'm asking for three more."

Before Lucy could speak, Peter said, "Two."

I took what I could get. "Two would be good."

"I've had a new idea." Lucy took off one mitten so she could tuck a stray lock of hair under her hat. "You know how the dancer Isadora Duncan died when her scarf got caught in the spokes of a car wheel? Well, I was thinking. Oscar always wears a scarf—"

"No plotting until I'm done investigating." I pointed a finger at her. "You promised."

"All right." The second word dragged in the way any kid reluctant to cooperate lets that fact be known. "But I'm going to look for a long scarf, so we'll be ready if in the end we have to handle this ourselves."

With a sigh, I acknowledged that readiness is good. "I've got an appointment with Oscar today, and I plan to meet the others at the firm as well. I'll text you this afternoon and let you know how it went."

"Oh, that reminds me. I did as you asked." Lucy took a sheet of paper out of her tote bag. Folded into thirds, it looked like a business letter.

Opening it, I scanned the handwritten text.

"Thanks. This will help."

As Peter took her arm and they crossed the street together, I sighed deeper and longer. How far could I stretch things before one or the other decided it was time to put their own plan into action?

When they'd gone inside, I crossed to the school and waited in the staff parking lot. I'd studied the photos on the academy's website, so I'd recognize Lucy's current teacher, Ms. Dixon. Lucy had been pleased to be raised a grade level after Christmas break, "—not because I'm conceited, but because Ms. Dixon's lessons are so much more interesting than that other woman's were."

Dixon arrived with only minutes to spare, exited her car, and dragged two cloth tote bags out of the back seat. One was obviously heavier than the other, so she listed a little as she bumped the door closed with a hip and started for the building. When I stepped into her way, she looked mildly irritated. Taking out the letter Lucy had provided, I showed it to her and watched her lips move as she read: *Mr. Dunham is helping Peter and me with a matter that is crucial to our survival. Please give him any information about us he requests.*

Dixon's wary look turned to a grin. "That's Lucy's handwriting." She read it a second time. "Survival, huh? What's that about?"

"I'm looking into the Gage children's home life."

She looked shocked. "Are they being mistreated?"

"No, but they've raised concerns that need investigating." I shrugged. "It's not like they have tons of experience with modern American life."

"So true. Lucy writes about how she grew up and I shake my head. Her father was wrong to keep them so isolated."

"Have you seen signs that they're adjusting?"

She twisted her hands, easing the burden of the tote bags. "Lucy's had trouble making friends. She's very...critical of America."

"I noticed."

"Once she offended the other kids with her, um, assertive opinions, they pulled away. Now she's an outcast, but she's pretty stoical about it."

"I understand Peter isn't much better off."

"He's had at least one fight. Our principal cut him some slack, figuring he was reacting to all the stress."

"You get along well with Lucy, she tells me."

She smiled grimly. "I've tried to explain that she doesn't need to express her opinions quite so strongly."

"One staff member told me she's dramatic and attention-seeking."

Dixon made a disgusted snort. "I bet that was her original teacher, Mrs. Keyes. She likes girls who simper and say, 'Yes, ma'am' and 'No, ma'am.' Lucy isn't capable of that, so they butted heads quite often." She chuckled as an example came to mind. "Before Christmas break, Mrs. Keyes asked the students to tell their favorite story about the holidays. When Lucy's turn came, she said she wasn't a Christian, so she didn't know much about Christmas, but she'd heard an interesting custom from the mountain villages of the Andes. On Christmas Day, people settle scores with those they've disagreed with over the last year by challenging them to a fight." Her eyes twinkled. "The way Lucy described it, there are fistfights everywhere, men punching men, women rolling on the ground, and everyone cheering for their favorite."

"Mrs. Keyes thought she'd made it up?"

"She accused Lucy of trying to 'ruin the holiday spirit.'" Shifting her tote bags again, Dixon finished, "Lucy was quite offended at being called a liar, so I looked it up. It's a real event." I saw her wage a brief battle with herself between truth and discretion. "They should never have put Lucy in that woman's classroom. With her strong personality, odd background, and recent trauma, she needs a little mothering. By the time I got her, she'd alienated almost everyone in the building."

"It sounds like you like her."

"She's probably the smartest student I've ever taught." She shook her head. "Still, behind that big brain, she's a little girl who's lost almost everything."

She hefted her bags as if to go, but I had one more topic to cover. "Did you know Lucy's had the police called in several times over the last few weeks? She claims she's seen a prowler, but there's no sign of one."

Dixon tilted her head, taking that in. "If Lucy said she saw someone snooping on my property, I'd go out and buy a better burglar alarm."

Thanking the teacher, I left the school, side-stepping the last few students as I exited the gate and returned to my car. Having plenty of time before my appointment with Oscar, I stopped at my office for the folder of printouts I'd forgotten.

It wasn't there. I searched my desk. Nothing. I combed the rest of the office, then the anteroom, and finally my apartment. Where had I left it? What was I doing when I had it last? Why would I have...?

Dodger. His coughing fit had sent me for water, giving him the perfect chance to snoop. He'd taken the folder out of my bag and hidden it somewhere on his person, probably stuffed down the back of his pants.

The material was still in my email and could be reprinted. But why had Dodger wanted it?

"Because he didn't know their names." I said it aloud, disgusted with both of us.

Lucy and Peter had given Dodger their Della Street and Paul Drake story. When the kids stayed over an hour at my office, he figured I'd taken the job. The next morning he'd stopped by, apparently on a whim, and lifted the folder. Technically the crime was petty theft, and a guy should expect no less from Dodger Ainsley.

I added an item to my mental to-do list: hunt down my old co-worker and warn him off the Gage case in the strongest possible terms.

When I showed up at the Coburn offices at 11:00, the receptionist informed me I'd been added to "Mr. Oscar's" schedule. In a comfortably upholstered chair, I watched the workings of the firm as I waited. Behind the reception desk was an array of doors, and people moved back and forth between them. Marla crossed once from an office on the right to one in the center. She came out again a few minutes later, reading as she walked, and I didn't think she realized I was there. Later a woman exited another office and spoke to the receptionist for a few moments. From her age and air of authority, I guessed she was Sara Dailey, the new head of the Coburn Law firm. Her website photo was of a much younger woman, but no one updates those things.

When Sara entered an office, I got a glimpse of Kevin Coburn sitting behind a large desk made of dark wood. The day before, he'd exhibited jealousy over Oscar's control of the kids' money. I didn't know if that made him more or less likely to be Oscar's confederate in his schemes.

"Please come with me, Mr. Portman."

I followed the woman to a door that had remained closed since I arrived. Knocking gently, she opened it to allow me in. I stepped onto Moroccan tile too valuable for a mere mortal's feet to deface.

The office was functional but elegant. On the shelves behind the massive desk were photos of Oscar with various celebrities: a former Tigers pitcher; a guy in a Detroit Lions uniform; and a rapper whose name I wasn't sure of. Each rested a friendly hand on the attorney's shoulder, and I wondered if he'd paid extra for that.

Oscar rose, extending a hand. "Nice to meet you, Mr. Portman." He gestured at a chair, and when we were both seated said, "Marla tells me you know the Gage children."

"It's been a few years."

"I'm pleased to meet someone who might help me understand them."

"And I'm pleased to meet the man who stepped up to take care of them. I admire you for that."

He nodded modestly. "I was under the impression the children had never had contact with outsiders."

"That's true with one exception. The anthropologist I worked for at that time, Dr. Alan Dover, studies traits common to uncontacted tribes."

"What traits would those be?"

It was a test, but I'd memorized an article from the internet that I hoped made me sound impressive. "In general, the world's uncontacted peoples operate without any form of currency. They work about twenty hours a week. They maintain peace by minimizing private ownership and competition. Each person's contribution, whatever it might be, is valued. Everyone gives away what they find, catch, or make without expecting anything in return. Despite the West's dismissal of so-called primitive cultures, those things usually result in a peaceful, contented existence."

"And for that contented existence, they give up everything I consider worthwhile in life: education, entertainment, labor-saving devices, and the satisfaction of owning nice things." When I didn't respond, Oscar asked, "Are you an anthropologist as well?"

"Me?" I waved the idea away. "I was a glorified bearer, schlepping the professor's equipment and washing his socks. Dover knew Ray Gage from U of M, and when he heard Gage had stayed on in Peru after his wife died, he asked if he might visit the Yarru village. The tribe said no, but Ray agreed to meet at a spot near the Brazilian border for two weeks and let Dover pick his brain. While the two geniuses yammered happily each day, I got to know the kids." I smiled. "They were pretty cool."

"Yes. I've grown fond of them, though we had a rocky start."

"The adjustment has been tough on them?"

"On all three of us." He shrugged, indicating he accepted the trouble willingly. "They're great kids, as you say, but they have some…residual behaviors we're working on."

"Used to living wild."

"That's putting it mildly." He chuckled. "For the first few weeks they both slept on the floor, claiming their beds were too soft."

How smug he sounded, sitting there with his expensive haircut and designer aftershave. "They've had experiences no kid growing up in Detroit will ever have."

"And sadly, that creates problems for me." Oscar's expression turned serious, and he adjusted his desk blotter so it aligned exactly with the edge. "They have absolutely no understanding of finance. If Lucy and Peter had their way, we'd hand their whole estate over to the World Wildlife Fund, tomorrow at the latest."

"They want to save the planet. Not a bad idea."

Oscar leaned forward in his chair. "I've tried to explain that they can be generous without simply handing huge sums of money to strangers. Wise donors maintain a say in how their money is spent."

"Their response to that?"

Coburn frowned. "Those two know far more about air currents over the Pacific Ocean than they do about managing wealth."

"Ray taught them the things he considered important."

"Oh, I have no doubt of that." Oscar sniffed. "Ray was a good friend, but I wish he'd been a little less…radical."

Oscar had once called Gage by the wrong first name, so I doubted the part about them being good friends. While I couldn't say that made him a possible murderer, it didn't exactly build trust.

"I'm sorry to hear you find the guardian role troublesome."

"I don't think of it that way." Coburn met my gaze for a second, and I sensed a shift in his approach. "Peter has issues with social interaction. I do what I can to help, but it's slow.

Lucy's more socially adept, but she's idealized her experiences in Peru, and she denigrates life here to the point that she aggravates everyone around her."

"Do you think they'd respond to counseling?"

"I haven't suggested it yet, but I might have to. Both the school and the local sheriff have been in my ear lately, telling me that this or that behavior is inappropriate and has to stop."

"Gee, they seemed like such great kids when I knew them."

His tone took on an edge. "I'm guessing you never had to ask them not to wipe their noses on their shirts."

"Well, no."

"I find myself making requests every day for behavior any five-year-old here in the states knows: Stay off other people's property. Don't tell your teacher her diet makes her fat and her voice is too loud. Keep quiet when people refer to the U.S. as 'America.'"

"It's a lot to remember."

"We're working on it." He checked his watch. "I have a meeting. Is there anything else I can help with?"

"I was hoping I could take the kids out for dinner or something, so we could catch up."

Oscar's brow furrowed. "I'd have to ask them. As you say, it's been years since they've seen you."

"I'll appreciate it." I handed him a slip of paper with the number of a burner phone I keep for such occasions. "Let me know what they say."

When I left Coburn's office, Marla Johnson stopped me. "I can't get away for lunch today." My mood drooped until she added, "But I'll make dinner reservations and text you when and where, if that's okay."

"Sure." She returned to her office, and I stood there, flooded with happy endorphins. Marla liked me.

My happy thought was interrupted when Kevin Coburn left his office and shambled in my direction.

"Hey," I said with sudden inspiration. "That woman said I might find a cup of coffee somewhere."

"It's down here." He led the way to a cubbyhole that contained a coffeepot, an urn of hot water, and a mini fridge. While I poured a coffee, he got himself a Coke. His shoes were Jimmy Choos, his belt was fine leather, and his cufflinks looked like real gold. Like his brother, the guy enjoyed the finer things in life. It didn't do much for Kevin. He came across as a dweeb in nice pants.

Popping his soda can with a hiss, Kevin took a long drink and then turned his attention to me. "First visit to the firm?" His gaze was intent, and he seemed to anticipate my answer with great eagerness, as if I were a celebrity who'd dropped in on the way to a Broadway opening.

"Um, yes. I met with Mr. Coburn."

A hint of resentment colored his voice as he said, "There are two Mr. Coburns. He's Oscar. I'm Kevin."

"I see." When you hear something in a subject's tone, you use it. "He's a very impressive attorney."

"Umm." *Thank you, Sibling Rivalry.* "You need representation?"

"No. I'm an old friend of the Gage family. I came to see how the kids are doing."

"Nice. When did you last see Dr. Gage?"

"Um, it was a couple of years ago."

"Interesting guy, right?" His gaze held mine like a tractor beam. "I often wonder how he managed to get the things he needed out there."

He might have asked Lucy that question, but maybe he wasn't into talking to kids. Or maybe Lucy had the same dislike for Kevin that she had for Oscar. That would make questioning her downright unpleasant. Whatever Kevin's reasons for seeking information from me, I was able to answer, since I'd read a few of Ray's reports. "They had a spot about a mile from the village where a helicopter dropped items they requested. Everything was disinfected before they took it anywhere near the Yarru."

"What kind of contact did they have with the outside world?"

"Each of them had an iPad. In their private hut, the kids could watch TV and movies, read books online, or listen to podcasts."

He frowned. "So they knew *about* things here but never experienced those things."

"Yes. That's why their behavior has been a little...odd."

Fixing his pale gaze on me, Kevin said, "If they'd never seen another white person in the flesh, how did they react to you?"

The man's interest seemed honest, but since I was lying through my teeth, it was unnerving. "Uh, they were curious about us, of course."

"Were they really integrated into that tribe? I mean, did they do voodoo stuff with them and whatever?"

"My understanding is they participated fully, but Ray explained to the kids privately that while ceremony is important, it doesn't necessarily represent truth." As if Lucy whispered in my ear, I added what she would have said. "That applies to every society, not just the Yarru."

Before Kevin could ask another question, I changed the subject. "What's your specialty here at the firm?"

He tapped his fingers on the Coke can. "I explain to prospective customers the advantages Coburn Law offers."

"I see you wear a wedding ring. Wouldn't a married man provide the Gage kids a more familial atmosphere?"

His lips tightened. "Oscar wanted the job, and most of the time, Oscar gets what he wants." Taking the last gulp of his Coke, Kevin tossed the can into a bin near the doorway and left. Stepping into the hall, I watched as he lumbered back to his office. Though his resentment of Oscar was plain, I didn't see how that affected Peter and Lucy's situation.

I wanted to meet the last Coburn lawyer before I left, so I hung around the lounge, sipping my coffee, until Sara Dailey's office door opened. A woman exited, zipping her jacket. Dailey followed as far as the doorway. After they said their goodbyes, I stepped forward. "Ms. Dailey? I'm an old friend of Ray Gage. Might we speak for a minute?"

Her face lit with interest. "You knew Ray?"

"In South America."

She glanced at her watch. "Come in."

I entered an office as tasteful as Oscar's with similar furnishings and the same Moroccan tile. On the wall were photos, but instead of an array of sport and music celebrities, Sara's showed her with the mayor, the past mayor, and two city councilwomen known for their stand on women's issues. She indicated a chair, and we sat. Sara was probably in her late forties, with perfectly styled hair and nails that matched her deep-green suit. She spread her hands on the desktop as if forcing them to be still. "What can I do for you?"

"I spoke to Mr. Coburn, um, Oscar, about letting me see Ray's kids. He seemed...cautious, so I wondered if I might convince you to put in a good word for me."

Her eyes turned icy blue, radiating distrust. "That depends on what you want with them."

"Only a chance to express my condolences. I learned of Ray's death last week when I returned from Malaysia. It's awful, but I thought maybe a visit from someone they knew in Peru would provide a little comfort."

"Are you a scientist, Mr., um…"

"Portman, Morrie Portman, and no, I'm more a facilitator. I travel with scientists and do whatever they need me to, from taking pictures to fixing meals. I plan to get a book out of my experiences someday." I met her gaze. "Ray Gage was one of the smartest guys I ever met, and a good man as well."

"He was." Her tone was warm, and her eyes went soft.

"Did you meet him through the firm?"

"No. I met Ray in college, twenty-odd years ago. In fact, I'm the one who introduced him to Amy."

"Really? I'd like to hear that story."

The receptionist knocked once and opened the door. "Mrs. Diller is ready to give her deposition."

Dailey's mouth pinched with irritation. "Get it started, will you, Anne? Have her sign the necessary paperwork and explain what's going to happen. I'll be there in a few minutes."

"Right." The woman left.

Dailey turned her attention back to me. "Amy Farrell was assigned as my roommate freshman year." She tapped a long fingernail on the arm of her chair, remembering. "At first, I had no idea she was the wealthiest girl on campus. Amy was serious without being dull, and stunningly beautiful, though to this day I doubt she was aware of it. She and I hit it off, and when I introduced her to Ray Gage, who was in my Speech 101 class, they hit it off too."

"Ray was in a speech class? I can't imagine that."

She smiled. "He was trying to overcome his fear of public speaking. Since I haven't got a shy bone, the prof asked me to

151

help. I tried, but in the end, Ray simply couldn't handle large groups. He dropped out."

"But by then you'd introduced him to your friend Amy."

"I've never seen a couple more suited to each other." She spoke in a wistful tone, and I wondered if she'd wanted a relationship like Amy and Ray's or simply wanted Ray.

Pulling herself out of her reverie, Dailey said, "We stayed close until we got our bachelor's degrees. Then I entered U of M's law school while Ray and Amy got doctorates and then headed off to the Amazon jungle."

"Did you see Ray after Amy's death?"

Her lids drooped, hiding her eyes. "A couple of years ago, Ray's father became ill. Ray came home, spent his dad's last few days with him, and arranged the funeral when it was over."

"How did he seem?"

She paused to frame her response. "He was…lost. I…um, did what I could for him." Her words offered a wealth of possibilities, but when she continued, it was with mundane details. "Ray never got over losing Amy. I doubt he'd ever have come back here if his father hadn't begged him to. The trip itself was a nightmare. He had to leave his children with the tribe, and while he insisted they were perfectly safe there, they'd never been without him. On his return, he had to quarantine for a time, so he didn't take any Western diseases back to those people."

"It's a very different life," I said, hoping I sounded experienced.

Dailey leaned forward, and I sensed I was about to be tested. "Give me your impressions of Ray."

That was tricky, but I used Peter as a substitute. "At first he didn't talk much at all, but once he decided he could trust me, Ray became a whole different person."

"Yes." Again, her tone hinted at more than casual interest in the man.

"I intended to stay in touch, but now…" I let my voice trail off.

She turned businesslike. "I'll speak to Oscar about letting you visit Lucy and Peter. I see no harm in it, but he's the responsible party. It will be up to him."

"I'll be grateful for your help. I don't know when I'll be back to Michigan, if ever."

As we'd been talking, I felt my phone pulse. Once I'd left Dailey's office, I checked the voicemail Oscar had left. *Mr. Portman, I spoke to Peter and Lucy, and they have only vague memories of your friendship with their father. I don't think it would be good for them to have a visitor from their past right now. They should focus on what's ahead.*

I'd stopped in the lobby to read the text. The receptionist was off somewhere, but on her desk were a half-dozen of those blank blueback forms used for legal documents. On impulse, I took one and stuffed it inside my coat. A guy never knows when something like that might come in handy.

Outside the building I texted Peter: *Where mt w U & L 2day?* Mom texts complete words with punctuation, claiming texting will be the death of the English language. I argue that it's progress, like moving from hieroglyphics to phonemes. Once I sent the text, I hit the drive-thru of a Burger King and got lunch. Eating as I drove toward Roger Ainsley's AAAA Private Eye office, I heard the chime that signaled a response. At a stoplight I set down my Whopper and read: *Miguels by skool 3:15.*

Dodger was not at his place of business, and the door was locked. Peering through the glass, I saw a desk heaped with unopened mail, a couple of chairs probably bought at Goodwill, a microwave stacked atop a mini fridge, and a couch with blankets and a pillow stacked at one end.

Dodger lives at his office. What a chump.

Oh, wait.

To make myself feel better and to burn up the time before school was done for the day, I went shopping. Most guys claim they hate buying clothes, but I enjoy having something new to wear. Besides that, I had a dinner date with an interesting and attractive woman. At TJ Maxx I found a nice dress shirt in a green that kind of matched my eyes and a tie that didn't have pizza sauce on it. Tossing my purchases into the back seat of the Mustang, I drove around Lawson Academy until I saw Miguel's, which, as I'd guessed, was a restaurant, or as the sign said, "Restarante." Don't blame me. Blame Miguel.

I had already chosen a table that allowed Peter a seat in the corner when the two entered. Peter had his odiferous backpack, which wasn't conducive to eating. A waiter led them to the table, his nose wrinkling when he got a whiff. I had asked for a soda. The kids chose water, which made me feel like I'd stepped wrong. Despite their earlier acceptance of pizza, I imagined they usually ate things like kale and edamame. Lucy said nothing about my unhealthy choice of refreshment, which I took as kindness on her part.

"Where do your keepers think you are?" I asked when the waiter had left us with menus.

"Peter has robotics three days a week after school. I texted Ilsa and told her I was going to watch them test their current projects."

When the waiter returned with the drinks, Lucy said, "We'd like to order food." To me she explained, "Oscar likes dinner at seven. He says it's civilized, but we're half-starved by then."

154

Since I'd chosen an unhealthy drink, and since I had a date with Marla later, I opted for a fruit cup. If I thought that would impress them, I was wrong. They ordered the large nacho platter with extra cheese.

"We'll pay," Lucy said once our orders were in. "In fact, we should discuss finances. We can't have you working for free."

"Pick up the tab today, and that will be good for now."

"We'll settle the question of compensation once the details of our arrangement are clear." Lucy fiddled with the silverware for a moment. "On that subject, we wonder if we should extend the parameters of the contract. Oscar's confederate could be part of the deal."

"Come on," I chided. "Now you're moving into 'Kill them all and let God sort it out' mode."

Without a hint of humor, Lucy replied, "We don't believe in God, Mr. Dunham. We'll only kill who we must, and we hope it's a small number."

After umpteen years of Sunday school, I got stuck on the first part. "You don't believe in God?"

"Not the way most people do. We don't attend church, nor do we expect that the right sort of prayer will bring about a miracle." Leaving the straw wrapped and untouched, she stirred the lemon wedge stuck on her glass into the water with a spoon, making the ice swirl and tinkle. "Peter and I invented a belief system we call Imperfect Deism."

"Deists believe an omnipotent power created the world and left it to operate by natural laws." Again, I was pleased with myself for knowing a little bit of what she was talking about.

"Yes. When a Deist sees the sun rise or feels a cool breeze on a hot day, she recognizes the Power that created the universe and feels grateful because she's able to experience it. We added *imperfect* because we don't feel living beings can grasp what

155

God is. If that's true, humankind has no way to define its obligations to Creation."

Unwilling to agree and incapable of arguing, I fell back on the vague but workable, "Interesting."

Our waiter appeared and unloaded his tray with practiced efficiency. "Thank you," Lucy said when he finished.

With a wink, he said, "Anything for a pretty little thing like you."

Lucy's expression changed, and I saw Peter shift in his chair. Her frown became a grimace, and she closed her lips, holding back whatever comment lay on the tip of her tongue. The waiter left, unaware how close he'd come to disaster. Lucy turned to glare at her brother, who examined the nachos with apparent interest. To smooth things over I said, "Tell me about last night."

"I woke up because of a noise at the window." Lucy took a chip from the edge of the plate, dunked it into the bowl of salsa, and bit it in half. "It was like before, something being dragged across the glass, over and over. After a few minutes I got up and pulled back the curtain. A man I've seen several times now was outside, wearing a ski mask and a dark hoodie." She dunked the remains of her chip in the guacamole then in the salsa. "He just sits there, staring at me. It's unnerving."

Lucy took another chip and repeated the process, dipping, biting, and then dipping again. It wasn't the way I'd been taught to eat from a shared dish, but I tried not to judge. That became harder when Peter loaded a bunch of cheesy, meat-topped chips onto one palm. Sticking two fingers into the tub of guacamole, he transferred a large blob to the pile of chips, and then inhaled the whole thing in one oversized bite.

I looked away. "What kind of build?"

"Stocky, I think, but I only see his head and shoulders." Gesturing at the plate between them she added, "Have some nachos, Mr. Dunham."

After watching you double dip? "No thanks. Late lunch." As they ate—the term *mowed down* seemed apt—I asked, "What did you do?"

"Closed the curtain." Lucy licked her fingers. "I know that was useless, but it made me feel better somehow. I went downstairs and told Ilsa that it had happened again. She called the sheriff's department, though I told her it wasn't necessary." Dipping another chip, she spoke around her chewing. "They found nothing, no footprints in the snow, no sign someone tried to force my window open." She shook her head. "I don't understand what he wants."

"I think he's there to scare you into calling the police."

After a beat, her eyes lit with understanding. "To make them see me as prone to hysterics."

"And it's working. The cops think you imagine this boogeyman."

"But why? Oscar can't have me declared incompetent because I imagine prowlers at the window."

Unready to share the more sinister part of my theory, I replied, "I'm not sure, but now that I'm at Mrs. Ellerson's, you can skip the cops and call me if he shows up. Leave the nanny out of it."

She nodded. "I won't tell anyone but you and Peter."

That led to the main reason I'd called the meeting. "What does Oscar say about this prowler?"

"First he said I'd had a nightmare and woke up thinking it was real. Last time, he asked Peter if he was scaring me as a joke." She made a snort of disgust. "Like he would do that."

"Who else was there when he asked?"

She frowned, and Peter said, "Kevin."

"Right. He'd stopped by to borrow the snow-blower."

"Has Oscar made any changes to the house in response to the threat of an intruder?"

"He mentioned adding window grills, but it hasn't happened yet."

In his terse way, Peter gave the information I sought. "Gun."

"Oh, yes. Oscar asked if we have experience with firearms, and of course, Dad taught us to load, aim, and fire a weapon if threatened." She smiled at her brother. "Peter's an excellent shot."

"Is he?"

"The first month we were here, Kevin's son Tim had his birthday party at one of those laser tag places. They were all still being nice to us then, so we were invited."

"Sounds like fun," I said.

"They explained the rules in quite a condescending way." Her voice turned syrupy as she mimicked the instructor. 'This is a gun. This is the trigger.' We went into the arena, eighteen of us, with our vests and our weapons. I was the twelfth player eliminated." Pantomiming multiple shots, she finished, "Peter beat everyone."

I put up a fist for Peter to bump, and he did, grinning. "Good job."

His smile faded, and he pulled another chunk of cheese-connected chips into his hand. "Didn't end up making me any friends."

"There was a lot of grumbling, and beginner's luck was mentioned multiple times." Dipping another chip, Lucy waved it, spilling salsa on the tablecloth. "People here claim to enjoy competition, but instead of recognizing Peter's skill, every one of those kids got jealous."

"We call people like that sore losers."

Lucy's head tilted to one side. "I hadn't considered shooting Oscar, but we could make it appear accidental." That brought another off-the-wall example to her mind. "Have you heard of Ronald Opus?"

"The guy who supposedly jumped off a building and got shot in the head as he fell past his parents' window?" I shook my head. "That's what we call an urban myth. It never happened."

"But it's an interesting idea." Lucy waxed dramatic, and I recalled the people who had described her as a storyteller, not in a good sense of that word. "Regretting his decision to raise another man's children, Oscar jumps off the roof of the house. As he falls, Peter shoots at a squirrel on a tree branch near an open window. His shot kills Oscar, but it can't be his fault because Oscar was already as good as dead."

When Peter and I turned toward her like disgusted bookends, Lucy became defensive. "It was just a thought."

The gun concerned me, but not because of some urban legend. Its presence in the house, and Oscar's inquiry into the kids' ability to use it, all but confirmed my theory of how he planned to get rid of one ward and bring the other under his control. If I'd figured out his plan, there was nothing the kids could do to stop him. That was up to me.

On my return to Dinah Ellerson's place, I found that she'd made a big pot of soup. "I can't make the stuff in small quantities," she confessed. "You'd be doing me a favor if you help me eat it."

It smelled great, the fruit cup hadn't been filling, and dinner with Marla wasn't until seven, so I accepted. Dinah set out crackers and spoons while I filled two bowls with potato-corn chowder perfect for a February evening. As we ate, I told her how I'd spent the day. Dinah listened eagerly, her nods and hums of interest indicating she enjoyed having someone around other than her elderly canine companion.

Fang, an ancient bulldog, was nearly deaf, so he'd slept through my earlier visits. Dinah had introduced us when I moved into the guest quarters, but I can't say either was impressed with the other. Fang ignored me completely, perhaps in hopes I'd disappear. As for my reaction: Think of the ugliest dog you can imagine, then add another degree or two of ugly. If Fang were human, he'd be over a hundred, which apparently excused his drooling, farting, snuffling, and vomiting multiple times each day. Dinah clearly loved him, so I looked the other way when he dragged his butt across the hallway carpet.

"I met your Mr. Coburn today," Dinah said when I'd caught her up on what I knew.

Getting up, I rinsed my bowl and set it in the dishwasher. "How did that happen?"

"He was leaving for work when Fang and I walked by. He was driving a snazzy little number much different from the car that Adam person came home in yesterday."

"Oscar seems to consider the BMW i8 Coupe his." Looking at her from under my brows I said, "Since it was probably still dark when this meeting occurred, I'm guessing you planned your walk to coincide with Oscar's estimated departure time."

Her grin admitted as much. "When he stopped in the gateway, I realized we'd met before, sort of. A month back, Fang and I were walking across the commons area, and the goofy critter took off after a squirrel." She looked fondly at the dog, who lay sprawled in the exact middle of the kitchen floor, snoring noisily. "Occasionally, he forgets he's as old as Methuselah. Since I wasn't expecting it, I lost my grip on the leash, and Fang disappeared around the community building. I went after him as best I could, but I'm old too." Her tone turned outraged. "When I caught up, that man was kicking at my dog. Kicking!" Dog-kickers were apparently near the top of Dinah's list of society's offenders, somewhere between assassins and women who go clubbing *sans* underwear. "I didn't know *who* he was then," she finished, "but I saw *what* he was."

"What did he do when he saw you?"

"He turned all jolly and said he'd been trying to catch the dog so he could return him to me." She huffed disgustedly. "As if a smile and a smooth line could fool me."

"I also spoke with Frank today."

"Frank?"

"The security man."

"Oh, yeah. Frank."

"He has a high opinion of Mr. Coburn, I suspect due to the tip he got at Christmas, but also because Oscar is 'civilizing' the Gage kids."

"Those kids are more civilized than—"

She raised a hand, signaling I was preaching to the choir. "Frank believes Lucy's sanity has been affected by her father's death. She imagines all sorts of dangers and insists that someone needs to save her."

Again I opened my mouth to argue, but it wasn't Dinah who needed convincing. "And I suppose Peter is a brilliant but hopelessly inept loser."

"Frank claims the boy teases his sister, making her more excitable than she already is."

"Peter is about as likely to do that as he is to appear on *The Price Is Right* in a Scooby-Doo costume."

She set her bowl in the sink. "When one can't speak for himself, reputation is created by his enemies."

I sighed. "Lucy's hysterical. Peter's emotionally immature. Those lies have to be part of Oscar's plan."

"Then you're beginning to believe this man really is planning some mischief?" Dinah poured us each a cup of coffee and I sipped at it, noting with relief it was plain coffee with no exotic additions.

Mischief was a mild word for what Oscar might be up to. "He's had a taste of real money, and I suppose it's difficult to face the prospect of one day giving it up."

"He's laying groundwork for a *non-compos mentis* ruling."

"Yes. The intruder at Lucy's window has convinced the local police she's a scaredy-cat."

"How does he think he'll get away with it?"

"How can they stop him? They're kids. They're different, which too many people equate with being wrong. He's got the court behind him, his firm to support him, and his "I'm doing the best I can" manner, which makes people take his side. The kids haven't helped with their pranks, but they believe they have to strike back."

"I don't blame them," Dinah said. "I'd smear peanut butter on his chair seat too."

"Oscar didn't foresee Lucy and Peter resisting his control. He assumed they'd be happy if he bought them stuff." I grinned. "He doesn't understand them, and he underestimates their determination."

Her eyes twinkled. "We all underestimate others at times."

I gave her a rueful look. "Like when I left here that first time thinking you'd believed every word I said?"

"To be fair, I have decades of experience on you. Also, my former occupation required that I learn how to judge people accurately."

"What did you do for a living?"

"The last ten years, I was District Attorney for Kent County."

A guy should never make assumptions when he meets a little old lady.

CHAPTER EIGHT

Marla met me at a restaurant about a mile from the area where I'd told her I was staying. When she entered the dining room, I rose and waved discreetly. As she approached, I noticed a figure that looked familiar in the bar behind her. His back was to me, and I told myself I was mistaken. That slumpy spine could belong to a thousand guys.

She looked lovely, having softened her daytime look by removing her jacket and letting her hair loose from the bun she'd worn at work.

We ordered drinks and chatted lightly as we waited.

A shout from the bar drew my attention a second time. A woman had recognized someone she knew, and they embraced. When the man I'd noticed before turned to watch them, I realized Roger the Dodger was indeed here, miles from his usual stomping grounds, sipping a beer and pretending he had no idea I was in the vicinity.

"What's the matter?" Marla asked.

"I thought I knew a guy at the bar," I said, "but on second glance, I don't think it's him."

But it was. Dodger had followed me here. He'd appeared at Dinah's too. How many of my other stops had he noted in the battered brown notebook he carried everywhere? I wanted to stomp over there and demand he stop dogging my tracks, but there was nothing to be gained by making a scene.

Dinner was pleasant. I'd told myself to let things play out naturally. If Marla mentioned Oscar, fine. If not, I was spending an evening with an attractive, intelligent woman, which hadn't happened for a while.

We exchanged information about our pasts. Mine was fake, so our relationship wasn't starting on a good footing, but if it came to a point where I had to confess, I'd claim client confidentiality. Lawyers understand that.

Marla's past included a stint in the army. "The military was my ticket out of a dead-end hometown." With a rueful grimace she went on, "But once I was in, I realized I prefer making my own decisions, not carrying out someone's orders."

"That's why I quit—" As soon as I said it, I realized I'd mixed up my real self with the pretend person Marla was getting to know. "—my first job," I finished. "Do you get to make decisions at the firm?"

"Not many yet," she admitted, "but I can see a time when I will."

"You're hoping to become a partner."

She shrugged lightly. "I get along with everyone, and it's doubtful old Mr. Coburn will be back."

"You fit in with them, I mean, ethics-wise?"

"Oscar and I don't always agree on procedure, but I can usually see where he's coming from. Kevin is…well, he isn't as skilled as Oscar nor as detail-oriented as Sara, but it's brilliant that they found a way to use his talents to benefit the firm."

"How's that?"

She hesitated, and I imagined her thought process. As far as Marla Johnson knew, I had no real interest in Coburn Law and would leave Michigan in a few days. "When clients look for legal representation," she finally said, "they have lots of choices. Kevin is…" She fumbled for a word but couldn't find it. "Oscar calls him The Client Whisperer. In ways none of us completely understand, Kevin convinces bereaved families and recovering victims that our firm is their best choice going forward."

"Do you mean he's persuasive?"

Taking up her wineglass and swirling the contents, Marla shook her head. "Kevin loves asking questions, and it seems like he listens to the answers with his whole being."

I recalled that Kevin had seemed fascinated by my every word. Question after question. The rapt look. "You're saying it's all faked?"

"Not fake. Shallow." She gave a disdainful laugh. "If you talked to Kevin yesterday, and I asked him about it today, he wouldn't remember what you said. He probably wouldn't even recognize your name."

"But he decides which cases the firm should take on?"

"No, he doesn't." She took a sip of the wine. "I'm told it was a real problem at first. Kevin got clients to sign with us, but when it came to what the case was about, he'd say, 'I think she had a car accident.' It was embarrassing to have to call the client and start the whole process over. Then Sara had the brilliant idea of having Kevin record his interviews. Now, our paralegals summarize the cases, and clients are assigned an attorney who fits their needs."

"The guy's got one talent, and they've figured out how to use it."

Setting her glass down, she put her elbow on the table and leaned forward, chin in hand, bringing her face close enough that I caught the scent of her perfume. "Sometimes, I still forget and tell Kevin things, because he seems so darned interested. To be honest, he only remembers times when he thinks he got a raw deal."

"Like he wanted to be guardian for the Gages and didn't get the job."

"Did he?" Marla looked surprised, and I realized I'd betrayed myself again. Maybe I should take lessons from Bobby on undercover work.

Breezing past my comment I said, "So Oscar isn't quite honest, and Kevin has some kind of memory dysfunction."

Marla sniffed and sat back. "Kevin means well, and I respect Oscar's talent. Most of all, I admire Sara."

Hoping she wasn't aware I'd met Dailey, I asked, "What's she like?"

"Ambitious, clever, capable. Sara knows what it takes for 'girls' to break into the system." Marla wriggled her brows. "She says once I have some experience and a decent client list, she'll help me make partner."

One of the realities of the legal profession is that junior lawyers don't get to choose their superiors or affect the tactics they engage in. Oscar was a risk-taker. Kevin wasn't a strong personality. Now that Carson Coburn wasn't there to rein Oscar in, Sara might see Marla as an ally who'd help keep her cousin honest.

That led to a question. "Have you ever seen Oscar break the law?"

I saw right away that I'd stepped too far. Taking her purse from the chair beside her, Marla rose. "I don't like being used, Mr. Portman."

"I didn't mean to put you on the spot, but I worry about Peter and Lucy." As she turned away, I said, "Those kids are alone in the world."

"And very wealthy." Her tone was icy, and I flinched at its force.

"My being here has nothing to do with the money. I'm looking out for their welfare. That's all."

Her expression softened, but she wasn't yet convinced. "I shouldn't have talked about my coworkers. I expected you to be...different."

"I am. I mean, I'm not what you're thinking. I asked you out because you seem like someone I'd like to know better." That was almost true. "Shall we keep the rest of tonight's conversation focused on us?"

Marla hovered for a moment but finally sat back down. We talked—well, for a while I talked, using every bit of persuasion I could muster to convince her I really was interested in her. Eventually, the mood turned pleasant again, and when we parted at our vehicles, she gave me a peck on the cheek. Taking out a business card, she wrote her cell number and home address on the back. "If you aren't busy Saturday afternoon, stop by and watch the Michigan game on my big screen."

I still clung to the hope of being on a plane to Mexico on Saturday, but I said, "Sounds good."

Marla opened the door of her sporty little Pontiac but paused to add, "The complex is big, and all the buildings look the same, so they painted animals over the entry doors. The easiest way to find my building is to look for the lion."

As I brushed my teeth in Dinah's pink-and-purple guest bathroom, my phone burbled. It was Mom, with a long list of things she wanted me to know.

"That nanny, Ilsa Dausman, is woefully unqualified. She was let go from her last job after a month."

"Do we know why they fired her?"

"No, but the former nanny, Denice O'Henley, would have been a much better fit. She's the Neil DeGrasse Tyson of nannies, while Ilsa is more the Elmer Fudd version."

"The kids go to school now, so I suppose the caregiver's IQ isn't as important as it was before."

"If you say so." Mom paused, presumably to consult her notes. "You asked about firearms. Oscar has a license for a Beretta 92, which I'm sure you know is a 9-millimeter handgun.

It's accurate and easy to care for, so a homeowner might well choose it for protection."

"I'll bet he's made sure people are aware that Lucy knows where the gun is kept."

"Why would he do that?"

"Because he plans to make it look like she shot her brother during one of her supposed panic attacks."

"Get outta here."

"It's a theory, but it's looking more and more likely."

"Wow." Mom paused to absorb the idea. "That makes the last thing I have for you a lot more interesting."

"Yeah?"

"Ilsa is a frequent texter, and I managed to get a peek at her cache."

"You can hack phone messages?"

"Not until yesterday, but it isn't as hard as you'd think. Most people don't have a lot of security on their phones, because it gets in the way of what they want to use them for."

"Okay, so you got at Ilsa's texts."

"I did. I had to run them through a translator, since she mostly texts friends back in Austria. Generally, her messages are about as interesting as your neighbor's blog, but she says 'they' have concluded the prowler is Peter playing jokes on his sister."

"Who's *they*? She's the one who calls the cops every time."

"The idea that it's Peter is new. Before yesterday she was all, 'Oh my God, someone's after us,' but this explanation came along, and she seems happy to accept it. Ilsa claims Peter is hard to deal with because, and I quote, 'He does not like that I can tell him what to do.'"

"That might be true, since his I.Q. is at least twice hers."

"Scaring people sounds like a stunt an unhappy teenager would pull," Mom said, "and you admitted they like pulling pranks."

"If that were the case, Peter would appear at Ilsa's window, or maybe Oscar's, though he's on the third floor and hard to get to."

Mom clicked her tongue a few times as she put it all together. "Oscar hires a flighty nanny, who calls the police a bunch of times. Now he's planted the idea in her head that Peter is the intruder. You think he did all this so something terrible can happen."

"Yes." I chewed at a thumbnail. "I wish I were wrong, but I'm almost sure Oscar is setting Peter up to die."

CHAPTER NINE

On Friday morning, I followed the BMW to the Lawson Academy and waited to see Lucy and Peter disappear into the building. Knowing they were as safe as they could be until 3:15 p.m., I got on I-75 South, headed for the courthouse and a day of waiting for my turn to testify in the case of the State of Michigan v Edward Farrell. I was a small but vital part of the prosecution, having seen Farrell purchase the handgun he used to kill his business partner.

I was replaying the memory, making sure I recalled the details, when metal hit metal and my car lurched sideways. Freeway traffic had been funneled to the right, and in the closed lane, a county truck sat idling while two workmen sealed cracks in the pavement. At the sound of the crash the men looked up, their faces registering horror as they saw my car send orange barrels flying as it hurtled toward them. Dropping their wands, they sprinted toward the median. The first man made it, diving over a bank of dirty snow, but the nearer guy slipped and landed on his rear directly in front of me. Wrenching hard on the steering wheel, I managed to miss him, but my new direction put me on a collision course with the truck. I couldn't miss it, but I turned the wheel back to the left, managing to achieve a sideswipe instead of a direct hit. My car scraped along the truck's heavy bumper, crumpling the passenger side like a stepped-on beer can. When the two vehicles parted, my Mustang slued violently. I tried to hold the wheel steady as I braked to avoid swerving back into traffic. For a second I was sure the car would roll, but it finally came to a stop, still in the closed lane but perpendicular to the highway.

It took a few moments for me to realize it was over. In the open lane, cars moved by as if everything were normal. The Mustang's engine made odd sounds, several kinds of metal in distress. I experienced the surreal moment that follows a traumatic event: *What happened? Am I okay?* And again: *What happened?*

"Idiot!" The man I'd almost run down strode toward me, his face a mask of anger and clothes caked with dirty snow. "You almost killed us."

I couldn't answer. My voice was frozen, and my heart and lungs worked overtime, dealing with the surge of adrenalin I no longer needed. Wrenching the car door open, the guy reached in and pulled me out. My feet slipped on the snowy ground, and I grabbed hold of his arm to remain upright. That seemed to make him even angrier, and he pulled back a fist. As I prepared myself for a blow, a voice from above and behind us called, "Cool it, Sanders. It wasn't his fault."

"Huh?" Sanders paused, his fist still cocked.

"I saw it," said a man in the truck cab. "Somebody hit his car and knocked him sideways. He did really good to avoid hitting you."

With a halfhearted, "Sorry, dude," Sanders let go of my jacket. The driver climbed down and asked if I was okay. I was, but my car was not.

An hour later, a young state trooper had taken my statement, which consisted mostly of, "I don't know," and, "I have no idea." The Mustang sat on the tilt bed of a tow truck, and I rode up front with the driver, a friendly type named Luis who said he could drop me at the courthouse. Aside from being shaky and dazed, I was okay. I texted the attorney and told her what had happened. She expressed concern but said I had plenty of time if I was sure I was up to testifying. My best option seemed to be doing my duty to the legal system and then arranging for a rental car.

It wasn't until I sat outside the courtroom, waiting to be called to testify, that I was able to analyze what had happened.

Three possibilities came to mind for what I'd experienced. The most believable was that I'd been hit by some numbskull who'd been checking his (or her) texts and drifted into my lane. Other explanations required intent. Either the guy I was testifying against had sent someone to waylay me, or someone else wanted me hurt or killed. I didn't think I was important enough to the state's case to cause Farrell to try to stop me from testifying. Nor could I think of anyone else angry enough at me to put my life in danger.

People who text while driving should be boiled in oil.

My appearance at the trial went well. First the ADA established that I was a former police officer with commendations on my record. Then she asked a question designed to establish my integrity. "Isn't it a practice of yours to donate time to a group called Bring Them Back?" She held up an obscure article she'd found in my hometown newspaper. "You track down homeless vets and reconnect them with family."

"That's true." I didn't mention that the director of the organization had convinced me to become their bird dog while we were seeing each other—in the best sense of that phrase. We'd both moved on from the relationship since then, but I still did pro bono work for them from time to time. "My dad's a vet, and with an investigator's resources, it's no big deal." Some of the jury members smiled, which probably meant they'd decided I was a decent guy. The ADA's expression revealed satisfaction as she turned to my eyewitness report that the defendant had purchased the murder weapon a week before the victim was shot.

When he got his turn, the defense attorney tried to portray me as a sleazy shamus who'd say whatever the prosecution wanted, but he didn't make much headway. I remained firm in my testimony and didn't rise to any of his attempted slurs. When he finished, the prosecutor didn't even bother with redirect.

My part done, I left the courthouse and walked through light snow to a nearby car rental place. I answered questions, showed my license, and was given a 2019 Fusion. After a few minutes spent learning where everything was, I headed north to Deer Creek Estates.

I stopped near the accident site to pose a few questions I hadn't had the presence of mind to ask earlier. The truck was down the highway some distance, and two men were again sealing cracks, one drying them out with a heat wand and the other applying patching material. The man I'd almost hit, Sanders, sat in the truck, ready to move it along when they were ready, and I gathered they spelled each other, two working while one warmed up in the cab. Pulling off the road, I waved to the guy who'd seen me get hit. He looked tired, and I realized that their cold, physical task, done as cars whiz by a few feet away, was stressful. My recent experience showed how quickly things could go wrong for road workers.

He recognized me right away. "You doin' okay, man?"

"I'm good. I came to ask if you can tell me anything about the car that hit me."

"You ain't gonna hunt nobody down and shoot 'em, are you?"

Smiling, I raised both hands. "No shooting, I promise."

He frowned, trying to bring the scene back to mind. "It was an SUV, a Honda, maybe. Your little 'Stang didn't stand a chance."

"Don't remind me." The repair estimate would be scary, and I was already dreading the possibility that my insurance company would declare the car totaled.

"It could have been a Toyota or even an Escape," he said. "They all look alike these days. The only thing kind of different was the color—that shimmery blue, like Lake Erie in the summertime."

When I returned to my rental car, there was a text on my phone from Denice O'Henley, the Gages' former nanny. I'd tracked her down (well, Mom did) at her current job, working for a family in Toledo. Using Lucy's name as an introduction, I'd texted to ask for a meeting.

O'Henley seemed eager to hear about the Gages, and since I'd asked to see her in person, she suggested we meet at three o'clock in a mall food court near her current residence. A public place made sense, since she didn't know me from Noah's uncle. Checking my watch, I figured I had enough time to make it if the southbound traffic wasn't too bad. I texted back that I'd be there.

When O'Henley replied with a thumbs-up, I exited I-75 north and went the opposite way, back through the city and on to Toledo. That meant I passed the scene of my accident yet again, and I shivered at how close I'd come to killing a man or being killed myself. And some careless driver had gone on rather than face responsibility for what he'd done.

Could it have been on purpose? I rejected that. Malice aforethought felt creepy, and I preferred the idiot driver scenario. During my years as a cop, I'd been in situations where dying was a possibility, but I'd never been targeted for death. I tried to imagine how the incident could connect to Lucy and Peter Gage, but I saw no way it could. Oscar didn't even know I was investigating him.

It was silly to think someone hated me enough to plot against me, follow me, and attempt to ram my beautiful Mustang into a large piece of road-repair equipment. Still, if Oscar did have something to hide...

Calling Baker, my buddy on the force, I asked him to check for recently stolen, Lake Erie blue SUVs.

"Lake Erie blue?" he asked incredulously. "Is that a real color?"

"My witness is built like a fireplug, but he has the soul of a poet."

"Max, you know I can get in trouble for this."

"I don't need specifics. Just tell me if a shimmery-blue SUV was stolen in the last twenty-four hours."

He sighed. "I'll get back to you, but not till Monday. I'm swamped."

"Thanks, buddy. I appreciate it."

The drive to Toledo was all freeway and traffic was light, so I was waiting when Denice O'Henley arrived. I saw why she'd chosen the location. The food court had a bounce house, and O'Henley had with her two lively boys of about four.

"Richard, don't kick your brother," she ordered as they neared. "Martin, it doesn't help when you trip him."

Rising, I introduced myself. O'Henley made the boys say, "Nice to meet you, Mr. Dunham," but the singsong quality made it clear neither of them meant it.

"You get the boys set up," I suggested. "I'll get drinks."

"Coke, please." O'Henley led the twins to the ticket booth, where she paid while the boys toed off their shoes. As I waited at the counter, I watched Richard loft one shoe high enough to smack Martin in the forehead. O'Henley stepped between them to quell the looming battle. Richard claimed it was an accident, but the smirk on his face said otherwise. Rubbing his head and shedding crocodile tears, Martin pled the case for Richard to be banned from the bounce house. Though O'Henley showed understanding for his pain, she rejected the suggestion.

As I carried our drinks to the table, Martin spat at his brother. The nanny intervened again, wiping Richard's face with her scarf before shaking a finger under Martin's nose and uttering what had to be a threat in tones low enough that only he could hear. When she escorted them to the entry ramp, the attendant made a low comment that appeared to be a warning. Nodding to acknowledge his concern, O'Henley took each twin by a shoulder. "One fight in there, no matter who starts it, and we go directly home. You'll stay in your rooms until suppertime, and I'll turn off the wi-fi and cable."

Experience must have taught them she'd follow through, because hostilities ended abruptly. In seconds, the boys were bouncing happily, calling out to each other to "Watch," and "Do this." O'Henley sat down opposite me with a theatrical sigh and a good-natured eye-roll. I pushed the Coke toward her, and she took a long drink, her gaze moving to the bounce house as if to assure that her time was her own for a few minutes.

The nanny was about thirty and as trim as a boot-camp graduate. Everything about her was neutral: her clothing, her hairstyle, her manner, as if she'd purposely erased any trace of personality. I wondered if nannies are expected to do that.

Nodding at the boys, I said, "They look like tough nuts to crack."

"They've had four nannies in the last two years," she responded. "The last one quit after Richard sneaked into her room one night and dumped his ant farm in her hair."

I rested an elbow on the table, which wobbled under the strain. "Let me guess. Mom and Dad see them as high-spirited lads who should not be subjected to any sort of discipline."

O'Henley folded a napkin several times and put it under the table's uneven foot, testing to see that the wobble was cured. Meeting my gaze, she said blandly, "Every child offers

177

challenges as well as blessings, Mr. Dunham. I'm here to learn how Lucy and Peter are doing."

"I need you to give me some background on them."

Her face went blank. "I don't gossip about my children to strangers."

Taking the letter Lucy had written from my jacket pocket, I set it before her. "She said to show you this."

As she read the document, O'Henley's guarded expression melted. "That's Lucy." Touching the signature lovingly, she handed it back. "What does she mean when she mentions survival?"

"The kids came to me with a story, which is why I need your input. Would you say Lucy and Peter are capable of dishonesty?"

"I suppose everyone is, given the right circumstances."

I took that as a yes. "If you don't mind, I'd like you to tell me about your experiences with them in the Rainforest."

"All right, if you promise that once I've answered your questions, you'll answer some of mine."

"I'll tell you what I can."

We fell silent while she considered that, which allowed us to hear Martin express pleasure at his current experience with a word that made O'Henley's lips go tight. "Excuse me for a moment."

Hurrying to the bounce house door, she reached in and, after a few unsuccessful attempts, grabbed the young man by the arm. Serious communication followed, in which she did a lot of talking and he did a lot of nodding. When she released him, O'Henley returned to the table, her cheeks pink. "My employers don't censor their children's 'natural vocabulary,' but I put my foot down when we're in public."

"I'm on your side on that one." I tried a little flattery. "Are you responsible for turning Peter and Lucy into little geniuses?"

"Hardly." Though she kept an eye on the bounce house, O'Henley launched into the story I'd come to hear. "Ray and Amy Gage planned to spend a year or two with the Yarru, but after Amy died, Ray stayed on."

"He was more comfortable in that culture than in his own."

"Exactly."

"Didn't he consider his children's safety? Life in that jungle was obviously dangerous."

She frowned. "That's true, and I did worry sometimes. The kids did whatever Ray did, whether it was climbing trees or exploring caves or wading through swamps full of snakes."

"You make Gage sound like Indiana Jones, but I think of science as mostly plodding work."

She shrugged. "While much of it is boring and repetitive, the best field researchers go places and do things most people wouldn't."

"Which is exactly what got Gage killed."

"I admit the kids are physically safer here in Michigan. I'm not sure what was right for them emotionally." She fiddled with her watch, an easily readable face with a plain black band. "If they'd come back after Amy's death, Peter might have gotten help with overcoming the trauma."

"He was there when she—when the crocodile—?"

"They all were, though Lucy didn't see the actual...death."

"Holy moly. For a kid with socio-whatever Peter's got, that's a heavy burden."

O'Henley nodded agreement. "Dr. Gage had learned to work around his issues, and he believed his son could do the same." She moved the soda in circles, leaving a series of damp rings. "Tolerant of individual differences, the Yarru accepted Peter's reticence as his way of being."

"No pressure."

"Despite what we Westerners perceive as deprivation, those people lead peaceful, happy lives."

"Lucy doesn't project peace. She hates everything about living here, and she antagonizes everyone." Thinking of Ms. Dixon, I amended, "Almost everyone."

"Lucy has an assertive personality."

"To say the least. How did the tribe deal with her?"

O'Henley paused, apparently trying to put a concept into words I could understand. "Among the Yarru, only insiders and outsiders exist. Members are accepted without question, and while they might be reproached for bad behavior, they're never shunned or rejected. Lucy was always free to speak her mind." She frowned. "She was outspoken, but never rude. If she's different now, it's most likely from unhappiness."

"She was their little sweetie, part of the tribe but special." I sipped at my drink. "Here she's just another little girl."

"Our society has many faults, as I'm sure you recognize. I can imagine that Lucy points them out with more honesty than tact." O'Henley watched the boys' faces appear and disappear at the windows of the bounce house. "Peter deals with unhappiness by pulling into his shell. Lucy lashes out."

"Shouldn't their dad have guessed they'd have problems adjusting to modern life?"

"You'd have to know Ray." O'Henley's tone was indulgent. "To his way of thinking, the kids had an idyllic childhood: a close-knit social structure, a healthy lifestyle, and an excellent education. They had access to the outside world, but they didn't have to deal with the stresses of that 'modern life' you mention."

I shook my head. "It seems odd to me."

"Ray spoke as if they'd always be with the Yarru. The kids would share the work as they were able and continue it when he got too old." She shrugged. "As far as I could tell, they were fine with that."

"How did you enter the picture?"

"When Ray came home to spend his dad's last days with him, the old man begged him to bring the kids back to Michigan. When he didn't agree, Ray's father insisted it wasn't fair to assume Peter and Lucy wanted to spend their lives in Peru. Because Ray loved his father, he compromised, putting an ad in the *Detroit Free Press*." She traced the imaginary headline: *"Seeking tutor willing to travel. Excellent salary.'* Having a bachelor's degree in literature with a minor in European history that wasn't getting me anywhere, I applied for the job."

"That was a big step."

Her expression turned wry. "I responded with visions of resorts in the Alps and beaches at San Moritz, but to his credit, Ray didn't sugarcoat it. He described a mud hut on a river with no name except 'the river.' But he made life in the village sound appealing." She waved, dismissing her naïve assumptions. "My actual arrival was a shock, of course, but before long I was in love with the hut, the river...and Peter and Lucy."

"Did you and Dr. Gage get along well?" I tried to keep my tone casual, but sexual attraction seemed the obvious reason a young woman might go into the Amazon Rainforest with a man she hardly knew.

A sharp glance told me she'd discerned my assumption. "Ray was my employer. Within a few weeks, we'd become friends, and within a month, I was helping where I could with the research." After a pause, O'Henley added, "He was attractive, so I can't say that didn't factor into my initial decision." Her lips twitched. "Whatever my subconscious motives were, I'm not sure Ray even noticed I was female."

"Were the kids pleased to have you join them?"

One brow rose. "There was a period of adjustment."

The same words Lucy had used. "They gave you a hard time."

"Lucy left a pile of lizard innards in my doorway, a spell to send me back where I came from." O'Henley grinned at my grunt of disgust. "She admitted later that she doesn't believe in spells, but she said it was worth a try." Her eyelids drooped. "As for Peter, he went into one of his long silences. He didn't look directly at me for months."

"They weren't happy to have an outsider show up."

"I told myself they'd get used to me in time."

"And did they?"

She rubbed her fingertips together. "There were some interesting experiences for a few weeks." Her eyes rolled up as she remembered. "First there was the snake in my sleeping bag."

I shivered. "That's horrible."

O'Henley shrugged. "I grew up with brothers, so it wasn't my first snake. And it was a harmless type."

"No such thing if it's in your bed."

Rather than argue the point, O'Henley went on with her list. "I found pebbles glued inside my hiking boots, bird dung in my clothing, and one morning, a spider the size of a tennis ball at the bottom of my coffee cup."

"They weren't happy to have you there."

"Exactly." When she spoke again, her tone was defensive. "I knew I couldn't demand the kids conform to cultural norms they saw as illogical or unnecessary."

Lucy's teacher had said something similar. If she could present a concept in a reasonable way, Lucy accepted it. "So you didn't work on things like making them chew with their mouths closed."

O'Henley seemed pleased that I understood her position. "I'm no computer genius, but without anyone to expose them to new technology, the Gages' skills had lagged. That put me in a position of strength."

"You became the guru?"

"I suggested Ray get tablets to replace their laptops. Soon the kids were asking for help with apps and browsers. They found opportunities to expand their knowledge they hadn't known about before. Their father had no interest in YouTube or TikTok, but they were fascinated." She blushed. "Once they decided I had value, the pranks stopped."

"It must have been weird for them, seeing things online that they'd never experienced, like flush toilets and KFC."

"I tried to show them the outside world without denigrating their day-to-day experiences in any way." She rubbed at her neck. "Despite my successes, I never got any of them, not even Ray, to practice social skills like table manners."

"That's apparently been a big disadvantage at school."

O'Henley shook her head. "If I'd had more time…"

"But Ray Gage died."

Her eyes reddened, and she blinked rapidly to dispel unshed tears. "It was horrible."

"What did you do when it happened?"

"I wasn't sure what was right. Lucy and Peter had no desire to leave Peru, but this lawyer appeared on Ray's laptop and ordered me to bring them to Detroit."

"Oscar Coburn?"

"It was a woman."

"Sara Dailey."

"Yes. She said the firm had legal custody, and they wanted the kids in Michigan as soon as possible." Her smile was grim. "Lucy refused at first, but Peter and I convinced her we had no choice. If they sent people to get us, the Yarru would fight, and that would be disastrous for them. Once Lucy agreed we had to leave, she contacted Sr. Diaz, and he made the arrangements."

"Those must have been hard days."

"At one point Lucy said it felt like she had to step into a movie she'd always considered fantasy."

Lucy's belligerence was not arrogance, but self-defense. She was uncomfortable here, scared and unsure where she fit. She had no support except Peter, who was fighting his own demons. She battled back the only way she knew how, by refusing to believe there was anything good in the change that had been forced on them.

"It would have been easier for them if you could have stayed on."

"They asked me to, and of course I said I would." O'Henley's face turned pink. "You might think it was because of the money, but—"

"I understand you had a family situation to deal with. Why didn't you contact them when it resolved?"

She glanced around the largely empty food court. "There was no family situation, Mr. Dunham. I was let go." O'Henley glanced away as if making sure the twins were behaving, but I sensed she was getting control of her anger. "We arrived in Detroit on a Friday afternoon. Mr. Coburn had arranged a hotel suite for us, and I got the kids settled in. They were exhausted and scared and grieving. We'd had a hard walk to the rendezvous point, a long ride in a crowded bus, and a week with the Diaz family, who are kind people but still strangers. Then the kids had their first airplane flight and a nerve-wracking ride to a hotel with a taxi driver who was more aggressive than most. Along the way they dealt with things they'd never experienced, from security pat-downs to wearing shoes and underwear."

"They must have been grateful to have you with them."

Her face contorted. "It was like moving a couple of robots around. They did as I said, but there was such pain in their eyes." She paused for a moment to banish that image. "In the morning, Mr. Coburn called and said he was coming to pick the children up. He wanted me to meet him in the hotel coffee shop. When he arrived, he told me I'd be given severance pay and a recommendation for a new job. He suggested I say goodbye to Peter and Lucy. He would take them out to breakfast, and I was to be gone by the time they returned."

A yell from the bounce house caught our attention, but the boys were enjoying themselves. The attendant stood stiffly at the entrance, giving them the Evil Eye. "They don't know what happened?"

"No. When Mr. Coburn and I went upstairs, he told them my mother was sick, and I had to leave so I could care for her." Her voice wavered as she finished, "They had no idea they'd never see me again."

I frowned. "You aren't allowed to visit?"

"Mr. Coburn claims it's best if Peter and Lucy cut ties with the past." She tucked a strand of sandy hair behind her ear. "I tell myself I could phone or email to explain, but he made it clear he expects me to stay away. He has the law on his side, and since I don't want to make things harder for the kids, I've done as he wished."

Oscar had deliberately separated Peter and Lucy from the person they trusted most and the emotional support they should have had. Further evidence that he was not only sleazy but also duplicitous.

O'Henley decided it was her turn to ask questions. "How are Lucy and Peter really? And why do they need a private detective?"

I looked down at my hands. "The kids believe their guardian is only after their money."

She put her hands on her cheeks. "I was afraid of that."

"It gets worse. Lucy insists he intends to actually harm one of them."

"Oh, no." After a moment she asked, "What does Peter say?"

"Almost nothing."

O'Henley looked shocked. "He doesn't speak?"

"He's apparently decided I'm okay, but everywhere else, he lets Lucy do the talking."

"That tells me he's suffering. Peter lost both parents, and now he's lost me." With a dismissive gesture she added, "I'm not saying I could replace his father, but I know how to get him through the rough spots."

"You've helped him with his issues before?"

Her expression softened. "People like Peter do better if they prepare for social contact ahead of time. A guide leads them through what might happen, and they decide how they'll react. Once they've rehearsed, they approach situations with less anxiety."

Recalling his practicing for an attack on Oscar, I agreed that Peter did seem to be a plan-ahead kind of guy. "Then with coaching, he'd be able to interact with people?"

"It will never be easy for him, but I think he'd do okay." She chuckled. "Those last few months in Peru, I noticed Peter behaving like a normal teenager, sarcasm and all."

"But now he's all walled off, and Lucy is determined to alienate everyone around her."

"The letter shows they trust you, Mr. Dunham. That's impressive."

I felt my face warm. "Which brings us back to the reason I contacted you. Do you think they're being straight with me?"

O'Henley sniffed. "I understand that Oscar Coburn is considered personable, even attractive, but since I'm not glamorous, powerful, or wealthy, he wasted none of his famous charm on me. When I asked to stay on for a month or two, he was cold and dismissive. But with the kids, he acted regretful that I had to leave so quickly."

Though it felt like O'Henley was honest, I tried to remain objective. I didn't approve of the way Oscar had shoved her aside, but I couldn't simply accept her version of the dismissal. From Oscar's viewpoint, she might have been an impediment to the job he'd taken on. O'Henley had accepted Ray Gage's unusual style of child-rearing. He might have felt they needed a clean break from their former nanny and their old, strange lifestyle.

"Here's my problem: Lucy and Peter have decided Oscar is a physical threat, so they're plotting ways to kill him."

"Oh, my."

I couldn't keep the sarcasm out of my tone. "Yeah. Oh, my."

O'Henley licked her lips, thought about what I'd said, and finally responded. "Among the Yarru, insiders are accepted wholeheartedly, as I told you. On the other hand, outsiders remain outsiders forever. If they are benign, as Ray and Amy were, they're tolerated. But if they're a threat, the tribe does its best to eliminate them, much like animals destroy interlopers in their territory. It isn't a question of morality. It's survival." She met my gaze. "There's no consideration of consequences, no holding back, and no mercy."

"That sounds like what I'm seeing. How do I get them to stop?"

She sighed. "Remove the threat."

"I'm not sure if I can do that."

"I wouldn't underestimate their determination," O'Henley warned. "They're very resourceful."

A buzzer sounded, signaling the end of the twins' bounce time. O'Henley rose and put out a hand. "If there's anything more I can do to help, please let me know."

"Shall I tell Peter and Lucy that you aren't allowed to visit?"

"Let me think about it. While I'd love to see them, I hesitate to make things uncomfortable for anyone." At a call from one of her new charges, she stepped away, then turned. "It was nice to meet you, Mr. Dunham."

Driving north, I took a call from Mom, who was uncharacteristically nervous. "Max, I found some information that scares me a little. It might be nothing, but I think you should be aware."

"What's that?"

"I've been reading articles on the internet at random, anything with Oscar Coburn's name in it. Three incidents with no obvious connection sort of clumped together in my head."

"Incidents?"

"Yeah. Taken by themselves, they're nothing much, but together they're kind of creepy."

"What do you mean?"

"In college, Oscar ran for student body president. His opponent was a guy a lot like him, personable, well-spoken, and popular. A week before the election, the guy fell down a flight of stairs. He ended up with a broken leg and a concussion, so he withdrew from the election, leaving the field clear for Oscar."

"And this was suspicious?" I asked.

"Not really, but that's Incident #1. The second one concerns a woman Oscar dated in 2009. They were quite the item, and people expected an engagement announcement any day. Then suddenly they split up. She wouldn't say why, but two weeks later she was found dead in her apartment, an apparent suicide."

"Any reason to doubt that?"

"She'd been an emotional wreck for most of her life," Mom said. "Oscar claims he begged her to seek professional help, but she refused. When he couldn't stand watching her deteriorate any longer, he told her the relationship was over until she took significant steps to get her head straight."

"That was accepted as believable?"

"The woman's sister claimed there was more to tell, said she acted 'weird' if Oscar's name came up. Before killing herself, she apparently erased her computer and burned her private papers."

"Not uncommon."

"No one could prove Oscar had anything to gain from his former girlfriend's death. In the end it seemed the sister couldn't accept what had happened and looked for someone to blame."

"Also not uncommon."

"Agreed," Mom said, "but here's the third incident. Three years ago, Oscar had a big trial, a so-called businessman who ran a prostitution ring on the side. The verdict pretty much hinged on one man's testimony, but a few days before he was slated to appear in court, he stepped off a platform and was hit by a train."

"Ending the possibility he could finger the client."

"That time there was an investigation. The body was a mess, of course, but the blood alcohol content was high. They concluded it was an accident with booze as a contributing factor."

"But Oscar's court case was dismissed."

189

"Yes. His client went free."

My mind replayed my recent accident: the sudden jolt, the shock, the desperate actions I'd taken to save my life and the life of another. I didn't share that with Mom, but said, "You're thinking Oscar Coburn arranges for people who get in his way to be removed."

"In each case, he had an alibi. When his college rival was hurt, Oscar was napping at his frat house. When the girlfriend overdosed, he was somewhere in Georgia. And when the witness died, he and his brother were fishing near Grayling."

"But each incident got Oscar something he wanted."

"Right. How many of us are lucky enough to have inconvenient people simply step out of our way?"

"Great work, Mom. It adds credence to Peter and Lucy's claim that he's willing to kill for what he wants."

"Since he's always somewhere else when bad things happen, he must have a helper. You need to find out who he was talking to on that phone call the boy overheard."

Candidates flooded my mind. People at the law firm. The Gages' domestic employees. Ex-con thugs Oscar had given a helping hand over the years. "I'll work on that. Thanks again for the help."

As I ended the call, a dismal thought occurred to me. Along with Oscar and his unknown confederate, I had to worry about Dodger. Had he gone to Oscar and offered information in exchange for money? What if Oscar had paid Dodger to impede my investigation? For the hundredth time, I tried to picture the car that had hit me or the person driving. I'd seen nothing. All I had was the worker's impression of the vehicle's size and color. I checked my messages to see if Baker had gotten back to me on recently stolen vehicles. Not yet.

If Oscar knew the kids were onto him, he'd be forced to act soon or give up his dream of easy wealth. If I was in his way, he might well be willing to hurt or kill me too.

Reluctantly, I canceled my plane ticket and hotel reservation. White sand, bright sun, and smiling bartenders would be replaced by dirty city snow, icy wind, and pedestrians with their faces buried in their coat collars. "Maybe next week," I told my iPad.

Plopping down on Dinah's floral couch, I put my unshod feet on the coffee table and let my mind work for a while. I needed to protect the kids. I needed to convince Oscar and his unknown confederate they couldn't get away with what they were planning. At the same time, I had to keep the kids from making their 'pre-emptive strike.' Not that I didn't empathize with their desperation. They were protecting themselves, since no one else would.

No one but me.

I called Peter. "Is Oscar around this weekend?"

"No. He's at some event in Grand Rapids."

That was good and bad. Good because he was out of my way. Bad because, if past practice was any indication, evil deeds happened at times when Oscar had a firm alibi. "Here's what I want you and Lucy to do."

CHAPTER TEN

At five o'clock, I appeared at the Gages' front door, dressed like a bush pilot and carrying a suitcase in one hand and a shopping bag full of exotic gifts in the other. Ilsa Dausman answered my knock, and her face puckered when she saw me.

"Hello there. I'm Morrie, your guest for the weekend." She looked blank. "I hope you heard about it."

"Um, no." She glanced at the suitcase. "No one told me ve were having company."

"Really." I feigned confusion. "I spoke to Mr. Coburn yesterday, and he said he'd let you know." After a moment I went on, "I suppose with the trip to Grand Rapids, he got busy and forgot to tell you."

All she could come up with was, "Um—"

"I'm Morrie Portman, an old friend of Ray Gage. I'm in Detroit for a few days, so I went to the law office and asked if I might visit the kids. Mr. Coburn suggested I spend the weekend, so we can catch up."

"Oh."

Right on cue, Lucy appeared behind Ilsa. "Hi, Uncle Morrie. I hoped you'd get here before dinnertime."

"You know this man?" Ilsa asked.

"He's not really our uncle, but we call him that because he and Dad were good friends." Stepping forward, Lucy gave me a hug. "Aren't you going to come in?"

Ilsa made a negative sound. "I had no notice from Mr. Coburn that company was invited. I'm not sure—"

With perfect timing, Peter hurried down the stairs. "Uncle Morrie."

I clapped him fondly on the shoulder. "Peter. It's good to see you."

Looking from me to Peter to Lucy, Ilsa said, "I can't. It isn't—" Her voice rose. "I don't know what to do."

"Call Mr. Coburn and check with him," I said, though that was the last thing I wanted.

"He wouldn't like that," Lucy warned. "He's at a banquet, and he hates being interrupted at social events."

"I can't let a stranger into the house." Ilsa's hands twisted nervously.

"You might call Ms. Dailey," I suggested. "I spoke with her after I met Mr. Coburn."

For a second, her expression turned hopeful, but then she said, "I don't have her cell number."

"Here." Peter took out his phone, made the call, and handed it to Ilsa. He'd turned on the speaker, which was brilliant.

"Ms. Dailey? This is Ilsa, the nanny for the Gage children."

Peter looked at the floor. Lucy's expression revealed anxiety. If Ilsa asked the wrong questions, our scheme might fail.

"Yes, Ilsa," Dailey said. "I'm in line to board my plane, so be quick."

"I have a man here, Morrie Portman, who says he is an old friend of the Gage family."

"Thirty-something, dark hair, bald spot?"

I took off my hat, leaning forward so Ilsa could see. "Mr. Portman says Mr. Coburn invited him to spend the weekend, but I'm afraid he forgot to mention it to me. I don't like to call him when he's away."

"I know they talked about it," Dailey said. "Oscar intended to check him out before making a decision."

"And did he do that?"

"We didn't speak about it again."

Thanking Dailey, Ilsa ended the call and handed the phone back to Peter. To me she said, "I'm sorry, but since she doesn't know what Mr. Coburn decided—"

"You know what?" I interrupted. "I have his message on my phone." Navigating to voicemail, I hit the button, and Oscar's voice came through clearly: *Mr. Portman, I spoke to Peter and Lucy, and they have memories of your friendship with their father. I think it would be good for them to have a visitor from their past right now.*

She made one more try. "He doesn't say you can stay here."

"We set that up when I called him back." I shook my head as if unsure where things would go from there.

Lucy scored the final point. "He must have left Morrie's name with security, or they wouldn't have let him in."

Ilsa sighed, her arguments defeated. I mentally thanked Bobby, who'd edited the message the way he often does to prank his friends. While cutting out Oscar's negative words, he'd told me all sorts of things about the development of voice recording: phonographs, magnetic tape, and...Bobby stuff.

Once she was convinced, Ilsa became gracious. "I have ordered Chinese food for dinner. There will be plenty for one more." The delivery guy pulled up as she spoke, and I fetched the bags and provided the tip.

Ilsa, Peter, Lucy, and I shared the meal. Lucy went out to invite Adam to join us, but he apparently had no use for food that wasn't American. Ilsa set an array of little white boxes on the table, along with real plates and silverware. Knowing Lucy's opinion of disposable dishes, I'd expected that.

The nanny made attempts at pleasant dinner conversation, but the topics she found interesting didn't suit anyone else. As we took our initial portions she said, "Lucy, I got a catalog today with some nice spring styles. Would you like to look at it?"

"No." Two seconds later she added, "Thank you."

Next, Ilsa told what she considered a shocking story. "I read today on Facebook that gang members from Detroit sneak up behind women and knock them out with a handkerchief soaked in chloroform. Once you're asleep, they can take your purse or...do whatever."

"It takes around five minutes for an adult to become unconscious from a cloth doused with chloroform," Lucy said, reaching for a crab Rangoon. "Not an effective method for rape or robbery."

Ilsa didn't answer for a few seconds. "I suppose if the attacker was very strong..."

Lucy rolled her eyes, and for a while there was only the sound of eating. Peter demonstrated his growing boy status by shoveling a second helping of everything onto his plate.

Unable to bear the silence, Ilsa asked, "Did you know that Dylan Bonner from *Married on TV* has filed for divorce from Alana Taylor?"

Her question brought more dead air, and I concluded I wasn't the only one at the table who had no idea who those people were. The lack of response made Ilsa's face go pink, so I made an attempt to fill the conversational gap. Sadly, the best I could come up with was, "Huh." It occurred to me that Peter's silent persona was useful in such situations.

Peter continued eating after Lucy and Ilsa pushed their plates away. I kept up for a while, but when even I had enough, he was still going.

In obvious desperation for the small talk that's supposed to be good manners at a meal, Ilsa informed us that the Vienna Boys' Choir might be performing in Detroit soon. I tried to appear interested, since I'd at least heard of them. Sounding bored, Lucy said, "Nice." Peter pointed at the next carton he'd like to dish from.

Finally, Ilsa hit on a topic of real interest. "I asked Mr. Coburn if ve might go to Paris over the Easter holiday." Her face lit with pleasure when we all turned to look at her. "He's thinking about it."

"I'll bet he is." Sarcasm dripped from Lucy's words like the sweet and sour sauce that was at that moment staining her placemat.

"You would love the Eiffel Tower, the cafes, and the shopping."

"I think the tower is ugly," Lucy countered. "Cafes are the same everywhere. And shopping is shopping."

Clearly disappointed, Ilsa tore the wrapping from a fortune cookie with her bright-orange nails. "At least you would not need to fear your night-time prowler for a while."

"A prowler," I said, apparently aghast. "What's been done about it?"

"The police come, but they do not find any sign," Ilsa replied.

"What does Mr. Coburn say?"

Ilsa glanced at Peter but didn't directly accuse him of being the culprit. "He says it is a...pervert, is that the word? He cannot get past the alarms, so he is an irritation, not a threat."

"I'd want him caught," I said in a tone of outrage. "I'd hire security."

Ilsa glanced at her fortune and tossed it and the cookie aside. "Mr. Coburn does what is best for the children. Ve must trust his judgment."

If that wasn't a party-line statement, I don't know what is.

We spent the evening playing euchre, a game Michiganders know well. Lucy talked shamelessly across the table to Ilsa, her partner. I didn't call her on it, because the woman needed constant reminding which suit was trump and reneged three times. Peter and I won every game.

When that was done, Ilsa suggested that she and Lucy give me a tour of the house. Lucy made no verbal objections, though she rolled her eyes as we walked through the wasted space that apparently suggests wealth. The kitchen was the size of a basketball court, and it was easy to imagine a team of cooks there, each working a station. When I wondered aloud why anyone would need that many ovens, Lucy snorted a laugh. "Ilsa doesn't even need one." She pointed at the refrigerator, where a dozen take-out menus were fastened with bright magnets.

"I will let you finish the tour and show Mr. Portman to his room," Ilsa said stiffly. Her apartment was apparently beyond the kitchen, because she disappeared down a hallway and I heard a door close a little more forcefully than was necessary.

"Oh." Lucy said with mock regret. "I wonder if I offended her."

A wide marble staircase took us to the second floor, where an open space held upholstered chairs, potted plants, and graceful pieces of statuary. There were double doors on either side, and on the left was the kids' living area: a common space with a kitchenette, large-screen TV, and shelves filled with more games, toys, and hobby kits than I'd seen outside a Toys"R"Us store. "Oscar ordered all this," Lucy said. "I guess so we can never complain that we're bored."

"Most of this stuff has never been opened."

She sniffed dismissively. "I told him to give it to kids in need, but he said we'd change our minds once we settled in." With an arched brow she added, "I haven't settled in yet, so I suppose it's still possible."

197

On opposite sides of the common area were the kids' private spaces. Each had a sitting room, and beyond it a bedroom with a bath and a walk-in closet bigger than my office. Peter had put some of the hobby stuff to use, turning his sitting room into a laboratory. Though the equipment was a mishmash of items taken from various kits, it appeared well-organized, with every drawer and each display carefully labeled. Despite his careless appearance and funky smell, Peter was no slob when it came to science.

Lucy's sitting room was lined with bookshelves, all filled. "I don't suppose I'll ever get around to reading everything that's here," she confessed, "but you never know." After a moment she added, "I'll gladly lend you any book you'd like to try."

"When I finish the book I'm reading now, I'll take a look." Since I started *The Tipping Point* in 2014 and it was still on my nightstand, that wouldn't be anytime soon.

The other wing was storage and guest rooms, which caused Lucy to snicker. "Not like we ever have company. Ms. Johnson sometimes stays over if she and Oscar have something going early the next morning."

I felt my brow furrow. "Stays over, like, with Oscar?"

That got me an under-the-eyebrows look. "Their relationship isn't sexual." When I raised a brow she added, "I'd know if they were sneaking around the house to get together."

I nodded, trying to look as if that information hadn't made me happy.

We reached the third floor via the left-hand staircase. "That side is Oscar territory," Lucy said, gesturing at the stairs that went up the other way. "We're encouraged to stay out."

The whole south side was open, with windows all around and a roof of insulated glass. "It's meant to be a conservatory,"

Lucy told me, her voice echoing in the empty space. "If we stay here, Peter and I plan to start growing a little bit of everything."

As Lucy mentioned the plants she saw in her imagination, I looked across at the doors to Oscar's apartment. There was a number pad at the right side. Oscar's "territory" was protected by an electronic lock. That disappointed me, since I'd intended to search his quarters during my stay. My options were to give up on the idea, get some inside information, or take a quickie course in breaking and entering.

The tour finished, Lucy led me back to the second-floor guest area and the room she'd chosen for me. She didn't follow me inside, which was a good thing, because past the bathroom and around a corner, I found Marla Johnson sitting on the bed. She did that little wave and said softly, "Hi, Morrie."

"Hey," I replied. I am so smooth in these situations.

"I came to pick up some papers Oscar needs revised and saw you having dinner with the crew. I decided to sneak up here and surprise you."

I raised my hands, framing my face. "I'm surprised." Lame, lame, lame. I was discombobulated. Gob-smacked. Whatever other word fits.

Marla's eyes narrowed. "I happen to know Oscar decided against letting you see the kids."

"Um."

Instead of waiting for my excuse, she went on, "Because you're cute and I kind of like you, I'm giving you a chance to tell me what's going on before I call him." After a beat she added, "Or the police."

I considered the ways the conversation might go from there. I could claim I'd talked Oscar into changing his mind, but one call to him would prove that was a lie. If I admitted I'd gone around him, said I felt it was my duty as Ray Gage's friend to see that his kids were treated well, she might take pity on me. To be honest, I had trouble thinking clearly with Marla in my bedroom, on the bed, her shoes tossed aside and her legs pulled up all comfy. The possibilities intrigued me more than I can say.

I made my choice. "I'm trying to keep Lucy and Peter safe."

Her expression turned from doubtful to confused. "Safe from what?"

"Lucy's seen someone on the grounds several times lately."

She waved that away. "I blame Ilsa for all that fuss. When a child sees a boogeyman, you don't call the police. You explain to her that sometimes we wake up confused, and a dream seems real." She made a disgusted huff. "Instead of acting like an adult, Ilsa flies into a fluttery panic every single time, making the situation ten times worse."

"You think Lucy imagines this prowler?"

Marla shrugged. "Four times, and there's never been a sign anyone was there."

"What if someone is scaring her on purpose?"

Her brows rose, and she made a grunt of disbelief. "Why?"

"To establish that she's unreliable."

"To what end?"

Having an attractive woman on my bed made it hard to think. Did I dare trust Marla Johnson? Should I offer evidence that a co-worker, who was in fact her superior, was deceitful and maybe homicidal? Would she call me crazy? Blab to Oscar? Laugh in my face?

Marla came across as honest and down-to-earth. We'd laughed over dinner. We'd talked about our favorite beers. Still, she knew Oscar much better than she knew me, so she probably wasn't ready to hear that he was plotting murder. She'd admitted that his ethics were sometimes thin, so I decided to try a grain of truth and see how she reacted. "I think he might be planning to have the kids declared mentally unstable."

"So he'll control the money." She said it softly, as if it had been lurking at the back of her mind and finally made its way to consciousness.

"Yes. Peter's disability makes it possible he'd be ruled incapable of handling his own affairs. If Lucy were declared unfit as well, Oscar would control their wealth completely."

Marla shook her head as if trying to banish the thought, but I could tell she was having a hard time with it. "Look," I said, "he's already spending their money on things that make him happy. Do you think he'll want to give up this lifestyle in three years, when Peter turns eighteen?"

She sighed. "It would be hard for him."

"Maybe impossible." I took a step farther toward the truth. "Peter heard Oscar on the phone one day, saying he'd like to get rid of one kid."

"What? That can't be right."

"He said life would be easier with only one, and he talked about which one he'd keep around."

Marla stared at me for a few seconds, her face frozen. Then she laughed. Not a giggle, but a good old roar of laughter. "Oh, my," she kept repeating. "Oh, my."

"What is it?"

"I know about that phone call," she said between gasps. "Oscar was talking to me, silly man."

Feeling my neck warm, I said, "Tell me about it."

"It was a week ago, give or take." Marla wiped her eyes. "The school had called to say Peter refused to make a presentation in English class. Ilsa had found vomit in the dryer. It turned out to be only plastic, but she didn't think it was funny. At breakfast, Lucy demanded he give fifty million to Amazon conservation for Arbor Day—fifty million! There was a sleety rain outside, and when Oscar opened his umbrella, they'd filled it with cornstarch, which dumped all over his suit. It turned to a gooey paste in the wet, and he had to go back inside and change. When Oscar called to tell me he'd be late, he was as grumpy as I'd ever heard him."

A looming cloud of chagrin descended directly onto my shoulders. "He vented to you about the kids."

She nodded. "He's usually tolerant of their shenanigans, but that day he'd had it. He said he'd never realized how hard taking them on would be." She laid a hand on her chest. "Trying to help, I asked if it might be easier if they were separated. Oscar said something like what you told me. They stand together against him, and that makes it hard to change their behavior. I asked if he might send one of them to a boarding school. He said that would be a hard decision to make, but he'd think about it." Marla met my gaze. "Does that sound like what Peter heard?"

"Yes," I admitted.

"Then all this was a big mistake."

"Maybe." In spite of the explanation she provided, my gut said Oscar was planning something worse than boarding school. I'd been run off the road. A prowler with no apparent motive kept showing up at Lucy's window. Denice O'Henley had been sent away. "Something isn't right."

Marla rose and approached me. "I knew I liked you, Morrie Portman. You're very thorough."

"Actually, my name is Max."

"And how did you become the kids' knight in shining armor, Max?"

"I'm a private investigator. They came to me for help, and I intend to make sure they're okay."

Her arms slid around my neck, and her whole front met mine. "Do you need an assistant?"

Immediate desire squelched thoughts of the future, and I pulled Marla tighter. She raised her lips, and I bent down—

And a rap sounded on the door. "Max? Peter and I decided to watch *Raiders of the Lost Ark* down in the TV room. Want to join us?"

I cleared my throat before answering. "Um, not tonight, Lucy."

After a pause she said, "Could you come and get it started then? We can never make it go from TV to DVD without messing everything up."

Marla stepped back, her expression signaling amused frustration. The intimate moment vanished, and I said, "Be right there."

"Thanks. You really should watch with us. I'm making popcorn."

"Um, sure." A minute later, after checking to be sure Lucy had gone downstairs, I left my room, signaling for Marla to follow. She came out, shoes in one hand, and said softly in my ear, "I have a conference call with Japan later that will take a while. Maybe next time we'll do better."

"Hope so." The promise of next time made the ruination of this time a little more bearable.

By the time Indiana Jones had defeated every Nazi in Christendom, it was after midnight. We climbed the stairs together, Peter and Lucy turning left while I went right. As I passed along the corridor, I wondered which room Marla stayed in when she slept over. Could I knock on doors until I found her? Turning, I saw Lucy across the open space, standing at her doorway, watching me. With a wave and a repressed sigh, I went on to my assigned space.

Going to my window to check the weather, I saw a hunched figure across the street from the gate. It could have been my already suspicious mind, but the guy was built like Roger Ainsley. As I closed the blind, I wondered exactly what Dodger would do for a hundred thousand dollars.

CHAPTER ELEVEN

Saturday morning, I woke to a text from Denice O'Henley. *Something I'd forgotten: when I packed up Ray's things, there was a sealed letter addressed to Carson Coburn. I found it at the bottom of my suitcase when I unpacked, so I mailed it to the law office with a note of explanation.*

Peter believed his dad had changed his will. I'd looked it up and found that Michigan courts may accept a document in the testator's handwriting that clearly states it's a new will and is signed and dated.

I checked the time: 7:40 a.m. Guessing O'Henley was an early riser, I called. "It's Max Dunham," I said when she answered. "I appreciate you letting me know about the letter Ray wrote."

"We know now that Carson Coburn didn't get it. One wonders who did and what the letter said."

"The kids think there was a new will in the works, naming you as their guardian."

"Do you think that's true?" There was a hopeful note in her voice.

It didn't matter at this point. If Ray wrote a will naming O'Henley as guardian, Oscar had surely burned it.

"If you were the kids' guardian, what would you do with them?"

O'Henley sighed. "I'd ask them to stay in the states until Peter turns eighteen. If they want to go back and live with the Yarru at that point, the decision would be theirs to make."

"Do you think they can adjust to life here? Peter's pretty unsettled, and Lucy keeps spouting off about Western decadence."

"Their whole lives, they saw this culture from the outside. Our crime, corruption, selfishness, and pure silliness gave them a negative view." O'Henley chuckled. "They used to ask questions like, 'Why do citizens ignore the lies their leaders tell?' or 'Why doesn't your government do more to stop pollution?' I said most Americans don't have a clue what pigs we are, and to that, Lucy responded, 'I don't think they care.'"

"She's probably right."

"Of course she is." O'Henley's tone turned pedantic. "With less than five percent of the world's population, we use one-third of the paper, a quarter of the oil, twenty-three percent of the coal, twenty-seven percent of the aluminum, and nineteen percent of the copper. And when we're done with it, we toss it into the ocean." I heard a smile in her voice. "Ray provided that information during my initial interview. With those figures before me, it was hard to justify the behavior of the average American."

"We aren't the only ones who use resources and generate waste."

She made a disdainful grunt. "That's an excuse, like a kid who steals candy and then whines that his brother took some too. Among the Yarru, each person is responsible for himself *and* for the tribe. If one is suffering, all must do what they can to help."

"Is it true there's no competition there?"

In answer, O'Henley told a story. "When I'd been there a while, I wanted to teach the children hopscotch. I drew squares in the dirt, and Lucy translated the rules. I had a whole mango to give to the winner as a prize. When the game was finished, the girl who'd won divided the fruit among the group. I asked Lucy why, and she translated what the girl said: 'How would the mango taste good to me if my friends had none?'"

"Interesting."

"Cooperation is the norm among the Yarru. Work and its results are shared, and no one fusses about who made the biggest effort. Here you're supposed to want to be the first, the best, or the most attractive. We don't realize the pressure that creates, especially for kids."

I was starting to see that Lucy and Peter's adjustment went beyond learning to navigate mass transit. "Their whole value system is different from the people they meet each day."

"And we tell ourselves they're the ones who are weird." I heard water running and guessed O'Henley was getting ready for work as we talked. "School must be torture for them, especially Peter."

I thought of Peter's blank stare and horribly smelly backpack. "He's developed coping mechanisms to make people leave him alone."

"He would." O'Henley spoke approvingly, but the coping techniques Peter and Lucy had chosen weren't particularly helpful. Oscar would have been smart to let O'Henley stay on to help them adapt. Then again, that might have been the last thing he wanted.

"I keep hearing that Lucy sometimes lies."

"Lies?" O'Henley seemed shocked, and the sound of running water stopped abruptly. "Give me an example."

"She claims she drove some poacher's truck into a swamp."

O'Henley sighed heavily. "That was foolish and dangerous, but she did it. You need to understand how hard it was for us to watch those people steal from the land and destroy its beauty."

"So the kids harassed them when they could. Do you think the poachers killed their dad?"

Her voice softened. "The poachers were wary of the 'white natives' that lived with the Yarru. They knew Ray's reports exposed their crimes. It's more than likely they killed him when the opportunity arose."

I moved on to another story the kids had told me. "Is it true that some Peruvian official wanted Lucy to marry his son?"

"Perfectly true. Since Ray's nerves knotted up when he had to talk to strangers, Lucy began making videos that reported conditions in the preserve to the Peruvian government. "Ray's old friend Sr. Diaz was impressed by her and proposed, in his quaint manner, that a marriage between Lucy and his second-oldest son might serve both families well."

"What did Doctor Gage say to that?"

Her giggle took me by surprise. "It caused some serious discussion around our fire pit, I can tell you. Ray didn't want to insult his old friend. Señor Diaz felt he was bestowing a great honor on Lucy, since his family has centuries of pedigree to recommend it. He praised her beauty to the skies and spoke of the 'fine grandchildren' he and Ray could expect."

"What did Lucy think of the offer?"

O'Henley giggled again. "She was beyond perturbed, since Diaz never once mentioned her intelligence. 'As long as I'm pretty,' she told us, 'it doesn't matter if I only use my brain for keeping my ears apart.'"

"I noticed she doesn't appreciate references to her looks."

"At least she had the good sense not to say that directly to the señor," O'Henley said. "He meant well, and we needed his political influence."

"How was the situation resolved?"

"Ray told his friend that Lucy is already spoken for. The son of a respected Michigan family."

"She's gorgeous and extremely wealthy," I commented. "Diaz won't be the last father with an unattached son who comes calling."

"Lucy has a good head on her shoulders. She'll be careful."

"Oscar complains that she wants to give away too much too fast."

"She's very philanthropic, like her parents. Ray believed wealth is a blessing if you use it for good and a curse if you only work to get more."

"Sounds like they didn't spend much time amassing more."

"No. Ray and Amy built a half-dozen hospitals in outlying areas of the world and endowed them, so care is free. Of course they also gave to environmental, social justice, and humanitarian groups." She sniffed. "I suppose Mr. Coburn has put a stop to that. He seems like the 'I've got mine. Go get your own' type."

That reminded me that O'Henley's loyalty was to the kids and their now-deceased father. While it was valuable to get her insights, I couldn't depend on her for objectivity. "I really appreciate the help," I said. "Now I'll let you get ready to deal with those rambunctious twins."

Marla was already downstairs when I went in search of breakfast. It's the most important meal of the day, Mom always says, and she claims I get grumpy if I skip it. Rummaging through the cupboards, we found a box of oat cereal, simple, quick, and full of fiber, another thing Mom highly recommends. Rather than using either dining room, Marla led me to a breakfast nook with full-length windows facing the back yard. It wasn't exactly a lovely view in mid-February: wrapped bushes, mulched tree bases, and the prison-like fence in the background, but the room itself was cozy. As we ate, we discussed the Detroit Pistons and whether the Mustang was the best muscle car ever. To my great relief, she said it was, though her last boyfriend had insisted it was the GTO.

"How could you date a man so misguided?" I teased.

"A big reason he's gone," Marla replied. "No grasp of reality."

I was amazed at how much we agreed on things. Marla preferred Eminem to Kid Rock. She agreed that the People Mover, Detroit's light rail system, was a good idea that hadn't been planned well enough to achieve a good result.

Movement outside the window caught my eye. "Who's that?"

She turned to look. "Oscar hired some guys to trim the trees. I guess it's better if you do it while they're dormant."

The men might have been brothers, both muscular and dark-haired. One set a ladder under a big maple while the other arranged saws and pruners on a tarp he'd spread on the ground. We watched for a minute before returning to our conversation about the benefits of Vernors ginger ale for an upset stomach.

When we'd finished eating and set our bowls in the dishwasher, Marla said, "I have to finish up some work Oscar left for me, but maybe this afternoon we could take the kids and do something fun."

Before I could answer, Peter appeared in the doorway, his face white. "Lucy's missing."

I was on my feet in a heartbeat. "What happened?"

"I don't know. She went to her room after the movie last night, but she isn't there now. I got up early and spent some time studying."

"In your room?"

"In the library closet." Looking embarrassed, he waved a hand at the men outside. "Those power tools make it hard to concentrate."

"Okay. When did you go looking for Lucy?"

"About ten minutes ago I realized she should be up by now. When I didn't find her, I asked Ilsa, but she hasn't seen her. Neither has Adam." His face was more expressive than I'd ever seen it. "Her coat is hanging in the closet, Max. Wherever she is, she must be freezing."

I started upstairs. Though I didn't doubt Peter's word, it's human nature to see for yourself. "Where's Ilsa?"

"In the living room, crying. She's afraid she's going to get fired."

Typically, Ilsa's concern was for herself. "And Adam?"

"He's cruising the neighborhood, hoping to spot her." We'd reached Lucy's room, which was empty. I tossed pillows aside and opened doors, aware it was useless but needing to do something. Marla, who'd followed us upstairs, regarded Peter with wide eyes. Before now she'd probably never heard him say more than one word at a time.

"Ms. Johnson knows why I'm really here," I told Peter.

His mind was on his sister. "Lucy isn't playing games."

"I know."

Marla touched my elbow. "Should we call the police, Max?"

That was a tough question. Lucy already had a reputation with the local authorities, so if she wasn't in danger, calling them would only make things worse. But she was outside on a winter morning, coatless. She wouldn't have gone out without telling anyone. Not voluntarily.

"Let's make a thorough search of the house and grounds before we bring in the cops."

"I'll drive around too," Marla volunteered. "Two pairs of eyes is better than one." We heard her steps on the stairs and a jingle as she swept up her car keys and headed out. *Efficient and attractive* flashed through my mind before I returned to the problem of Lucy's disappearance.

While Peter started a thorough search of the interior, I went outside to speak to the men we'd seen in the back yard. One of them stood on a stepladder, lopping limbs off some sort of fruit tree. The other held the ladder steady and handed up tools as needed.

"I'm wondering if either of you saw the girl who lives here this morning," I said. "She's nine years old, brown, curly hair."

"Real pretty, right?" His jacket said "EverTree" in large letters and beneath that, "Jack" in smaller script. "Haven't seen her today." The other man shook his head, indicating he hadn't either.

"Well, we can't find her."

"You want us to help you look?" That was the second man, whose coat patch said "Jay."

"That would help." Though it was conceivable they'd had something to do with Lucy's disappearance, I doubted they'd hang around trimming trees if they'd recently kidnapped someone. Suggesting they search the grounds and outbuildings, I went back inside.

Ilsa was about as helpful as the tissue wadded up in her hand. She hadn't seen Lucy since we finished playing cards the night before. She had no idea where she could have gone. She wondered if I would tell Mr. Coburn that none of this was her fault.

Leaving her to her selfish fears, I joined Peter, who was inspecting the guest rooms on the second floor with grim determination. Though neither of us believed Lucy was hiding, we looked in every spot we could think of where a slim girl might be concealed. We didn't address the fact that she'd have to be unconscious—or worse—not to give some sign of her presence. When we'd assured ourselves she wasn't there, Peter led the way upstairs. After a quick search of the empty conservatory, he turned to Oscar's apartment.

"I can probably get in there," he said. "Oscar's codes are always some combination of his birth date: 11-15-1976." In the tone of a born techie he added, "His computer illiteracy works for us right now."

I nodded like a wise old owl, since I never use my birthday for my passwords. I use Mom's.

"Go ahead and try to break the code," I said. "I'll keep looking."

Returning to the ground floor, I went to the closet for my coat. Ilsa slumped on the couch, keying letters into her phone at a frantic pace. As I passed behind her, I looked over her shoulder. It wasn't in English, but her sniffles hinted that the message was *Poor me. Poor me. Poor me.* Noticing stairs near the back door that descended to the basement, I went down to check the space. There was plenty of dust but no sign anyone had been there in weeks, perhaps months.

Convinced Lucy wasn't in the house, I joined the tree men, Jack and Jay. They moved along opposite sides of the property, their expressions serious. I crisscrossed between them, checking under bushes in a search doomed to futility. Peter joined us a few minutes later with a helpless gesture. "Not there." Taking that to mean he'd been in Oscar's apartment, I filed the numbers he'd mentioned, 11-15-1976, in my memory.

Outside the gate, I found four cigarette butts atop a light layer of snow that had fallen the day before. Someone had stood out here, watching the house. Someone who looked a lot like Dodger.

When we'd been all over the house and grounds without finding any sign of Lucy, I said, "The temperature is dropping. Time to call it in."

Eight minutes later, a sheriff's car pulled into the drive. A tall, raw-boned deputy got out, his face a polite mask. "I understand the little girl has gone missing."

"No one's seen her since last night," I told him. "We've done a thorough search of the property. The chauffeur and a friend are driving around, hoping to spot her, but neither has called." Sensing his resistance I added, "Lucy's coat and mittens are inside. She's in danger of freezing."

His expression didn't warm. "Girl living in a place like this probably got more than one coat."

Peter glared, but I put a hand on his arm and said to the deputy, "We need an organized search."

Another vehicle pulled into the drive, and my gut clenched when I saw the Deer Creek Estates logo on the side. Frank emerged, closing his door with a definitive slam, and swaggered toward us. Seeing me, he demanded, "What are you doing here?"

"I'm staying with the Gages."

His mouth twisted. "Weren't you staying with Mrs. Ellerson?"

"I was."

"Now you've moved here?"

"Turns out I knew the kids' dad years ago."

He set one hand on his hip, fingering the Taser that hung there. "Mrs. Ellerson's cousin from Maine is also an old pal of a guy who's dead and can't confirm the so-called friendship."

"Ask Peter."

Huffing a laugh, he turned to the boy and said in a mock serious tone, "Tell me, Mr. Chatty. Do you know this guy from before?"

Peter came through like a champ. "He's b-been a friend for years." I wanted to pat him on the back, but I settled for a grateful glance.

Just then a car pulled into the drive. It was Adam, and he leaned out the window to shout, "I found her!" Beside him Lucy sat, wrapped in his jacket, her face expressionless.

Minutes later we were inside, Lucy beside Ilsa on the couch, swathed in a microfiber blanket. Peter and I stood beside them, and the boy's eyes never left his sister. Adam hovered near the doorway, as if being in the house was uncomfortable for him. Frank stood in the entry, arms folded as if to discourage someone, probably me, from making a run for it.

The deputy took a notebook out of his pocket and clicked his pen to writing position. "You found her at the playground?"

"On a swing." Adam shook his head. "I got a flash of something red as I drove by. Turns out it was her shirt. She was acting funny."

She still was. Lucy looked like she'd been asleep and wasn't fully aware yet. When Ilsa asked why she'd gone outside, she shook her head, unable to say. Lucy was not Lucy-like at all.

The deputy clearly considered his job done. She was home and safe. His report would detail yet another instance of the Gage girl's weirdness.

I wanted to tell him he was wrong, but it wouldn't have helped. I counted myself lucky when Frank announced in an irritated tone that he needed to get back to his post. Best if he left without pressing for further information as to how I'd gone from Dinah Ellerson's cousin to the Gages' houseguest.

When the deputy said all the right things and left, Adam went out to put the car into the garage. "Glad you're okay, kiddo," he said in farewell. Lucy didn't answer, didn't thank him for perhaps saving her life.

The rest of us accompanied Lucy to her room. I wanted to question her, but Ilsa chose that moment to impress us with how caring she was. After fussing with the blankets and the thermostat, she asked, "Should I sit with Lucy until she goes to sleep?" The question only underlined her lack of commitment. If she cared about the kid at all, a tornado couldn't have made her leave her side.

Peter made a terse comment. "I'll do it."

A decidedly Teutonic sniff indicated irritation, but she didn't argue. "All right then. I'll be in my room."

Texting, no doubt.

When she'd gone downstairs, Lucy sat up in bed. Her face was pale, and she kept a hand on her stomach as if she felt nauseated. "You were drugged," I told her.

"I assume so," she said in a matter-of-fact tone. "When I came up here after the movie, I got really sleepy. The next thing I knew, I was sitting on a swing in the park." She shivered. "I was really cold, but then Adam was there. He put his coat around me and carried me to the car."

She remembered nothing of how she'd left the house or ended up in the park hours later. Knowing what I did of drugs like Rohypnol, I guessed she'd been given a dose and led away in a state of confusion.

"What did you eat or drink after the movie last night?" Peter asked.

She thought about it. "Ilsa left a piece of fudge on my nightstand."

"Ilsa made fudge?" I asked incredulously.

Lucy's smile was thin. "It's her only kitchen talent, but it's really good." She glanced around. "There was a note."

Peter and I looked but found nothing. "What exactly did it say?"

Her brow furrowed. *"I made fudge for a T-R-E-E-T.* I chuckled a little at the misspelling."

"That doesn't sound like something Ilsa would do," Peter said. "You got fudge, but I didn't. She doesn't usually play favorites. And I've never seen her make a spelling mistake before."

"You're right." Lucy rubbed her forehead as if forcing her thoughts to organize. "But who can't spell to save his soul?"

"Who?" I asked.

They answered together. "Adam."

Though she tried, Lucy could remember nothing more. "We should have had the deputy take you to a doctor," I said. "Checking your urine would have convinced them you didn't disappear voluntarily."

"Wait." Peter left the room and returned a few seconds later with an empty, stoppered test tube. "We can take one now. You could get it tested at one of those independent labs."

"It won't be legal proof without a proper chain of evidence," I said, "but it might help us build a case."

I handed the test tube to Lucy, who went into her bathroom, her gait slightly uneven, and closed the door. A minute later she came back with the tube wrapped in a washcloth. "I'll get this tested as soon as possible," I said, pocketing it.

It was time to put the kids on guard, even if it meant they'd bring up the "Let's kill Oscar before he kills us" argument. Pale and groggy, Lucy seemed too fragile to face the fact that her worst fears were coming true, but I knew how she'd react if she learned later that I treated her like a child. "You both need to be careful what you eat and drink. Something's in the works."

"You think Oscar hired someone to kidnap Lucy?" Peter asked.

"No. This was done to build the fiction that she's mentally unstable." When Lucy frowned, I explained, "If you'd been out in the cold all night, you'd be dead. Someone drugged you, kept you inside until daylight, and set you on that swing. He came back a while later and 'rescued' you."

Peter's expression was grim. "Adam."

Lucy seemed sad. "He's no Einstein, but he's funny. He calls me Lucy-Loo and teases Peter about having to fight the girls off with a stick."

"Money makes people do bad things," I told her.

Lucy nodded, stoically accepting one of life's hardest lessons. "What should we do about it?"

"I'm going to go after him right now, while he hasn't got Oscar to protect him."

Peter took a step forward. "Do you want me to back you up?"

"Watch Lucy." Before she could object, I added, "And she'll watch you. You're a team, so get ready for whatever they've got in mind." I waited for a suggestion, even a demand, that I find them that hitman, but neither kid went there. Peter nodded, and after a moment, Lucy did too.

Going out to the garage, I climbed the stairs to Adam's apartment. He answered my knock with a belligerent, "What do you want?"

I shouldered my way inside. "I know what you did. I know what you've been doing for weeks now."

He took a step back, but his reply was even more belligerent. "You don't know jack."

"You've been climbing up to Lucy's window at night to scare her. Last night you came into the house, left her a 't-r-e-e-t' with some kind of drug in it, carried her out once she was under the influence, and kept her until morning. Then you put her in the trunk of the car and pretended to go looking for her. You set her on that swing long enough to get good and cold, and then you 'rescued' her."

"She told you this?"

"She doesn't remember."

He crossed his arms. "Then you got a story nobody's gonna believe."

Though he was right, I didn't give up. "You're making Lucy seem unreliable to the local cops."

"Prove it." Adam's confidence undoubtedly came from knowing Oscar would defend him every step of the way. "What would I get outta something like that?"

"Money."

"Buddy, I ain't even got a bank account."

"So Oscar pays you in cash."

"Mr. Coburn is a good guy that gives ex-cons a second chance. You're a low-life chiseler that wants a slice of the kids' money." A grin belied his sincerity, but that was exactly how the world might see things.

The purr of an engine outside distracted us, and Adam looked over my shoulder. "Who's that?"

Turning, I saw Denice O'Henley getting out of a Ford Fiesta. Her expression revealed nervousness, but it settled into determination. She closed the car door with a firm clunk, and I realized she'd come to see for herself how her former charges were faring.

Adam's puzzled frown told me he didn't know who she was. With her plain black coat, sensible boots, and hand-knit hat and gloves, she looked like a worker bee from some government office, which gave me an idea that bordered on genius—or it would if it worked. "We're up here," I called.

Maggie Pill

O'Henley turned, and recognition lit her eyes. Hurrying down the stairs, I reached her before Adam got close enough to hear. "Follow my lead," I said urgently. "For the kids' safety." Though her brow twitched, she gave a single, jerky nod.

As Adam joined us, I said, "This is Ms. Turner, your parole officer."

He shook his head like a horse with flies. "Nope. Mine is a guy."

"Well, this one is the boss of your old one. When I realized you're part of Oscar's scheme I called her, and she graciously agreed to give up a few hours of her weekend to come out here and see what's going on."

Adam eyed O'Henley warily. "Ain't nothing going on."

"If CSI techs examine your apartment, they'll find evidence that you've been harassing Lucy Gage. Maybe it will be her hair on your couch. Maybe there'll be scratches on the sill from where you crawl out your window to get to hers. They might even find the Rohypnol you used to knock her out last night."

"You can't search my place without a warrant."

"*I* can't, but if she suspects you're in violation, your P.O. can."

Adam turned to O'Henley. "Is he telling the truth?"

She hesitated, and I coached mentally, *Come on, Denice. Come on.*

To my great joy, she pulled out her phone. "If I call it in right now, there'll be a crew here in thirty minutes." Her eyes turned hard. "You could be in handcuffs in an hour."

Adam seemed to melt a little, like the icicles hanging off the garage roof. "What do you want from me?"

"We want you to tell the police what Oscar is up to."

He gave a single bark of laughter. "I got nothing to tell. Sometimes I find an envelope stuck in my door. Inside is money and a note that says something like, *Stay somewhere else Tuesday night but come around 2 a.m. and scare the girl at her bedroom window.*"

"And yesterday?"

"I got specific instructions and the, um, medicine."

"Do you have the notes?"

"It always says to burn them."

"But you know who they're from."

Adam gave a mighty shrug. "Even if I did, how you gonna prove it?"

Again, he was right. If the police found the evidence I'd mentioned, it would prove Adam's guilt, but not Oscar's. Disgusted, I told him, "I want you to leave here today. Right now, in fact."

"They'll hunt me down and shoot me in the head."

The reference to "they" hinted he knew more than he'd admitted, but he feared them more than me. "Oscar and his helper will be behind bars soon. If you leave now, I'll keep your name out of it if I can."

He glanced up at his apartment. "Give me fifteen minutes."

"Do not contact Oscar." I put as much steel into my voice as I could muster. "He's going down for attempted murder and more, and you know that if he can shove the blame onto you, he will."

The look on Adam's face told me he hadn't known murder was part of the plan. He opened his mouth to speak, but in the end, he merely turned and hurried up the stairs.

"You did great," I told Denice, "especially since you had no idea what's going on."

She gave another of those giggles that belied her nanny persona. "It was kind of fun, but what did I do?"

I pointed upstairs. "That guy has been setting Lucy up to look like a scaredy-cat." Feeling I could trust her with the rest, I added, "I think Oscar intends to kill Peter and blame her for it."

"What?"

I summarized what I knew and what I'd surmised. "I'm letting Adam leave because I don't think he knew the murder part, and I hope it will disrupt Oscar's plans."

"How can we stop this?"

"The kids use what Lucy calls guerilla tactics to harass the guy whenever they can. I'll do the same until we find a way to stop him for good. We'll delay, distract, and discombobulate."

Denice took it in calmly, but I suppose someone who lived in the Amazon jungle for a year had faced dangerous situations before. "He said *they* would hunt him down. Who else is involved?"

"I'm not sure. It could be the nanny, or one of the other lawyers, or someone still in the woodwork. There's also a shady fellow investigator interested in what's going on out here."

"Would this investigator take Mr. Coburn's side?"

"He generally leans toward whoever offers the best deal."

"I see." Denice ran the information through her mind and reached a conclusion. "Whether Mr. Coburn knows who you really are or not, he can't proceed without dealing with you in some way."

The memory of my recent accident returned. "I won't go quietly."

"Nor should you," she said approvingly. It occurred to me that any other woman I knew, except maybe Mom, would by now be demanding I be careful and not take chances. This one seemed to understand that life presents unavoidable dangers if you're set on doing the right thing.

Not sure how to wind up that conversational thread, I said, "As soon as Adam leaves, I'll take you inside to see the kids."

When an Uber showed up a few minutes later, Adam came down the steps with a single bag so hastily zipped that a bit of sock protruded from one end. Once he was gone, a joyful reunion was held in Lucy's bedroom. She'd begun to rebound from the drug and the scary experience. When I announced that Adam was gone from their lives, she shook her head. "I still can't believe he did all those mean things to me."

Sitting down on the bed, Denice took her into her arms. "He's a bad apple, but you've got three people right here in this room who'd fight a shoal of piranhas to save you."

"Four," said a voice from the doorway, and we turned to see Marla, holding an extra-large fast-food bag. "After Peter's all-clear message, I hit the drive-thru so we can celebrate Lucy's return with sausage burritos." Setting her burden on the nightstand, she extended a hand to Denice. "Marla Johnson. I assume you're the former nanny."

Denice rose and shook hands. "Denice O'Henley."

"She's going to be our nanny again," Lucy said. "Oscar said she quit, but she didn't."

"Oh!" Ilsa stood in the doorway, one hand pressed to her chest.

"Lucy," Denice cautioned. "We can't know that. Your guardian—"

"Is a liar," Lucy interrupted. "You and Max will tell people what he's really like, how he's planning to get our money." In an emcee-like tone she finished, "Oscar Coburn is going down."

Ilsa seemed about to speak, but after a moment, she turned and left.

"Is she going to make trouble?" Lucy asked me.

"Probably."

"Let me talk to her," Marla suggested.

As she started for the door Lucy said, "Ms. Johnson, offer her ten thousand dollars if she leaves and doesn't tell Oscar what we know."

Marla grinned. "That will serve as incentive, I would think."

"Max will bring the money down in a minute."

Marla left, and we heard her call, "Wait a second, Ilsa."

At a nod from Lucy, Peter left, crossing the common area to his own rooms. Denice glanced after him, bewildered, but I guessed his purpose. Strolling casually to the doorway, I looked across and saw him, down on one knee as he emptied his smelly backpack. Along with a couple of textbooks and some loose papers was a carton of what I guessed was specially prepared stinky stuff, aerated to let the smell escape. Under all that were the stacks of hundred dollar bills he'd showed me the day we met. Turning, I found Lucy glaring a silent accusation at me. I returned to the foot of her bed, blushing as if I'd done something wrong.

Peter came back with a single bundle of bills. "Tell Ilsa we never want to see her again," Lucy ordered, and I left to do as she said.

Ilsa and Marla stood at the bottom of the staircase, Ilsa in tears and Marla speaking in low tones. "Is she okay with the deal?" I asked.

"Well?" Marla prompted. When Ilsa hesitated, she added, "You can have money for a new start, or you can have trouble with the police. They'll probably deport you."

"All right," Ilsa said resentfully. "I will go."

When she turned away, I murmured, "Watch her until she's gone."

"I promised her a letter of reference," Marla said, "though Heaven knows what I'll say that's good."

Going back upstairs I reported, "I think it's under control."

Denice seemed less confused, which meant the kids had caught her up. "What happens now?"

"You go back to Toledo," I replied. "It will be a few days before we get things squared away here."

"I'll help," Denice said. "I'll tell how Mr. Coburn lied about my situation."

"That doesn't prove anything," I said gently. "He'd say he felt it was in the kids' best interest."

Though she was reluctant to accept my argument, Peter and Lucy agreed. "Give your two weeks' notice," Lucy advised. "You'll be back with us before you know it."

It was nice that they were optimistic, but I still wasn't sure how we'd end Oscar's term as guardian. We had no proof he'd planned murder, while he had considerable legal skills and the support of his firm and the courts. Since the day had already been stressful, I hid my concerns for the moment.

Once Denice had hugged the kids and started south, I announced, "When Oscar comes back, we'll tell him Adam and Ilsa ran off together."

"What if he doesn't believe us?"

"What can he do about it? Their absence will force him to delay his plans, so you'll be safe for a while."

"All right." Lucy got down to business. "How do we get him fired?"

"We approach Sara Dailey," I said, "though I'm not sure how we'll make her listen."

"She'll listen." Lucy's tone was firm. "We found out some things."

"What things?"

"Peter has started deleting Dad's online presence." Lucy pushed a hand through her hair. "We were slow to do it, because

225

it felt like we're erasing him." Her eyelids reddened, but she went on. "Anyway, he found some personal messages between Dad and Ms. Dailey."

"You mean they…"

Lucy raised her brows. "After Dad returned from his father's funeral, he said in an email that she should have told him something. He wasn't specific, but he said he'd never have done what he did if he'd known."

"Is there a Mr. Dailey?"

"Yes. Not only is she married, but she hopes to have a political career someday." Lucy's eyes narrowed. "If she won't help us, we'll threaten to make the emails public."

"That's blackmail, Lucy."

She shrugged. "If you don't want to do it that way, we can return to our original plan."

"Blackmail it is." I suggested something I knew wouldn't be popular. "I should be the one to approach her." Before Lucy could object, I added, "We don't want her angry at you or Denice, but it won't hurt a thing if she gets mad at me."

"What should we do then?"

"On Monday, go off to school like it's a normal day. Pretend life is hunky-dory."

Lucy chuckled. "Where do you get those expressions?"

"It means you don't let Oscar know we're onto him."

"I got the meaning," she replied. "But sometimes you sound like an old lady."

Marla had Ilsa packed and ready to go within an hour. When the taxi left and she came inside, I explained what we had in mind.

"Do we pretend we don't know what Adam did?"

"Yes. If he knows about the latest incident, we claim to believe Lucy's begun sleepwalking due to stress."

Marla sighed. "He isn't going to be happy to see you here."

"True, but he's also going to need someone to look after the kids. If I volunteer to fill in as nanny-slash-driver, he'll have to let me stay on."

Her lips curled in a smile. "I don't see Oscar rearranging his schedule to drive them to school or make their dinner."

"My presence should keep the kids safe. Monday morning, I'll visit the law office and talk to Sara Dailey." Recalling she'd been boarding a plane Friday night I asked, "She'll be back by then, won't she?"

Marla's answer came slowly. "Oh, sure. But if you show up, won't Oscar realize something's going on?"

"I was hoping you could sneak me in."

"I don't think that will work." She paced for a moment before turning back to me. "I could talk to Sara."

"You?"

"I belong at the office, so it won't raise any eyebrows if I see her privately. And I can bring up her fling with Ray Gage as kind of a girl-talk thing, whereas you'd come across as a stranger making threats."

Whereas. She was cute when she spoke lawyer. "Can you convince her Oscar's the wrong guardian?"

"I think so. Like I said before, Sara and I are a lot alike."

"Will you call me as soon as you talk with her?"

"Right away."

"Great." It felt good to have a plan. "If we can get through the rest of the weekend, things will work out."

Marla touched my arm, and I felt a tingle of warmth. "Like I said before, Max, you're a good guy."

With Adam and Ilsa gone, things seemed different in the house. Peter talked more. Lucy suggested we skip leftover Chinese food and attempt to cook a real dinner. "We've got candlesticks and everything. We can make it fancy." She excused her enthusiasm by adding, "The Yarru always hold feasts to celebrate their victories, and getting rid of those two feels like a win to us."

When neither the kids nor I had an idea how to begin making a feast, Marla became the hero. She found pork chops in the freezer and demonstrated how a microwave oven can be used to defrost meat. Peter peeled some slightly shriveled potatoes he found in the pantry. Lucy wanted to recreate her favorite dish from school, broccoli salad, but most of the ingredients she needed were missing from Ilsa's kitchen.

"I can fix that," Marla said brightly. Using an app on her phone, she ordered the items Lucy wanted and asked for delivery. An hour later, a kid from a nearby Meijer store pulled up outside with several bags of groceries. I knew a person could get meals delivered from a dozen different places, but it amazed me to learn that someone will bring raisins and sunflower seeds to your door just because you ask.

Marla had added to Lucy's list, so the delivery included dinner rolls, several kinds of vegetables, and a yummy-looking cake for dessert.

As we unloaded the bags, Marla seemed pensive. Finally, she asked in a low tone, "Max, do you really think Oscar is behind all this?"

"Who else?"

"Everyone at the law firm gets a cut from his management of the estate. Maybe it's Kevin or even Sara who doesn't want that to end. He always needs money, and she'd like to run for office, which takes a lot these days." She batted her eyelashes. "You might even suspect me, since the extra in my paycheck does wonders for my credit card bill."

"Oscar gets the lion's share. Besides, there are incidents in his past where someone who stood in his way was hurt or killed."

Marla's eyes widened. "You've got to be kidding."

"I can't prove it yet, but I think Oscar's already guilty of murder."

The sound of the front door closing caught our attention, and we left the kitchen to look. Oscar was setting his bag down in the foyer, and the kids stood rigidly at the bottom of the stairs, their arms almost touching. "Uncle Morrie," Lucy said in an overly bright voice, "I was about to tell Oscar what's happened since he left."

"The sheriff's department called to tell me you went missing but were later found," Oscar said. "It would have been nice if someone here had informed me." His gaze lit on Marla, who seemed to wilt under it. I put a hand on her back, letting her know we'd get through this together.

"We didn't want you to worry," Lucy said. "What you don't know is that Adam and Ilsa have run off to Niagara Falls to get married."

"What?"

"I know. It's very irresponsible of them. Luckily, Uncle Morrie was here to stay with us." She gestured at me, but her arm was stiff, like a puppet's. "We ran into him Friday night and invited him to stay with us for the weekend. Adam and Ilsa must have figured it was a good time to go, since we had a chaperone."

Oscar sniffed suspiciously, as if testing the scent of my truthfulness. "And Ms. Johnson? Are you chaperoning as well?"

Marla seemed flustered and tongue-tied. "I came—to get those—papers you wanted me to get ready for Monday, and M—the kids asked me to stay and help them cook dinner."

"How nice."

I stepped forward, putting on my best non-threatening manner. "I know you weren't in favor of me coming here, Coburn, but now you need someone to see that the kids are fed and taken to school. I'm between jobs, so I can help out until you find replacements for your missing staff."

It took a minute, but finally he said, "That's kind of you…Morrie."

"We call him Uncle Morrie," Lucy said sweetly. "Back in the day, he and Dad were like brothers."

CHAPTER TWELVE

Our dinner turned out well, but Oscar's presence was like a damp blanket dropped over the gathering. We congratulated each other on the food. We talked about movies and music. He made no attempt to join in. When it was finished, he rose from the head of the table and said, "I'm going up to bed. Marla, you should stay over. We need to go north early tomorrow morning and interview Mr. Middaugh." His eyes rolled slowly toward me. "That is, if Morrie doesn't mind staying with Peter and Lucy."

"I'd be happy to," I replied as if he'd nominated me for a Pulitzer. "I was thinking I'd sleep in the hallway outside Lucy's door tonight. That way if she sleepwalks again, I can stop her."

"I hardly think that's necessary." Oscar's gaze turned to Lucy, a challenge in his eyes. "Are you afraid you might wander away again, Lucy?" The subtle emphasis on the word *afraid* indicated he understood her reluctance to admit to fear.

"I'm not—" Her expression revealed sudden pain, and she glanced at her brother before finishing her reply. "I suppose it's a good idea."

Oscar shook his head. "Seems a bit much to me."

Marla disagreed, though I noticed her tone was falsely cheerful. "It will be good for everyone's peace of mind."

Peter and I pushed an oversized rocker-recliner from the common room into the hallway, and Lucy brought me a pillow and blanket. "I feel like such a baby," she said through clenched teeth.

"Oscar's a tricky guy," I responded. "We can't give him a way to get at you."

"What about the window? He could turn off the alarms and come across the breezeway just like Adam did."

"I could rig the sash," Peter offered. "Anyone who touches it will get a jolt of electricity."

I stopped with a blanket half unfolded. "Nothing fatal, right?"

He was already sorting through his lab for materials. "No. Unless he falls off the roof from surprise."

Taking out his phone, Peter disabled the alarm system so he could work. As he ran wire along the window base I asked, "Where did you learn this?"

"Physics class."

"A teacher showed you how to set a booby trap?"

"Actually, the students did. The teacher was the target." After a moment he added, "It's the only demonstration I've seen at Lawson that was the least bit informative." Connecting the wire to a 6-volt battery, he closed Lucy's window. "If anyone touches that, we'll hear the yelp."

As the house settled down, I reclined the chair to its fullest and pulled the blanket over me. It wasn't too uncomfortable, and I was settling in nicely when movement down the hallway brought me to attention. My dread turned to something nicer when Marla came into view, index finger pressed to her lips. Before I knew it, she was in the chair with me, and I realized that while I was sleeping in my clothes, Marla was not. "I borrowed one of Oscar's t-shirts from the dryer," she whispered, her lips against my ear.

Like the gentleman that I am, I covered her with the blanket, and things went swimmingly for a few minutes. Marla was a great kisser, and my whole body appreciated her efforts. Part of me was aware that we lacked privacy, but my seamier side answered, "Everybody's asleep." The kissing went on.

Until the door behind the chair opened. "Max?"

Marla quickly curled herself into a ball, and I pulled the blanket over her head. "Um-hmm. Hey, Lucy."

"I know it's late, but I'd really like a cookie and some milk. Will you go downstairs with me?"

"Um, sure." I fumbled for a delay. "Do you have your slippers on?"

"No, why?"

"The tile floor will be cold. Get your slippers, and then we'll go down together."

Lucy did as I suggested, and Marla slipped away while I got myself together. When Lucy and I returned from the kitchen after Oreos and two percent milk, I had the big chair all to myself.

The kids slept late on Sunday, but Oscar and Marla were up and gone when I came downstairs at seven. He'd mentioned a town to the north and a client unable to travel. "At least you won't have to worry about him trying something," Marla had whispered while we snuggled in the chair. "He'll be a hundred miles away."

Though I didn't contradict her, I wasn't able to relax. Oscar being gone seemed more dangerous to me than Oscar in the house. If he had something nasty in mind, he'd arrange for someone else to take the blame. I hoped we'd delayed him by getting rid of Adam and Ilsa. While Oscar drafted Plan B, Marla would be ratting him out to Sara Dailey.

After a bowl of some kind of Chex, I sneaked up to the third floor and started trying combinations of Oscar's birth date: month-day-year, then day-month-year, and so on. I hit on my fourth attempt, which was good, because usually there's a limit for how many combinations can be entered. The numbers turned green, I heard a soft click, and the doorknob turned in my hand.

Oscar's apartment brought Sherlock Holmes' digs to mind, with Victorian décor and an honest-to-goodness fireplace in case he wanted to warm a long February night. I wondered who'd lugged the pile of fat logs up three flights of stairs and stacked them so neatly. Probably the now-absent, unlamented Adam.

There wasn't much in the place to help me understand the man. After scanning his sitting room, kitchenette, bath, bedroom, and closets, I decided the pay dirt had to be in his office.

I was wrong. The office was as empty of clues as the rest of the place. No papers. Books that appeared to have never been opened. (I almost sneered at that until I remembered the shelves of unread volumes in my own office.) There was a lovely oak filing cabinet in a corner, but every drawer was locked. I searched for a while but couldn't locate its key.

As I stood there, frustrated, a noise sounded behind me. I turned to the window and saw someone peering in. We were face to face, and I recognized Jack, the tree-trimmer, straddling the sturdy branch of a large oak tree that grew close to the house. He recognized me at about the same moment I placed him. Waving the pruners, he said something I missed, then "….branches laying on your shingles, you got problems."

I gave an exaggerated nod of understanding, grateful he didn't seem suspicious to see me on the third floor, where only Oscar should be.

When I went back downstairs, Lucy and Peter were in the breakfast nook. "Would you two like to see a Lions' game?" Peter's face lit with interest. Lucy's turned dour, but I'd already made the arrangements. "I want you somewhere Oscar doesn't know about."

"But why would I watch grown men in tight pants beat each other up?" Lucy asked. "It's medieval."

"It's safe," I countered. "I need a few hours to get some things done."

"Then you won't be coming with us?"

"If all goes well, I'll make the second half."

"But how are we supposed to—"

"Don't worry. I have the perfect guide for your first experience with American football."

"USian football," she corrected. "Remember the other Americans."

"USian football," I said to placate her. "Try it. You might like it."

We picked Bobby up at his place, and you can probably guess how he looked. He wore a coat with a roaring lion pictured front and back, a cap with the same logo, and mittens with maps of Michigan all over them, each with the rampant lion showing Detroit's location.

"Hey, guys," Bobby said as he launched himself into the car. "Max says you've never been to a football game before."

"I doubt we've missed much," Lucy said in a cool tone.

Her mood had no effect on Bobby's. "No, you're in for a real treat. The Lions are a little off right now, but they're about to roar back in a big way. Today would be great, because we hate the Vikings, right, Max?"

"With a passion." In the rearview mirror, I saw Peter's lips quirk at my deadpan voice.

"Anyway, I'll explain the details as we go, but the main object is to get the ball over the goal line."

"In civilized games, players don't knock each other down to do that," Lucy opined. "They use finesse to take the ball where they want it."

"Finesse?" For a moment Bobby seemed at a loss for words, then he said, "Wait till you see a running back pick his way through a crowd of three-hundred-pound linemen. That is the height of finesse, Ms. Gage."

"Here you are," I told them. "I'll join you as soon as I can."

Once they'd gone inside, I navigated my way out of the parking lot and headed for Inkster, where I hoped to find Dodger Ainsley at his office-slash-residence this time.

Dodger was in, but he didn't look pleased to see me. He wore a worn bathrobe and flip-flops, and his hair had not been anywhere close to a comb lately. "The place is a little messy," he said, blocking the doorway with his chunky body. "I don't usually see anybody on weekends."

"Why don't you get your coat, and I'll buy you a beer?"

That pleased him, though he also needed to put on a shirt, shoes, and pants. Ten minutes later we were seated at a BWW not far from the free clinic where Dodger rented rooms on the second floor.

"I'm going to ask questions, and I need you to tell me the truth."

He considered taking offense, but in the end said, "Sure, bro. Shoot."

"Two kids came to you with a proposition." Dodger said nothing, and since I hadn't asked a question, that was okay. "I'm not sure how you decided they weren't lying about having money, but you did."

He showed no more than mild interest, so I said, "You followed them to my office, and later you stole the information I had on them."

Dodger raised a finger. "I did not break in, Maxie, and those papers were easily replaced."

Trying to hold my temper I said, "You weren't entitled to them, so that makes it theft." I let him ponder that for a second. "It won't help your reputation to have that on your record."

"I gave you a chance to make a deal." Dodger curled a paw around his beer mug. "Soon as I found out who those kids are, I knew we were in like Flynn."

"Would you really have killed their guardian for them?"

The look he gave me said I'd cut him to the quick. "Of course not. They told us a fairy tale. We make them think we scared the guy into leaving them alone, and we walk away with a generous paycheck."

"It's not a fairy tale."

"Wow." He took a long drink while he processed that, his Adam's apple bobbing as faint *glugs* emanated from his throat. "Okay. You and me track the guy down. We tell him we know what he's up to. We make sure he knows we'll be watching him. The kids pay us, and we split the money." He spread his hands. "Five thousand each. A piece of cake."

"You went to his office, didn't you?"

"You went there first."

"*I* had a cover story. I bet *you* went in there like an ape in a tearoom and made him suspect someone's investigating him."

"He wasn't even there." Dodger pointed a stubby finger at my nose. "Look, I didn't hurt nobody. I didn't have an intention of hurting nobody. I saw a chance for a fat payday and took it, like any businessman would."

"You put those kids' lives in danger, Dodger. Oscar was in no hurry before, but now he's got to act before things get beyond his control."

My voice had risen, and our waitress paused in her route to a table farther down. "Trouble here, guys?"

"No, no," Dodger assured her. "We're discussing politics. You know how that gets."

She met my gaze, tacitly asking if I agreed, and I waved to signal things were okay. When she went on, I rose from the seat. "Stay away from Lucy and Peter Gage. Stay away from the Coburn Law Firm. And stay away from me." Tossing some bills on the table, I left, stepping into blinding sunlight as the door closed behind me. The air felt good on my skin, cooling my anger somewhat.

Then a hand grabbed my shoulder. "Listen, bro—"

Wheeling to face him, I said, "Dodger, I am not your bro. I'm not your friend. I'm trying to save a kid's life while you're looking to score. Now get your hand off me before I smack you one."

Dodger stood frozen for a few seconds, taking in what I'd said. In the end, he chose to respond to the least emotional part of what I'd said. "You really believe Coburn would kill a kid for money?"

"He plans to kill the boy and blame the girl for it."

He seemed genuinely angry. "What a jerk."

"Well, yeah. That covers it."

"Listen, Br—Max, I didn't know. Your guy in the office said you were going on vacation, so I figured once you were gone, I'd offer to help those kids." His expression was as earnest as I'd ever seen it. "If I'd known Coburn was a scumbag, I wouldn't have..." He had a hard time saying the word. "...interfered."

Dodger seemed legitimately contrite, but I wasn't ready to forgive and forget. Leaving him mumbling on the sidewalk, I went on to my car.

By the time I found my little party at Ford Field, it was after half-time. In my absence, Lucy had done a complete turnaround on the topic of American football. "This is fun," she said as I took my seat. "Do you see the guy with the ball down there? He's the quarterback, and he's really good. Watch and you'll see."

I glanced at Peter, who gave me a shrug and an amused grin. Beyond him, Bobby looked pleased at having made a convert. When we stood up to stretch during a time out, I maneuvered to a seat next to Bobby. Once play began again I said, "Tell me about Dodger Ainsley."

"Roger? Nice guy. Do you know he can pare an apple and set the peeling down so it looks like the apple is still in there? He showed me."

"He's a man of many talents. When did you and he meet?"

"Well, he came in on Tuesday, when I was minding the store. He told me about you guys being friends on the force for years." Bobby gave me a look. "He makes it sound way more exciting than you do."

"We've all got our stories. Dodger asked about Lucy and Peter?"

"He said he needed to contact their guardian, but he lost the note where he wrote down his name."

"So you gave it to him."

"Yeah." His eyes went wide. "Was that wrong?"

"Bobby, P.I.s don't share information on their clients with anybody."

"Not even other P.I.s?"

"Not even."

"Jeez, Max. I'm sorry. He seemed to know all about the case, and he told me how you stood up for him with the other cops. How you always had his back."

"I did?"

Bobby frowned. "That's what he said. Like when some cops were giving him grief about something, you told them to back off."

It took a minute for the incident to swim out of my memory. Several cops had cornered Dodger in the locker room, angry because he'd pulled some stunt that made us all look bad. Sensing that harsh words, even a punch in the nose, wouldn't change the guy's view of life, I'd told them to stop acting like punks in an alley. The way to handle a dishonest cop is to lodge a formal complaint, and I suggested they do that.

"He said I took his side?"

"He said you were his best friend on the force."

That was sad. Dodger had interpreted my intervention as a kindness, since it saved him a beat-down from the others.

After we dropped Bobby off at his place, Lucy cleared her throat in a way that indicated what would follow was important. "If your talk with Ms. Dailey doesn't work out tomorrow, Max, we feel that we have to go ahead with our original plan."

I'd been dreading this moment. Since I now knew they were right about Oscar, the kids hoped I'd come around to accepting their solution. "Look," I said reasonably, "we can't kill him."

"Then we have to at least injure him." I opened my mouth to object, but Lucy held up a finger and went on. "As long as Oscar is physically able to come after us, Peter and I are in danger."

"I don't think he'll try anything with me there."

That was my hope, but Oscar had to be getting desperate as his dream of controlling millions of dollars faded. Nightmare scenarios nagged at my brain, and I wasn't sure we had the ammunition to stop him. Still, I didn't want to replace "Let's kill Oscar" with "Let's maim him." Trying to sound certain of my abilities, I said, "I'm watching his every move."

The look that passed between them told me Peter and Lucy had their own ideas about how the next few days would play out.

When we got to the house, Oscar and Marla were there, apparently finishing up paperwork needed for the client they'd visited in Bad Axe. Marla suggested a movie marathon. "Oscar can go get McDonalds, and we'll spend the night in a bunch in the den." Though she spoke lightly, Marla held my gaze, and I realized she was suggesting a way to keep us all together. I shot her a grateful smile. While she wasn't convinced Oscar was evil, she wasn't willing to take chances with the kids' lives.

When he returned with more food than we could ever eat, Oscar declined to share movie night with us. Lucy, Peter, Marla, and I hauled blankets and pillows down to the TV room and made ourselves little warrens. Lucy made a tent out of blankets and an end table, where she lay on her stomach, watching *Shrek* through a slit. Peter tipped two upholstered chairs on their sides and draped blankets atop them, using the cushions as his mattress. That left the adults with two couches, Marla on one and me on the other. After *Shrek* we watched *My Spy* and then *Guardians of the Galaxy*. Twenty minutes into that one, the kids were asleep. Dragging her blanket along, Marla joined me on my couch. We didn't do much more than kiss, in case somebody woke up, but once again, Marla proved that she is a very good kisser.

CHAPTER THIRTEEN

As I left the breakfast table Monday morning, Lucy commented in a tone that sounded a little too innocent, "If you're going to drive us to school, we need to get going. Peter is already outside waiting."

Oscar hadn't yet come downstairs. We had a good forty minutes to drive five miles. A good detective has an ear for duplicity, so I said, "Go ahead. I need to visit the bathroom."

When she left, I began a search for the booby trap I was sure I'd find. It turned out to be a length of cord tied across the second-to-last step on the staircase to the third floor. They'd chosen a color that blended well with the steps, and the unsuspecting Oscar would have gone sprawling onto the landing. It probably wouldn't have been lethal, but it fit the kids' new goal, incapacitating him until the wheels of justice ground out a new Gage family guardian.

I removed the rope, extending a life I didn't find particularly worthy, and went outside, where Peter had started my rental car and turned on the heater. I didn't admit I'd foiled their little plot, and Lucy, focused on the prospect of Oscar's fall, told the story of a Portuguese footballer who'd stepped through some elevator doors without noticing the carriage wasn't there, fell five floors, and died. "One can't predict how a fall will end," she finished as if wrapping up a fable.

"I'd prefer Oscar is arrested and has to go through the humiliation of a trial that reveals his evil intentions and black heart."

After a moment Lucy said, "We'll get back to you on that."

At 8:02, my phone rang. I put the call through the car's speaker, demonstrating the proper way to handle driving while communicating. "Hi, Mr. Dunham, this is Shelly at Lifesaver

Insurance. I'm really sorry, but your Mustang has been declared a total loss. We'll cut you a check and send it—"

"No," I interrupted. "I'm having it fixed."

"We can't offer more than the estimated value," she warned. "It will cost far more than that to repair it."

"I'll figure out a way."

"What happened to your car?" Lucy asked when I ended the call.

"Someone sideswiped me on the freeway." Angry with the insurance company's decision, I added, "It isn't like it was a head-on collision or anything. It's mostly body work, and the Mustang is a classic."

As I watched Peter and Lucy enter the school building, I checked my messages. The urine sample we'd had analyzed showed Rohypnol in Lucy's system. While that proved she was a victim, not a drama queen, it didn't implicate anyone but Adam. I was pleased we'd managed to get rid of Oscar's on-site accomplices, but it bothered me that we didn't know who else was in on his scheme. Telling Sara Dailey might be a mistake, and I hoped Marla was careful. Even if Sara was honest, she might tell Kevin our suspicions, and who knew what he might do to get his hands on more of the Gage wealth?

It occurred to me there was someone who could tell me a lot about the Coburn Law Firm. Carson Coburn was, according to Mom's research, a decent man. If he believed the Gage kids were in danger, he might give me something I could take to the police.

Carson was now a resident of an exclusive care facility called Fox Homesteads. I had trouble finding his exact address, since people paid Fox large amounts of money for privacy in addition to assisted living of the finest kind. The place had a sliding system, so a client might enter as a mostly functioning member of society and proceed along a continuum of decline, all needs met until the day he finally fled this mortal coil.

Places like Fox Homesteads don't let strangers simply waltz in, so when I got to the security booth, I showed the guard the blue envelope I'd stolen during my visit to the firm. It was tastefully emblazoned with "Coburn Law" at the top, and I explained that "we" needed Mr. Coburn's signature on a document he'd begun months ago. Such requests had no doubt become common since his stroke, and I had no trouble getting in.

I was checked twice more on the way to Carson's apartment, but each time my story held up. At the door of #217, I knocked lightly. A young woman answered, a bottle of protein drink in one hand. "Yes?"

"I have a document for Carson Coburn to sign."

She looked annoyed. "His niece said they're caught up on his cases."

"This client took a long time deciding whether to go ahead with it, but now she's ready to file."

"We're almost done. Wait here for a minute." She backed away, allowing me inside. Returning to the bedroom, she said, "You have a visitor, Mr. Coburn. Drink up, and I'll get you ready for company."

I caught glimpses of the old man as the woman moved around him, holding the straw so he could finish his drink and then removing the napkin she'd tucked into his pajama top. Taking a wet wipe from one of those warmer things, she gently cleaned his face, paying particular attention to the area around his mouth. He submitted to her ministrations stoically, eyes lowered and face impassive.

When the woman finished, she invited me into the room and said formally, "Mr. Coburn, this gentleman needs to see you about a legal matter you worked on a while back. If you need me, your call button is there by your good hand. All you need to do is press this red circle, right here. You can do that, right?"

"Yeth." The word snapped with resentment. A man who'd once ruled his world was reduced to dependency and reminded of it by over-simplified instructions. This young woman might never understand how he felt, how far he'd fallen in his own estimation.

As the aide picked up a bag of trash and left the apartment, closing the door softly, Carson examined me critically. I did the same, noting the slack musculature on his right side: drooping mouth, lazy eyelid, and an arm that lay useless along his body. There was a glint of anger in his eyes, but I read somewhere that's common in stroke patients. With the brain's emotional center impaired, they experience bursts of anger that aren't really aimed at anyone.

"Mr. Coburn, my name is Max Dunham, and I'm not really here for a signature. I'm a private detective, hired by Peter and Lucy Gage."

"Uh?"

"Doctor Ray Gage died in November. His children, Peter and Lucy, became wards of your law firm."

His lips twitched—well, one side did. I interpreted that as surprise. Had he forgotten Gage's death? Was he unaware of the terms of the will? Or did he know Ray had meant to name Denice as guardian?

His gaze focused on me, waiting for further explanation. "The kids are in Detroit now, and they came to my office to ask me to protect them."

"'Tect?"

"They think someone intends to kill one of them in order to gain control of the estate."

His gaze sharpened, and he demanded, "'Splain."

"Your firm is their guardian, but one individual was appointed to serve as a parent figure."

"'Anny."

After a beat I translated. "No, not the nanny. One of your attorneys." He glared at me, waiting. "I suspect Dr. Gage changed his will, but the new one was never registered."

A *g* sound came out twice, and then "dun?"

"Oscar."

"Na nanny?"

"She was sent away. Oscar bought a big house, and he keeps the kids there. He spends their money on expensive items they hate. He's told people the girl is hysterical, and he claims the boy scares his sister to torment her. Neither of those things is true." Taking a breath, I took the plunge. "I think he's going to kill the boy and blame the girl for it. Then he can medicate her and lock her away in a wing of the house while he enjoys her money."

"Nuh." He made a dismissive gesture with his working hand.

"You know your son, Mr. Coburn. Which part of that do you think Oscar isn't capable of?"

"Nun. Osk wouldn't…" He stopped, unable to complete the lie.

Though I felt sorry for him, I couldn't let him off the hook. "Are you sure, Mr. Coburn?" I asked. "Are you willing to let the firm you built over three decades be used this way? And worse, are you willing to bet the life of a child that Oscar won't kill to control millions of dollars?"

My questions bothered him, and though the frown remained, I saw his resistance fade. "Tried…tell 'im."

"Oscar? You tried to tell him what?"

"Law's fah gud. Osk uses 't fah h-self." His eyes turned watery. "Osk…wants all."

I nodded. Oscar Coburn did want it all, and he was willing to do terrible things to get it.

"I'm sorry." And I was. What must it be like for a father to know that his son was rotten to the core?

"Will Sara help replace Oscar if she knows the truth? She heads the firm now, so—"

Carson made an angry growl in objection to that revelation. "No women. Too…emoshun'l."

"They all agreed to it." I gave him a second to absorb the blow. "Will Sara help the kids?"

"Yeth." He turned his face aside. "Wan' me t'can 'im. Crook'd, she said."

It was what I'd come to learn. Carson trusted Sara more than he trusted his own son. Which reminded me: "What about your other son? Would he side with Oscar or with Sara if it came to a fight?"

His head twisted on the pillow. "Needer," he spat. "Boyz c-coward."

"Even if there's a lot of money involved?"

The old man's expression turned sad. "Dunno."

Reaching out with his good hand, Carson grabbed my arm. "Ge' me outta here. I…fix it." Pulling at me with surprising strength, he repeated, "Ge' me out. Still got it."

Gently, I pried his grip loose, took his hand, and shook it in the time-honored gesture of a gentleman's agreement. "When you're ready, when you're well," I said, "I'll tell them it's time for you to return to work."

Leaving Fox Homesteads, I called Mom. "How goes the research?"

"Nothing new on Oscar. If he kills people, he's good at it."
I heard papers shuffling. "Have you met the associate, Marla
Johnson?"

"Um, yes." I don't know what most guys tell their moms
about their romantic relationships, but for me, it's zilch. There
wasn't much to tell anyway, though it wasn't for lack of trying.

"Are you aware of her military background?"

"She mentioned being in the army before she went to law
school."

"She was asked to leave when she failed a psychological
review."

"What? How?"

"The report cites traits that are, quote, 'deceitful and
amoral.'"

Two things smacked me right in the brain. First, Marla
wasn't what she seemed. Second: "Mom, you hacked into U.S.
Army records?"

"That would be wrong, Max. But your boy Oscar isn't as
ethical as I am. While hacking *his* records, I found the report he
dug up before he recommended the firm hire her."

"Before? You mean he wanted someone deceitful and
amoral?"

"My theory is no one in his family would play Coburn's
dirty games, so the guy cozies up to ex-cons, men he knows will
walk on the wrong side of the law if the reward is enticing
enough. Then along comes this new lady lawyer with deceitful
tendencies, and he sees an opportunity. You need to steer clear
of her, Max."

"I will, Mom, and thanks. You're the best."

When we ended our call, I saw that I had a text from my
cop friend Baker. *Sorry—crazy wknd. Blue SUV taken fr*

Miradale Apartments in Ferndale Friday a.m. Found later with extensive damage FL side. Officers suspect local teens.

Miradale Apartments sounded familiar, but not in the sense I'd been there. It was a name I'd seen recently, but I didn't remember where. Since it wasn't far, I decided to take a run over there.

Following GPS commands, I entered what resembled a bee colony: building after building, alike and characterless. In an apparent attempt to make finding a particular building easier, animal faces had been painted on the street-facing ends: a tiger, an elephant, a zebra, and a lion.

Marla Johnson lived in the Miradale Apartments.

Mom was right, and I was an idiot. Marla had been snuggling up to me to learn what I knew and what I was going to do about it. Her kittenish cuteness hid a scary underside, someone who'd locate a car suitable for a hit and run, maybe even someone who'd do the deed herself.

A guy was chipping ice away from under his eaves with rhythmic, patient strokes. I came up the walk as if I intended to enter the building and then stopped and commented, "Good day to get a handle on that."

He leaned on the spud. "The sun's my friend at the moment."

"My girlfriend Marla says somebody got his car stolen the other day. That's not cool."

"Mrs. Blanchard. They found it, but it ain't in very good shape."

"Did they hot wire it?"

"No. She had an extra key in the wheel well in one of those magnetic boxes. Cop said thieves run a hand under there looking for them."

I shook my head at the sad state of the world, and the guy pointed a crooked finger at me. "You tell Marla to watch out. She parks right next to Mrs. B, so her car might be next."

"I will." I went inside, waited until the old guy disappeared through his sliding door, and returned to my car. Marla was not next on the list of possible car theft victims. She was the perp.

Angry and embarrassed, I made my way to the Coburn Law Firm and told the receptionist I needed to speak to Marla Johnson.

"Ms. Johnson is gone for the day."

"It's only one o'clock." The look she gave me said it was none of my business what time Ms. Johnson came or went from work. "All right. I need to speak to Sara Dailey then."

"Ms. Dailey is on vacation this week."

"I was told she'd be back after the weekend."

Her attention to stacking some files more neatly on her desk signaled I wasn't entitled to know Ms. Dailey's comings and goings either.

Marla had lied to keep me from contacting Sara, but Peter had her personal number. I could still speak to her. If Sara knew about the plot, Oscar would have to give up on it.

I texted both kids, asking for Sara's contact info. Neither answered.

The trip to Lawson Academy took longer than I wanted, even though I broke a few rules of the road on the way. I didn't endear myself to the school secretary when I hit the entry buzzer more times than necessary. "It's an emergency," I called. "Let me in."

"Please stand back for a moment."

I did, raising my arms and turning once so she could see I wasn't carrying a weapon. The door buzzed, and I hurried into the office. "I need to see Lucy and Peter Gage right away."

When she started a canned spiel about privacy, I had to hold myself back from grabbing and shaking her. Remembering Lucy's letter, I took it out and handed it over. The woman read it once, looked up at me, and read it again. "That's Lucy's handwriting, but I don't under—"

"I haven't got time to explain. Can you please get them down here?"

"They're gone. Their guardian sent a car for them. I can—"

She was still talking when I pushed my way out the door and hurried down the steps.

I was almost ready to back out of the parking space when my phone rang. The ID said *Peter*, but I knew who'd be on the other end of the call.

"Hello."

"Max, it's Marla."

"Where are Peter and Lucy?"

"Here at the house." She sounded concerned, though I knew better. "Oscar couldn't reach you, so he asked me to pick up the kids and stay with them until he returns." She lowered her voice. "I'm worried about Lucy. Peter thinks it's funny when she gets…riled up like she does."

"What do you want, Marla?"

"I think it would be good if you joined us."

Marla sounded innocent, caring, and a little desperate. If the conversation was replayed at some point in the future, it would seem she'd done her best when the guy responsible for the kids, fake Uncle Morrie, failed to show up.

"I'm calling the police."

"Why would you do that? The kids are here, and they're safe. I'll stay with them until you return."

I got the underlying message: *Show up or bad things will happen*. What if I refused? Would they proceed, knowing I was aware of the plot?

That led to some disturbing truths. What parts of the so-called plot could I prove? Oscar was clever. Marla seemed honest. Lucy and Peter had been cast as kids who, because they couldn't adjust to the tragedies life had thrown at them, acted out and told lies. I had to assume the plan had been adjusted to make me a bad guy who'd taken advantage of their weirdness.

With that in mind, I pushed the red button, ending the call. The least that Marla deserved was to sit there and wonder what I intended to do next.

CHAPTER FOURTEEN

Though it wore my nerves raw, I stayed away from Deer Creek Estates until it was dark. I entered the property via my stealthy route, unwilling to run the risk that Frank and his ilk would either delay me or alert Oscar to my presence. At a dollar store along the way I bought black jogging pants, a sweatshirt, and dark running shoes. Parked behind a Burger King, I changed into my ninja outfit and then picked at fries and sipped on a root beer, waiting until the sun disappeared behind a fat bank of gunmetal gray clouds on the horizon.

As I waited, I called Dinah to check in. I didn't tell her how bad the situation was, since she'd probably suggest calling the sheriff in to sort things out. Knowing how well Oscar and Marla operated as a team, I didn't think I could beat them with my unproven theory and the testimony of two kids known for peeing on their neighbors' lawns when they felt it was necessary.

Dinah sensed my anxiety. "Are you sure you're all right, Max?"

"Fine, except I'm eating fast food instead of your wonderful, home-cooked meals," I replied. "I'll call tomorrow, when things calm down."

I slid my phone into a pocket, aware that Dinah suspected trouble. I hoped she didn't interfere, because Oscar could no longer allow the Gage kids to speak to anyone in authority. A cop showing up at the door was likely to cause dire consequences.

Parking my vehicle at the same car dealership as before, I left my bulky coat behind, figuring activity would keep me warm. I took along only my phone, silenced, and a Swiss army knife Mom had given me for my last birthday. So far, I'd used it only for non-lethal tasks like scraping chocolate off my car seat. Scaling the estate's stone wall, I dropped into the play area, threaded my way between a swing set and a slide, and headed for the Gage house, keeping to the shadows.

Staying at Deer Creek had given me time to scope out alternate ways to get onto the Gage property. The lot behind theirs was uninhabited, its residents having jetted somewhere warm for the winter. On his midnight rambles, Peter had discovered their security cameras were fakes, meant to deter crime, not record it. Crunching my way through the old, crusted snow in their yard, I reached the fence, scaled its ice-cold metal bars, and dropped at a spot behind the garage with minimal noise.

Security on the Gage estate was potentially a problem, but I was betting on one of three positive prospects: I could avoid the cameras, since I'd made it my business to know where they were; they were turned off so Oscar could prowl the estate without setting off his own alarms; or Peter had turned off the system, hoping I'd come to their rescue.

I got as far as the open garage door when the first surprise hit. I'd been on the lookout for Marla or Oscar, but the figure I came upon was too large for her, too short for him. Flattening myself against the outer wall, I waited. When the man turned, the garage light gave a good view of his face. It was one of the tree-trimmers. John? Joe? No, Jack. The other one was Jay.

After a few seconds he was approached by a tough-looking man I'd never seen before. "Anything?"

"Nope. I bet he's scared to show his face."

It was a good news-bad news thing. The alarms had to be off so the men could patrol the area, but…the men were patrolling the area.

"Keep an eye out," Jack ordered.

"We will." The second man went off, leaving me wondering how many "we" meant.

The answer wasn't long in coming. Rough hands grabbed me, one at my collar and one at my belt. "Hey!" the man who'd come up behind me called out. "I think we got him."

Jack came toward us. "We been waiting for you, snoop."

The hand at my collar twisted it tight, so I struggled to breathe, much less speak. I fought to escape, but my efforts only made my captor snort derisively. "Stop that." Jack back-handed me so hard that my head reeled, and I stayed upright only because of the other man's grip. "Shut up and stay still." Searching my pockets, he took the knife and my cell.

"What do we do now?" the voice from behind me asked.

"Boss said don't hurt the guy, just hold him till he gets here. And the woman just called to say the girl is on the loose in the house. We need to make sure she doesn't leave."

"Who watches my spot if I'm stuck guarding this yahoo?"

Pointing to the garage, Jack ordered, "Take him in there and tie him to something. There's stuff in there you can use." When my captor turned me in that direction, Jack cautioned, "Don't leave marks. Boss wants him in good shape when the cops get here."

Oscar has to know I'll tell the police everything, I thought, but that was immediately followed by an unpleasant correction: *unless they find me dead.* The new plan was for Max Dunham, deceased, to be blamed for the terrible things that were going to happen at the Gage home tonight.

I had to stop it, but my chances didn't look good. I was held in an iron grip. My head still rang from the swat I'd received. Propelled toward the garage by sharp jabs to my spine, I made only a few pitiful attempts to resist. The man was strong enough to pull me onto my toes, so my choices were to trip along like a ballerina or stumble and end up being dragged to where he wanted me.

Inside, the man took stock and made his decision. "Over by the stairs." On the way, he picked up some zip-ties from the workbench. "These will keep you in one spot," he said. "I ain't no babysitter."

A minute later I was spread like a scarecrow, my wrists fastened to the spindles of the stairway railing. Tearing up a rag that smelled of car wax, he made a gag, tying it so tightly I thought my lips might split. I felt helpless. I felt hopeless. I'd failed the kids, and Oscar was winning.

The man stood back to check his work, nodded satisfaction, and left. Did he know—did any of them know—that Oscar planned to kill me? If they did, would they care?

When I was dead and it appeared I was a criminal, my mom would protest that her boy was honest. But Dodger would report that I knew the kids had a hundred thousand dollars in cash. Bobby would try to defend me, but my interest in Oscar and the kids would be obvious from my recent activities.

Marla would swear to whatever Oscar said, and Oscar would report that I'd come under false pretenses. He'd blame himself, claiming he'd suspected all along that I was shady. He'd bite his lip and curse the day he'd let the kids talk him into allowing me to enter their home. I'd forced the two hired caregivers out of the way. I'd look like a man guilty of greed and possibly worse.

My death would be easily explained. Oscar would say I tried to kill him and he fought back. The tricky part would be including Peter's death—two in one night. Whatever the final scenario, I was going to die by Oscar's hand, and there was nothing I could do about it.

My defeatist thoughts were interrupted by a tap on my shoulder. Turning, I found Lucy crouched on the stairs behind me. She had a pair of tinsnips, and with them she deftly cut the zip-ties, releasing my hands. I pulled the gag off, took a deep breath, and looked out to see where Oscar's thugs were. Jack stood outside the doorway, his back to us, his head on a hundred-eighty-degree swivel. No way to get past him and make a break for it. Even if we did, others were out there in the dark, between us and freedom.

Touching my shoulder again, Lucy mimicked climbing with her fingers. Nodding, I tiptoed up the stairs behind her. Adam's apartment felt almost as cold as outside, and I saw that the window at the east end was wide open. "I was trying to figure out how to get across the roof without being seen when you came along," Lucy said softly. "While they were busy with you, I made the trip."

"Where's Peter?"

"Marla's got him."

"Can we get back over there?"

"I think so, if we're patient." She knelt by the window and peered out cautiously. "Jack is a coffee fiend. When he works in the yard, he comes inside about once an hour to use the bathroom. Now tonight, he isn't supposed to leave his post, but USians have a phobia about peeing in public. He'll have to go soon, so he'll step around the corner of the garage to relieve himself in the dark. When he does that, we'll go." She craned her neck for a better view. "He's already looking uncomfortable."

"Okay." I sat down on Adam's couch. "While we wait, catch me up on what happened today."

"Someone called the school saying Oscar was sending an associate to pick us up due to an emergency at home. When we came outside, Marla was there. She said you needed our help to convince Sara that things weren't right." Her brow narrowed. "I should have known something was up when she started flirting with you."

The interruptions that had kept Marla and me apart were not the innocent events I'd assumed they were. "Why should you have known?"

Lucy pursed her lips. "*I* like you, Max, but you aren't in Marla's league. She had to be after something."

While that was deflating, it wasn't the time to defend my sex appeal. "We should have refused to go with her," Lucy said regretfully. "It's not like she could have pulled a gun on us right there in the school's circle drive." She leaned forward, checking on Jack. "He's starting to pace." Sitting back against the wall, she returned to her story. "Once we were away from the school, Marla started telling these huge lies. It wasn't Oscar who was the bad guy, it was you. She claimed Oscar was hurt that we doubted his concern for us."

"I know you didn't fall for that."

She frowned. "We probably should have pretended to, but I told her it was a bunch of garbage. Marla stopped pretending to be nice and locked the back doors so we couldn't get out. I said I was going to call you. Peter grabbed the seat, ready to crawl over and stop the car. That's when Marla showed us Oscar's pistol. She pulled the car over and made us give her our phones. She said if we tried anything, she'd shoot one of us." Disgust made her voice harsh. "All we could do was sit there like victims while she drove back here."

"What did Marla do once you were in the house?"

"She called you and then Oscar." Lucy made a disgusted sound. "She's talked to him about six times today, griping that her role wasn't supposed to be this active. Oscar told her she can leave as soon as he gets here, and she seemed relieved." She sniffed. I couldn't tell if she felt disdain for Marla or was fighting tears. "Oscar's up north, establishing an alibi. When he gets here, I don't know what happens."

It was time she knew the worst. "Peter and I will both end up dead. Oscar's going to make it look like you shot your brother by accident."

Lucy swayed as if she'd been slapped. When she finally spoke, her voice was soft with grief and dread. "Only the crazy girl who makes up lies will be left, and the fact that I'm responsible for my brother's death will cause a breakdown I'll never recover from."

"Yes." I didn't voice my suspicion that after her 'breakdown,' Lucy would be isolated and medicated into idiocy. She was smart enough to figure that out for herself.

Her voice got stronger. "Max, we can't let that happen."

"We won't."

"How long have you known this?"

"I don't *know* it," I said. "It's a theory that fits what's gone on here. Returning to current concerns I asked, "If Marla has a gun, how did you get away from her?"

"I used the whiny kid ploy." Lucy's tone changed to sharp nasality. 'There's nothing to do down here. I'm so *bored.*' After an hour of that, she took us upstairs and said we should play with our toys." Lucy huffed a bitter laugh. "She actually said that. Holding a gun. Waiting for a killer to arrive. 'Play with your toys.'"

"What did you gain by getting her to take you upstairs?"

"In our own territory, we have resources." She said it as if it were obvious, but I didn't understand at the time. Looking out the window, Lucy smiled. "Jack's looking for a private spot."

I was thinking I should persuade her to let me go to Peter's rescue alone, but Lucy had more to tell. "Marla insisted we had nothing to be afraid of. Oscar would straighten things out when he got home. I told her it would take some doing to explain why we were held prisoner at gunpoint, but she insisted Oscar had learned things about you that made it necessary for him to cut off communication. We finally pretended to believe her, and she relaxed a little."

Knowing Lucy's ways, I said, "Which is what you were hoping for."

"Yes. Peter asked if he could measure and chart the progress on some of his experiments. Marla said okay, as long as we were all in the same room. I took a book from the shelf and said I'd read while Peter worked." She interrupted herself again. "Jack's definitely looking for a spot." Still peeping outside, she went on, "I sat in a chair near Peter's worktable and pretended to read while he fussed with beakers and Petri dishes. Marla stood in the doorway at first, guarding it, but after a while she dragged a chair over and sat down." I saw Lucy's head move in the shadows. "I can't imagine why women wear those ridiculous heels on their shoes, but it worked for us."

Used to pulling Bobby back on topic, I did the same with her. "What was Peter really doing?"

"Making some surprises." She didn't elaborate. "By six-thirty, Marla was bored and hardly paid attention to us at all. She called Oscar again, and I think he was driving. His voice had that tinny sound it gets when someone's on speaker phone."

I checked the clock on Adam's nightstand. Eight ten. Oscar had to be getting close.

"He asked if you'd come around, and she tried to disguise what they were talking about so we wouldn't understand." In a clever imitation of Marla's clipped manner, Lucy said, "'No, the package hasn't arrived yet.' Give me a break." Lucy finally got back to answering my question. "After a while I stood, like I was interested in what Peter was doing. Marla looked up, but he just kept on measuring and pouring until she lost interest. When she went back to scrolling on her phone, Peter dumped a pile of baking soda on his worktable and wrote a message in it, telling me how I was going to escape."

"Just you?"

Her voice got shaky. "I was supposed to go next door and call the police. He said it had to be me, since I'm smaller and less likely to be seen crawling across the roof."

"It's a good plan. If you're free, they can't go ahead with...what they intend to do."

Now her voice had a hopeful note. "That's right. They can't kill Peter without me there to blame for it."

Though there were other possibilities, I chose to agree, hoping it would convince her to do as Peter wanted. "Exactly."

"Marla had started thinking you wouldn't show up, but I knew you would." I was about to be flattered when she added, "Not that coming here alone is the smartest thing you've ever done."

"Hey!"

"I appreciate your concern, but some backup would have been nice."

I'd spent hours worrying about Lucy, climbed two walls, been hung up like a Christmas ornament, and now she was criticizing my decisions. Anger and fear pushed a burst of words I shouldn't have said, certainly not in that time and place. "Who should I have brought, Lucy? You're considered a nutcase, because you treat everyone like dirt. Our way is always wrong, and *your* way is always right. Maybe our society is full of nervous wrecks, but we don't die from infection in a puncture wound. Maybe we're too focused on work and money, but we've figured out those things up in the sky are stars, not lizards and serpents. Your culture is your culture, Lucy. There are good things and bad things in each one, and you…" Lucy sobbed, only once, but it was so deep that my anger dissipated like smoke. "I'm sorry. I didn't mean…I'm worried about you. About Peter." I sniffed. "About myself, for that matter. We're in trouble, and it doesn't pay to second guess the decisions any of us made."

"I know." Her voice was so small I almost couldn't hear it. "I'm sorry I was mean."

I recalled her teacher's words: *Behind that big brain, she's a little girl who's lost almost everything.*

"I'll go help Peter. You climb the fence and get the security guys."

She shook her head. "As you just pointed out, I have no credibility with them, or with the local police."

"If you report that Peter's in danger, they have to at least come and check to see if he's okay."

"And Marla will meet them at the door, frantic because the crazy girl took off again. By now she might have given Peter some of that stuff they used on me. She could take the cops up to his room and let them see him in bed, sleeping peacefully. They'll turn me over to her, shake their heads, and go back where it's warm to gripe about those impossible Gage kids."

"Okay, but once we're sure Peter's safe, get to a phone and call for help. Say there's a fire or a bomb or wolves in the basement. Just get someone here."

Lucy turned to the window. "Jack should be moving any time now."

"You didn't tell me how you got away."

"Peter set his wastebasket on fire. He hollered and then kicked it over, like he'd panicked." She snorted a laugh at the idea her brother would become hysterical over a trash fire. "When Marla ran to help him put it out, I slipped out the door, went to my bedroom, and opened the window." Chuckling, she confessed, "I forgot about Peter's booby trap, so I got quite a jolt. That was good though, because when I stopped to disconnect the battery, I saw those men patrolling the yard below." Her tone revealed the frustration she'd felt. "I was stuck there until you came along."

"Marla didn't come after you?"

"Peter told me he'd delay her as much as he could, and I heard her yelling at him to let her go. We also guessed she'd need to shut him in somewhere before she could go looking for me. It should have given me enough time to get away."

"But Marla called Oscar's thugs and told them to watch for someone leaving the house as well as for me coming in."

Lucy held up a finger. "Jack just went around the corner."

"Okay, go. I'm right behind you."

"She'd better not have hurt him." For the first time since I met her, Lucy sounded scared, but not for herself. For her brother.

I followed Lucy through the window and across the breezeway roof, testing each spot for weakness before I set my weight on it. Behind us, Jack's footsteps crunched along the garage as he looked for a private place to take a leak.

The trip took less than a minute, but it felt like hours. The air was so clear that we heard Jack's zipper drop, the liquid hitting the ground, and the clink of his belt as he re-buckled. His feet scraped on the concrete as I slithered headfirst through the opening, braced myself with my hands, and pulled my feet inside. Rolling onto a shoulder, I completed my ungraceful entry. Lucy closed the window with a whisper of sound.

While I got back to my feet, she hurried out the bedroom door. I made a frantic grunt in an effort to stop her, but she ignored me. Exiting her sitting room, she crossed the common area and tried the door to Peter's space. The handle didn't turn.

Lucy came back, softly closing the doors to her sitting room and her bedroom. With three walls between us and Marla Johnson, it was safe for us to talk in low tones. "Marla has locked herself in there with Peter. I suppose she's going to wait until Oscar comes to decide what to do."

"I should talk to her."

"Why?"

I imagined Marla pacing back and forth, upset that things had gone wrong on her end. Had she called Oscar to tell him Lucy had escaped? Had the men outside let him know they'd had me and lost me? I guessed not. Fearing Oscar's wrath, they'd try to get Lucy and me back under control before he learned they'd screwed up.

It seemed like a good time for the old Divide and Conquer technique. "I'll talk to Marla," I told Lucy. "I'll tell her you've gone to the cops, but she can still walk away and claim she had no idea what Oscar was up to." After a pause I added, "There's the money in Peter's backpack. I could offer her that."

"You know Oscar has promised her some outrageous amount. I don't think she's the type to settle for a little money when there's a possibility of getting a lot of it."

Hoping I knew Marla better than Lucy did, I said, "We should try."

"I suppose so." She turned businesslike. "You go ahead with that. I'll arrange impediments for anyone who comes looking for us." At my confused look, she explained, "We made some booby traps. We hid them at the back of a linen closet, because Ilsa was always snooping." With a smirk she added, "Not that she'd have recognized a booby trap, even if it was labeled in large, block letters."

"Show me."

I followed her to a closet near the top of the stairs, where she removed a large bucket filled with what appeared to be rags. She went to the staircase, peered briefly over the railing, and knelt, removing the bucket's contents. I looked down, trying to plumb the darkness below. "Is it smart for us to wander around like there aren't murderers on the premises?"

Setting various items out around her, Lucy spoke in a low tone. "Aside from Oscar, they aren't violent types. Jack and Jay, for example, got drunk, broke into a Walgreens, and took all the beer and cigarettes they could carry. The police followed a trail of empty bottles to Jay's apartment and found them both passed out."

The story didn't allay my fears all that much, but Lucy went on. "In addition, Oscar's henchmen—and henchwoman—were told to capture us without physical injury. That means they can't hit us over the head or toss us down the stairs."

"Great." I tried not to sound sarcastic, but I did.

Lucy ignored it. "Once Oscar arrives, things will change, but right now, those are our advantages." Her practical resolution brought an image to mind of the Gage kids dealing with other situations in which danger was real and close. Poachers. Snakes. Daily threats of living in a hostile environment. They'd learned to act logically and save emotions like fear for later.

Still, Lucy was nine years old. "We can't fuss with thingamajigs. We need to find you a place to hide. Oscar could arrive anytime, and I should talk to Marla before he does." When she rolled her eyes, I realized her perception of Marla was different from mine. While I saw her as misguided, Lucy took a harder view. Still, the important thing was to get her out of danger. In an urgent tone I said, "Remember, if they can't find you, everything they're planning has to stop."

"Yes," she said impatiently. "I'll hide soon, but these 'thingamajigs' will help. Trust me."

From the bucket, Lucy had taken bottles, cans, and tubes of various sizes, a spool of fishing line, a small pair of pliers, and some books. Choosing several items, including a can of furniture polish, she hurried to the bottom of the stairs and sprayed the lemony stuff on the tiles around the landing. Coming up a few steps, she set four books at one side of a stair, as if someone had left them there to be put away later. Behind them she set a can with a megaphone-shaped top. She laid a fifth book at a careful angle, so it hid what I now realized was an air horn. Tying a length of monofilament line to the opposite post, she stretched it across and tied it around the slanted book. Someone coming up the stairs would trip the wire, which would drop the book onto the air horn and cause that awful noise they make. No one was going to sneak up on us.

"Clever," I whispered, and Lucy made a mock bow of humility.

Sounds from below stopped us cold. At the back door, men's voices floated up to where we crouched. "—lost the girl, but we made sure she didn't leave the house."

"How did Marla lose her?" It was Oscar's voice.

"Something about a fire. Like I said, we're sure she's still here."

"But there's been no sign of the man?"

There was a long pause. "Nope." I smiled at Lucy. Oscar's goons were afraid to tell him they'd had me and then lost me.

"He should be here by now." Oscar sounded more angry than worried. "I need to get something from Marla's car. You two find the girl."

"Okay." We heard footsteps and the opening and closing of the front door. That was followed by a whispered conference between Jack and Jay, no doubt discussing how to proceed. One of them said, "Okay," in a tone that indicated they were ready. A second later we heard, "Oh-h-h!" followed by a cry of pain.

Lucy shook her head as a string of profanity reached our ears. "Such language."

"Come on," I ordered. "You promised you'd hide."

"Not just yet," she whispered. "We have time for a machicolation."

"A what?"

"You might know them as murder holes." Peering over the railing, Lucy set the empty bucket in a spot she judged suitable while I struggled to recall what murder holes were. Castles. Right. They'd had openings where they could drop stuff down on invading enemies: hot tar, boiling oil, manure, or whatever. Lucy and Peter's version involved a bunch of rags and newspaper torn into strips. Beside the bucket was a tube of bathtub caulk and a bottle labeled "Bondo Resin."

"Squeeze that caulking into the bucket," she ordered. "I'll add resin."

I obeyed. Below us, Jack assured Jay he'd be okay. He wasn't buying it, and I heard him moan, "My frickin' shoulder's broken."

"Stay right there. I'll find something we can use for a sling."

Lucy ignored them, using a ruler to stir the glutinous mess. "Peter calls this Russian Krazy Glue," she said in a low voice. "I wish we had the ingredients for more, but we can make one of them uncomfortable."

We waited in silence until I saw Jack and Jay through the bannister rails, the latter with one arm wrapped in a Christmas-y scarf, its ends tied around his neck. They stopped in almost the exact spot Lucy had guessed they would and looked up, obviously wary. Before Jack could comprehend the danger, Lucy dumped her concoction on his head.

The swearing we'd heard earlier was multiplied by ten. I had an urge to put my hands over Lucy's ears to shield her from the unpleasantness.

Jay did what he could to help Jack, using his good arm to clear away some of the sticky mess. Bits of rag and newsprint clung to Jack's hair, and when Jay pulled, he swore even louder. "Stop," he ordered. "You'll pull my damn scalp off."

Fascinated, I crouched there as the two men backed into the hallway, one hunched like a chimpanzee and the other littered with debris he'd have a hard time shedding. Lucy touched my arm. "Come on."

The next surprise involved the same bucket, used for a new purpose. Leading the way to the common room, Lucy removed two doorstops that held the double doors open. Hurrying to the kitchenette, she got an assortment of condiments from the mini fridge and set them on the table. I got the idea—I did go to summer camp as a kid—and began squirting mustard and ketchup into the bucket. Lucy added pickle relish and mayonnaise. When the bottles were empty, she pushed the bucket toward me. "You're taller. Will you do the honors?"

I dragged a chair into place, opened the privacy doors a little, and balanced the bucket between them. As I did, Marla called from behind the door, "Who's out there? What's going on?"

I looked at Lucy, who shook her head, indicating I shouldn't answer.

"We won't stop them with these stunts, Lucy," I whispered.

"We're leveling the field. An enemy afraid of what will happen next is vulnerable."

I was afraid of what might happen next too, but I wouldn't admit it. I had to emulate Lucy and think less in terms of being outnumbered and more in terms of how we might win the fight.

"Who's out there?" Marla called. "Oscar? Is that you?"

Turning toward Lucy I said, "Let me try to talk to her."

Though she clearly didn't see the point, Lucy said, "Okay. I've got a few more traps to set." Pulling up her shirt, she took a firecracker from the waistband of her pants. It had a dozen safety matches taped around its body, and folded tent-like over its fuse was a two-inch strip of fine-grit sandpaper. Through that was threaded a zip-tie and some fish line. I didn't see its purpose until Lucy pantomimed what would happen. When tripped, the line would pull the sandpaper across the match heads, igniting them. They in turn would light the firecracker fuse, causing a bang and some smoke that would warn us and temporarily unnerve Jack and Jay. It probably wouldn't deter Oscar, who had better nerves and months of experience with Peter's tactics.

"Be careful," I whispered as I tiptoed toward the locked door.

Lucy responded with her own bit of advice. "Stay to one side. She might shoot right through the wood and kill you." With that, she sidled carefully through the space between the double doors, leaving the bucket of goop in place overhead, and disappeared.

CHAPTER FIFTEEN

Obeying Lucy's warning, I stood to one side and called, "Marla?"

"Max. We knew you'd come." She tried to sound casual, but I heard stress in her voice. I had to work quickly, before Oscar came to shore up her fading confidence.

"Where do you think this is leading, Marla?"

"To a million dollars, silly man."

"Oscar can't be trusted. He kills people who get in his way."

Her tone turned cool. "Not being as naïve as some I could name, I have safeguards in place."

"Like Ray Gage's handwritten will."

"I took care of Carson's mail. Oscar told me to burn it, but it's tucked away in a safe place."

"Marla, you realize that whether you kill anyone or not, you'll be as guilty of murder as Oscar is."

"He should be here by now."

"He must still be establishing that all-important alibi up in Bad Axe. How will that work, anyway?"

"Oscar rents a motel room, uses the key card, and props the door open while he messes up the bed and dampens some towels. Then he leaves. Their records indicate he was there all night. In the morning, he opens the door again, making a record of his time of departure."

"How will he get back here without being seen?"

"We took two cars up there yesterday and left one in a parking lot. He wears a hat, turns his collar up—incognito."

"If you find her, Lucy gets a dose of Rohypnol, so she's confused."

"Oh, we'll find Lucy. She can't get away."

"I know what Oscar's plan is for her, but the police will analyze the room and figure trajectories. Something won't add up."

"The local sheriff already thinks Lucy's nuts. He'll accept the conclusions we hand him on a platter."

My jaw was so tight I could hardly spit out my threat. "You won't get away with it."

"Oh, I think we will." Her voice turned hard. "Despite the trouble you caused us."

"Did you know from the start that I wasn't Morrie Portman?"

"No, but later in the afternoon on the day we met, this creepy man in a bad suit came to the office. Since Oscar was in court, the receptionist had me talk to him." She made a clicking noise with her tongue. "Two men asking about the Gage kids in one day was a tipoff."

"You played me." I couldn't help sounding resentful, because I was.

"Oscar thought you'd believe me if I vouched for him. When I saw that wasn't going to happen, I pretended to join your side."

"You also wrecked my Mustang trying to get me out of your way."

"Maybe." She sounded almost proud of herself.

Anger warmed my neck, but I focused on inserting a wedge between Marla and Oscar. "Don't you worry he'll turn this onto you somehow?"

"You're the one who should be worried, Sweetie."

A touch at my back indicated Lucy had returned. Without another word, I backed away, leaving Marla talking to herself for the second time that day.

I managed to follow Lucy through the gap in the double doors without dumping hamburger extras on myself. She led the way to the east wing guest room farthest from the stairs. As I looked around for a spot Lucy could hide in, I muttered angrily, "I can't believe I trusted that woman. She's evil."

"True," Lucy agreed, "but it wasn't a complete waste of time."

"Peter is in there with her, and we can't get to him. That puts us at a disadvantage."

"I suppose," she agreed. "But Peter has a weapon, and I think he'll know how and when to use it."

"Wait. Peter has a weapon?"

"As I said, we guessed Marla wouldn't come after me until she had secured Peter. The easiest way to do that is to barricade him in his closet."

"Yeah, put a chair under the knob. That's what I'd do." I checked under the bed. It was high enough for Lucy, but searchers always look under the bed. Same for behind the door. "While Peter arranged the trash can fire," Lucy was saying, "I tidied his room, like a sister who can't abide her brother's messiness. I hung up his jacket and put things in drawers. In the process, I took a small bag from a shelf and set it in the closet. Marla saw it all but didn't suspect a thing. Then Peter shouted, 'Fire!' and she ran to take care of it."

"And you slipped out the door." My attention was drawn to a high shelf in the closet where some extra blankets and pillows were stored.

"Exactly." Lucy sounded confident. "When things start happening, Peter will defend himself."

The space I was looking at was dimly lit, which was good. "What is this weapon you gave him?"

"His paintball gun. It only holds ten rounds, but those things sting like mad, especially up close."

Lucy's faith in Peter was strong, but what if Marla didn't open the closet door until she had backup? How many direct hits would it take to defeat her, Oscar, and whoever else showed up?

The air horn sounded. Our gazes met, reflecting mutual dread. The horn stopped abruptly, and for several seconds, all was silent.

"Up you go," I said. When she hesitated, I added, "They don't expect me. That puts the odds in our favor."

"You can't fight three of them at once."

"One is disabled, so it's more like two and a half. I'll hit the first one who comes through the door and then push past the others. They'll chase me, and you'll be safe."

"I can help. I have skills."

"Lucy, I'll do better if I know you're safe. Now get up there, and I'll hide you with extra bed linen."

She didn't argue. There wasn't time to, since we heard Jay whining about his shoulder while Jack muttered threats about bratty kids. Oscar spoke calmly, assuring Jay they'd see to his injury soon and telling Jack, "You'll shave your head. Women think that's sexy. Until then, focus."

Jack said, "Look. There's her shoe. She's down here somewhere."

I turned to Lucy, who indeed only wore one shoe. From her arched eyebrow, I guessed it was by design. A few seconds later there was a loud *crack!* in the hallway. It startled me until I realized it was one of Lucy's firecrackers going off. She held up three fingers to indicate there were more, and I heard Oscar warn, "Watch where you step. They've set booby traps everywhere."

A few seconds later Jack said, "Here's another one."

"Good. They're trying to make us jumpy. Take your time, and you can avoid them." Oscar sounded smug, and I almost smiled to hear him underestimate Lucy. Still, he was a deadly foe, and it was my job to stop him.

Going to the closet, I made a stirrup with my hands. Lucy stepped into it, and I boosted her up to the linen shelf I'd cleared. She stretched along its length, and I replaced the blankets, hiding her from sight.

As I worked, I heard Jay say, "Oscar, I gotta see a doctor about this shoulder."

"Maybe I should take him to the ER," Jack said. Unhappy with unexpected events, the hired help wanted to leave.

No doubt realizing they'd come to a delicate point, Oscar turned conciliatory. "I have to find Lucy before she hurts herself or someone else." He paused for dramatic effect. "The kids have a hundred thousand dollars in cash hidden in their rooms somewhere. Help me get them under control, and the money's yours."

While Oscar didn't understand Lucy and Peter, he knew about greedy ex-cons. Jack and Jay didn't know the end game was murder, and that much money was sure to convince them to cooperate.

Jay did have one question. "What about Uncle Morrie or whatever his name is?"

"He's probably home in bed." Oscar paused. "If he shows up, I'll handle him."

I waited for Jack to admit I was already on the premises, but he remained silent. That's the downside to being the boss. No one wants to tell you things are more screwed up than you know.

For the next couple of minutes, doors opened and closed along the corridor. The sounds got closer, and finally Oscar spoke from outside the door. "It figures she'd choose the last room for her last stand." I turned to Lucy, who peeked from behind a blanket and gave an "I'm okay" head bob. I backed up to the wall behind the door, holding an inverted lamp ready. With a weapon and the element of surprise, I had a good chance of disabling the first guy through. The other two would be problematic.

The knob rattled and rattled again. "Locked," Jack said. "She's in there." A shoulder bumped against the door, but a shoulder does the job only in movies, unless the door happens to be made of cardboard. A second later, Jack changed tactics, kicking the door just below the handle. A splintering sound signaled it was giving way. Before he could launch another blow and disengage it entirely, I heard screams of pain from the opposite end of the house. Marla shouted, "You—" That ended in a squeal like a stepped-on puppy, and then, "Stop that. I'm going to—Ow!"

"Get the girl," Oscar ordered Jack and Jay. "I'll go see what Marla's problem is."

I used the time provided by the interruption to move a dresser in front of the door, but Jack was soon pushing it back toward me. "It's the guy," Jay said in a hushed tone.

"I know it's the guy, dimwit. Help me push the door open."

"My shoulder—"

"Help me, or I'll break the other one."

From far away came a crash, a wet splash, and a loud curse. Though I was struggling to hold the dresser in place, I turned to glance at Lucy, who peeped out, mimicking a dropped bomb with one hand.

With two against me, the dresser slid back, inch by inch. Reconciled to losing that battle, I picked up the lamp again. When Jack's hand appeared in the opening, I whacked it hard.

"Ow! Ow! What the—" It didn't stop him, but it served a purpose. He came in angry and careless, and I met him head on, swinging the lamp. Seeing the blow coming, Jack ducked, taking it on his back. Though he yelped in pain, he didn't retreat. Wriggling his shoulders to release the pain, he faced me with a look that indicated I'd be sorry.

Jay entered the room, cradling his bad arm like it was a newborn baby. He stood back, watching, apparently confident that Jack could take me. I wasn't sure he was wrong.

Besides his advantages in height, weight, and musculature, Jack was a street fighter. He used every dirty trick in the book, starting with an attempt to knee me in the crotch. I managed to twist away, and the blow landed on my hip bone, which I hoped hurt him as much as it hurt me. Jack leaned in and took a swipe at my eyes, but I knew enough to keep my head low. Next he tried a head butt that would have broken my nose, but I avoided that too. Cops don't get a lot of training in hand-to-hand combat, but I'd seen my share of down-and-dirty tactics. Still, it's different when you're not trying to break up the fight but to win it.

I was holding my own, dodging blows and landing a few, when an assault to my back sent me staggering forward, directly into Jack's fist. My head reeled, and I dropped the lamp, grabbing Jack in a bear hug to hold myself upright. I couldn't see Jay, but whatever he'd hit me with felt like the proverbial brick bat. I couldn't turn and deal with him, since Jack was all I could handle.

When I looked back on the event later, I imagined I heard the *pffft!* of something whizzing out from the closet, but that's probably my brain filling in the blanks. I did hear Jay's howl of pain. He retreated a few steps, which was a great relief. Seconds later, Jack recoiled, grabbing at a spot on his back. Taking advantage of the opportunity, I landed a solid blow to his chin. With a growled curse, he returned to trying to beat my face in. Moments later Jay shrieked, "I got stabbed!"

Jack's hands dropped, and he flinched in pain. When he turned to see where the invisible attack had come from, I saw a tiny dart stuck in the soft flesh at the base of his neck. Staggering out of my reach, he fumbled for the missile, pulled it out, frowned as if he'd never seen anything like it, and flung it away.

"It's the girl," he said. "She's here somewhere, throwing stuff." The break in the action allowed me time to bend and reclaim my weapon. When Jack came at me again, I raised my lamp like Lady Liberty, ready to send him to the floor. That was great, except I saw, in my peripheral vision, Jay approaching with the twin to my lamp in his upraised hand. I was about to be felled by the other half of a matching set.

That's when a yell like nothing I'd heard outside the movies sounded from the closet. Jack and I turned to see Lucy land on Jay's back like a rodeo cowboy on a bronc. She put her hands over his eyes, and Jay screamed like a...well, not at all like a girl. He screamed like a guy whose broken shoulder is under stress and who's got a big problem on his back. Lucy's intervention neutralized one enemy, and the distraction allowed me to give Jack a blow to the head that made his eyes go funny.

Overbalanced by Lucy's weight and disoriented by pain, Jay fell flat on his face. When he hit, Lucy lost her grip and rolled off. Before she could grab him again, Jay was up and out of the room. A few seconds later a *pop!* and a curse indicated he'd tripped a wire they had bypassed earlier. The shout he emitted was a combination of anger and frustration.

At that point, Jack recovered his wits enough to decide that joining his companion was better than fighting on. Pushing himself to his feet with a clumsy effort, he gave me a shove that knocked me back a few steps and then bolted from the room.

I helped Lucy to her feet. "What was that?"

"Blowgun." She held up a carved tube with tiny darts attached to it. "I didn't have any curare, so I used hydrogen peroxide on the tips. Full strength that stuff feels like fire in a cut."

"I don't think those two will be back."

"Agreed. Now let's go rescue Peter."

We left the room cautiously, me holding the lamp like a ball bat and Lucy ready with her dart gun. She made straight for their wing, but I grabbed her arm and formed my hand into a gun shape to remind her of the danger. Though departing from their plan would be messy, I guessed Oscar and Marla were past worrying about that. They'd kill me on sight and concoct a story to fit the situation.

The double doors that led to the kids' living quarters were now closed. Behind them was silence. Lucy peered through the crack and shook her head, indicating that she saw no one. Slowly, I pushed the door open. The floor looked like the counter at a paint store, a mess of reds, greens, and yellows. The bucket lay on its side against the wall. No attacker stood waiting to shoot me, so I stepped around the spill and into the common area, with Lucy at my heels.

The door to her rooms stood open, and she tiptoed in. Seconds later she came back with a head shake that told me they were unoccupied. We froze when we heard low voices in Peter's room, and like two cartoon characters with synchronized movements, we leaned toward the door, listening. Oscar offered assurances. Marla whimpered. "Come with me," Oscar said, and Lucy and I hurried into her sitting room. Through the crack, I saw Oscar escort Marla out.

The bucket had caught him on one shoulder, and the whole side of his dark, tailored suit was caked with goo. Though he was no doubt uncomfortable, Marla's experience had been twice as messy and painful as well. Paint splotched her hair with green. Her blouse had a large orange stain on one shoulder. Her navy skirt sported an irregular white blob at one hip. And her hand—the hand that had once held the gun—was smeared with yellow. The thumb looked swollen, and I rejoiced a little at the mental image of a direct paintball hit. She spoke in a whiny tone. "That homely P.I. showed up, so I figured I should move Peter to another room. When I opened the closet, things went to hell. He hit me about six times before I got the door closed again."

I hoped every single one had hurt a lot.

Oscar was too distracted to provide the sympathy she was looking for. Everything had gone wrong, and he was already adjusting. "Okay. Here's the new story. Some men broke in, intending to kidnap the kids. Morrie was the inside man who shut down the security system for them."

"How do I explain this?" She indicated her stained clothing.

"You won't be here. I returned from Bad Axe early, due to a bad feeling about Uncle Morrie." He led her toward the stairs, and I strained to hear. "Can you make it home on your own?"

"I—I think so. What are you doing?"

"Texting the others to tell them to get out. I'll finish this myself."

"But look at me. I can't—"

"With your coat and hat and the dark, the guards won't notice."

"But Peter's room is a mess, and there's that." I guessed she pointed back at the condiment-smeared floor.

"The kids fought Uncle Morrie in the best way they knew." I heard the smile in his voice. "I arrive too late to save Peter, but I get to be the hero who rescues Lucy."

"Does she still shoot Peter?"

"Yes. Even if I don't find her tonight, anything she says when she does emerge will seem like a hysterical child rationalizing her mistake."

"And the P.I.?"

"To make this work, the boy and Uncle Morrie have to die at about the same time. Peter is safely locked in his closet. I'll deal with him as soon as that nosy detective is dead."

"Are you sure you can do it all by yourself?"

"You'd be surprised at what I can do all by myself." Oscar's voice receded as they went downstairs.

"Let Peter out," I told Lucy. "Leave as soon as the men below are gone."

A flash in her eyes told me she considered refusing, but in the end, she didn't. I was still trying to figure out my own plan of action when she came back. "He's not there."

"What?"

"The hinges are off the closet door. He must have done it as soon as Oscar and Marla left his bedroom. And his window's open."

"He climbed down?"

"With those men on the grounds, that might not be a good idea," she said. "Maybe he went up."

A step sounded on the stairs. "I'll find him," I promised Lucy. "Go."

Her obedience was a surprise. A bigger one came when she was gone and I turned to find Oscar standing at the double doors. "Well, well," he said. "Here I was waiting for you, and you're already here."

I moved to one side, putting an overstuffed chair between us in an effort to find cover. It didn't help. In his left hand, Oscar held a pistol in a manner that showed he was at ease with it. Looking closer, I saw a bulge in his jacket pocket. A second gun to leave beside my corpse, proving I was the bad guy.

"You can't get away with any of this now," I said. "Too many people are aware of what you're up to."

"What are they aware of, exactly?" Oscar asked. "Once you're dead, everything people 'know' will turn against you. The scummy detective who's been following you will blab about the bagful of cash, which explains how you got interested. You talked your way into this house so you could look for it. Jack can testify that he saw you searching my apartment. I've already expressed doubts about you to my fellow attorneys, but…the kids are stubborn, and I'm reluctant to deny them the pleasure of an old friend's company."

"The kindly guardian will hang his head and wish he'd been firmer with two headstrong children."

"Exactly."

"I know of at least three people you've hurt or killed, Oscar. If I die, that will come out."

The threat stopped him for a moment. "Well, well. I have to admit you've done your research."

"I know someone." You don't tell your archenemy that your mom does your background work. I counted his victims on my fingers. "The rival at college who took a bad fall. The witness hit by a train. The girlfriend who committed suicide." I paused. "Why kill her? The others were in your way, but she wasn't."

"Clare was insecure, which made her nosy. She was sure I was cheating on her, so she snooped where she shouldn't have."

"You *murdered* her." Unsure if I was curious or trying to delay my own death, I asked, "How'd you manage it from Tampa?"

"Guts and Red Bull. Do you know how sleepy you get driving from Atlanta to Detroit and back in thirty-three hours?"

"My sympathy for your discomfort is boundless. I wouldn't have guessed you do the wet work yourself."

"I believe it's best not to trust others with big crimes. Subordinates make mistakes. They get religion. They turn state's evidence. The men who were here tonight may suspect, but they can't testify to anything."

With an effort of will, I took a step toward him. "Someone will question your luck eventually, Coburn."

"Too late for you, I fear." He waggled the gun a little, making my skin crawl. "Where's the girl?"

"Off the property by now."

"I doubt that. As long as her brother is here, she'll hang around."

I'd been trying to figure out how I could live through this. If I stayed where I was, Oscar would shoot me and put the second gun in my dead hand. If I ran, he'd shoot me anyway, claiming he'd been defending the kids. Though fully aware that outrunning bullets isn't easy, I was unwilling to die standing meekly before him.

A muffled thud from Lucy's bedroom caught Oscar's attention, and he looked that way for a second. Grabbing a pillow from the chair, I used it to swat his gun hand aside. He didn't drop the weapon, but the unexpected move gave me a chance to push past him and run.

As I careened toward the double doors, concerns popped in my head like Lucy's firecrackers. Had she escaped? Had she even tried, with Peter somewhere in the house? And where was Peter?

A bullet zinged by my head, and my body made a decision my mind didn't contribute to. Using the bannister as a fulcrum, I swung myself onto the staircase and started up.

A second shot pinged off the railing, and I turned, catching a glimpse of Oscar paused on the second-floor landing, trying to get a bead on me. Crouching to make myself a smaller target, I waddled forward. The keypad, which would have slowed me down, was not a problem. The doors to Oscar's apartment stood open.

As I rose from my crouch, Peter stepped into my field of vision, hands raised. "Don't come in!"

I stopped, relieved to see him but confused by the order. "He's right behind me, Peter."

"Then jump." When I hesitated, he repeated, "Jump, Max. Jump through the doorway."

A tripwire. More firecrackers? Another air horn? Neither was enough to stop a killer with a gun. As I hesitated, Oscar's footsteps sounded on the stairs, crisp scratches that indicated speed.

"Jump!" Peter said one more time, and I obeyed the command in his voice. Pushing off the bannister, I propelled myself through the opening, aiming for a gazelle-like leap. Since I was out of breath and scared out of my mind, the move was more Guernsey than gazelle. Still, I cleared whatever Peter had wanted me to miss. Landing hard, I staggered into a sofa back and somersaulted over it, ending up sprawled full-length on the cushions. As soon as I caught my breath, I raised myself to a position where I could see the doorway. Oscar stood looking in. I saw something he couldn't, but in my excited state, it didn't register.

"Don't come in," Peter warned. "If you do, you're going to prison."

For a second Oscar froze, surprised to hear Peter speak at such length. Then he grinned. "You little jerk." He raised the pistol, but Peter disappeared behind a recliner. I huddled on the couch, expecting a bullet to come tearing through the upholstery at any moment.

"We have quite a list of witnesses," Peter called. "Adam, Ilsa, Jack, and Jay, for starters. They'll swear they had no idea murder was the plan. You know when things get hot, people protect themselves."

"They'll keep their mouths shut once you and the detective are dead," Oscar said. "I'll have the money to see that they do."

"You can't kill both of us." Peter's tone was mocking. "If you come after me, Max will jump you, and if you go looking for him, you have me to worry about." Peter shot from the cover of the recliner and disappeared behind a partition dividing Oscar's kitchenette from his living room. Though I couldn't see Oscar, I heard a shot, a half-second too late. It hit wood, not flesh, and I breathed a sigh of relief.

Where did the kid get that kind of courage?

And how many rounds did Oscar have left in that gun?

I was ashamed to huddle in safety while Peter baited Oscar, trying to make him angry enough to do something dumb. Until now Oscar had killed only unsuspecting victims. He might not do as well with head-on opposition.

Rolling off the couch, I hit the floor and moved into the open, letting Oscar get a glimpse of me rounding his coffee table before I dived behind an ottoman. He took a shot, but he was late by a half-second and wide by a yard.

The ottoman wasn't as big as I'd thought, and all of me didn't fit behind it. I looked around for something close that was bigger, but it was too soon to move again. My rear stuck out, which worried me, but there was nothing I could do about it. I had to hope darkness would hide the protrusion.

Then it wasn't dark anymore. Light flooded the room, and I looked up to see Peter standing at the switch. Oscar's gaze landed on me, and he took a step forward, aiming for the kill shot. When he did, he tripped the wire across the doorway, releasing two large fireplace logs rigged on ropes at either side of the door. They came together with Oscar's head between them, and his eyes crossed exactly like a cartoon character's do. As he slumped to the floor, I imagined little birdies twittering and singing around him.

A week ago, I'd never have thought two kids could save themselves from a killer. At that moment, I became a believer.

A commotion outside the room put me back on alert, but a familiar face appeared in the hallway. "Are you guys okay?" Bobby asked.

I should have been surprised to see my intern in Oscar's doorway, but I was beyond shock. "We're good. Can you find something to tie this guy up with?"

"Dinah has the duct tape. I'll go get it."

"Wait. Dinah?"

"She called us because she was worried about you. When we got to her house and you still hadn't contacted her, she insisted on coming here with us."

"Us?"

"Roger and me."

"Roger."

"Yeah. So we got here a few minutes ago, and while we were trying to figure out a plan, this guy came flying out the front door. He ran right into Roger, which sent him sprawling. He's all like, 'My shoulder, my shoulder,' and we grabbed hold of him and were like, 'What's going on in there?' and then he's like, 'Those kids are crazy,' and I'm like—"

"Bobby. Did you stop him?"

"Well, yeah. And the other one that came along a minute later. So a few minutes after that, this woman comes sneaking out, and Roger says, 'Excuse me, Ms. Johnson. Where are you headed?' Real polite, like they teach you in cop training. She gave us this cock-and-bull story about having to do an errand for Mr. Coburn, but you know how they tell you in training to look people over and notice stuff? So I asked what happened to her clothes, and she says it was an accident, but then here comes Lucy. She says all three of them are co-conspirators, and you and Peter were taking down the ringleader. So Dinah has this little gun, which I told her to point at them while Dodger duct-taped them up like mad. They put them in Dinah's car." I must have looked puzzled, because he explained, "They're criminals, yeah, but we can't let them freeze to death. Anyway, I was coming to help you out, but it looks like you handled the guy."

"Actually, Peter had a lot to do with it."

"Cool beans, Pete!" He raised a fist to Peter, who stood over Oscar, holding a fire iron in case he tried to get up. Without taking his eyes off his nemesis, Peter fist-bumped Bobby with his free hand.

Dodger ducked under the logs and joined us. "Is this the last one?"

"Yeah."

Ripping a healthy quantity of duct tape off the roll he'd brought along, he bent to grab the half-conscious man's wrists. "We called the cops, but this will hold him until they get here." He examined the bloody scrape on Oscar's head. "I always wondered if that log trick would work. Guess we know now."

Oscar groaned, and Bobby leaned over to speak into his ear. "So when you're up to it, can you tell us how it felt? I mean, my interest is purely professional, but it would be good to know."

While the others greeted the police, I found a moment to speak to Peter and Lucy about how much to tell. Only Dodger, Mom, and I knew they'd planned to hire a hitman. Mom wasn't a problem, and Dodger wouldn't mention the money he'd hoped to scam the kids out of. "Be honest," I told them, "but leave out your plan to...you know."

"Kill Oscar," Lucy said. "We see where that could lead to problems."

"We'll say we hired you to protect us," Peter said.

"Which was my intention all along."

Pointing an accusing finger, Lucy drew in a breath, undoubtedly ready to scold me for being less than honest with them. Peter sent a meaningful look her way, and she dropped her hands into her lap. "And we appreciate everything you did for us."

Good, I thought. *She's starting to understand how to live among the USians.*

CHAPTER SIXTEEN

Five of us sat down the next morning in the Gages' breakfast nook to compare notes and make plans. Denice came from Toledo, saying she could stay until one o'clock, since the twins were in preschool. Dinah walked from her house, carrying a coffee cake crusted with pecans. She'd left Fang asleep, she said, which I didn't mind one bit. The kids seemed to like her, probably because she didn't talk down to them and listened with interest to what they had to say.

"I still have friends in the system," she said when we'd covered everything. "If the law firm is willing to name this young woman as your guardian, it can be done quickly."

"I spoke to Sara Dailey on the phone. With two of their people going to prison, they'll do whatever it takes to get this mess out of the news as soon as possible."

"Are you sure they're going to prison?" Dinah asked. "Oscar's a competent attorney."

"True, but the evidence is stacked pretty high against him."

"He could blame the woman—Marla. Say it was all her doing."

I turned to Lucy. "Tell her what you did."

She grinned. "I recorded him, like Dad used to record poachers." Both Denice and Dinah made little "Ooh" sounds.

"I had specifically told her to go out the window," I said reprovingly, "but instead, she hung around to eavesdrop."

Lucy took over the story. "I'd seen where Marla put our phones, so I got mine back and called 9-1-1. Then I waited to see if I could help Max. Oscar started bragging about how clever he is, and I got most of it." She took a pecan off the coffee cake and ate it. "I made a noise to distract Oscar, hoping Max would take advantage." Her dimples appeared. "I never guessed Oscar would end up in Peter's best booby trap ever."

"That was awesome," I said to Peter.

"I had things ready, in case, um, in case." He remembered my warning about keeping their "Let's Kill Oscar" plan private. "I was going to call him up there, but then I heard the shots."

"You got to the third floor by climbing through the trees?" I asked.

He beat his chest in a comical parody of Tarzan. "Jungle boy, remember? I'm pretty good at getting around that way."

My phone, which Peter had found on a shelf in the garage, signaled a text. "Baker says the police found Adam Saracco. He'll testify in exchange for a deal."

"They can charge Oscar and Marla for conspiracy to commit murder and a bunch of other crimes," Dinah commented.

"Including wrecking my beloved Mustang," I added resentfully.

"Don't worry about your car," Lucy said, "I called the garage and told them we'll pay to fix it."

"Well—I—Thank you."

The doorbell rang, and we all hesitated. The press had been at us already, trying to get statements. Various members of the local police had been by to express regret that they hadn't taken the kids more seriously. Lucy was magnanimous for once, commenting only that she hoped Oscar's case would be handled efficiently and with all possible speed.

Frank, the security guard, had made a stumbling apology on behalf of Deer Creek Security, admitting they should have believed Lucy "from the get-go." He gave me the evil eye, and I guessed I was to blame in his mind for the lecture he'd no doubt received from his bosses. I didn't deserve his anger, but it's like they say: haters gonna hate.

Peter went to see who was at the door this time, and I was surprised to hear him let out a whoop of joy. Rising, we all went to the foyer, where a dark-eyed man of about fifty embraced the boy fondly.

Lucy got a hug too. Then she turned to us. "This is Sr. Alberto Pablo Quispe Diaz, our friend from Peru. Please, señor, come in. You know Denice. This is Mrs. Ellerson and our...friend, Max Dunham."

The next hour was interesting. Diaz had been in D.C., where he'd seen a news report of Lucy and Peter's trouble. "I came," he told us, "to assure myself that my old friend's children are well and safe, and to offer my home to them if they desire to return to my country. Now, tell me how this travesty of justice could happen."

Lucy gave him an abbreviated version of events, minimizing the danger they'd faced and maximizing my role to the point that I felt my neck warm. "Oscar is a bad person," she concluded, "but Max saw to it that his plan failed."

"I had spoken to your guardian several times about coming to visit," Diaz told us. "He always refused, saying I should wait until you had 'fully adjusted' to your new lives."

"It's wonderful that you're here now." Lucy turned to me with a look I couldn't have imagined on her face until that moment. "And I'm pleased that you got to meet Max."

"I too am pleased to meet Max," Diaz said meaningfully.

I cleared my throat, unsure why everyone was smiling at me like I'd received the Congressional Medal of Honor.

Diaz was personable and entertaining, and the time passed quickly. When his watch beeped discreetly, he said, "I must go. I'm due back for an important meeting on climate change."

"Please come again when you can," Lucy said warmly. "It's good to know we have friends."

Outside, the kids went to say hello to the ambassador's driver. As we watched, Diaz said, "I commend you, Max, for protecting Lucy from her enemies. Such things are a man's duty to those he loves."

"I don't—Ow!" A sharp pain above my shoe-top shortened my reply. Denice stood beside me, apparently unaware she'd severely injured my left ankle.

"Mr. Dunham is very protective of Lucy," she told Diaz.

I got that I was supposed to go along, though I wasn't sure with what. Smiling, I kept my throbbing ankle to myself. When the ambassador stepped to the car, Denice said out of the side of her mouth, "Life will be easier for Lucy if His Excellency believes he's met her intended and found him an upright and courageous man." She gave me one of those grins that turned her from plain to pretty. "He really was quite determined to have her for his son."

Dinah had come on foot, so I walked her home, meaning to pack my things. The sidewalks were clear, but knowing old bones don't mend easily, I hovered near her elbow in case she hit a slippery spot. When we reached her door, she turned to me. "Max, you're welcome to stay here for as long as you like."

"That's very kind, but I don't want to impose."

"Impose?" She put a gloved hand on my arm. "It was fun having someone to cook for and talk with." She frowned. "I didn't go on too much, did I? Old people do that."

"Not you. And your cooking is awesome."

"Then stay." She made an amused grimace. "You don't have to answer to me or look out for me." A note of longing crept into her voice. "It's nice to have someone in the house besides Fang."

"If I stayed a few more days, maybe we could go to the shooting range together."

"That sounds good, and my calendar is pretty open." She went inside, her step a little lighter. I found myself looking forward to it too.

Of course, I told Mom everything, and within a few hours, she knew more than I did. "Ilsa Dausman will be a witness for the prosecution," she said when she called back.

"If Oscar doesn't have her murdered to keep her quiet."

"He's been denied bail, so arranging a hit would be tough." Mom's voice took on a triumphant tone. "Thanks to Lucy's video, they're looking into the case of the missing witness."

"New evidence?"

"Just before the witness disappeared, a clerk saw him talking to an unknown person in a Chevy Colorado pickup. No one saw the man get into the truck, but the brother..."

"Kevin."

"Kevin has a Colorado. He and Oscar were up north hunting that weekend, but Kevin remembers finding his truck squeaky clean when he woke up the next morning. Oscar said he did it to surprise him, but now that his pattern of establishing false alibis has come to light, the police wonder why Kevin's truck required such a thorough scrubbing."

"Blood?"

"Techs are going over it inch by inch as we speak."

"You've been reading police communications again, Mom."

"Plausible deniability, Max. Anyway, if they find blood in the truck, Oscar can be charged with murder along with everything else." She sounded satisfied as she added, "He'll never get out of prison, which serves him right for trying to hurt my boy."

"Well, I'm glad Peter and Lucy will soon have a new guardian."

"Denice O'Henley. What is she like?"

"At first she seems dull, but when you get to know her, she's nice."

Mom's voice took on an odd tone. "Will you be seeing more of her?"

"Um, I guess so. I'm staying at Dinah's for a while, so I'll be close."

"That's nice, Honey."

"The kids are trying to decide what they want to do. Keep the house or sell it. Leave Detroit or stay."

"Whatever they do, they'll do better without that awful man working against them."

"Yes. Denice will keep them on an even keel."

"And what are you doing now?"

"Planning my delayed vacation." As soon as I said it, I realized I was in trouble. "I, uh, I've always wanted to visit Mexico."

"But you can come to Florida for practically nothing. We've got the spare bedroom. Your dad will have to move his tools out of there, but that won't be a problem. You could meet Derrick and Sandy, I told you about them, and Mark and Linda. You'll love them. And we could take you to this restaurant we like. The portions are huge, and they put your drink in these cute mugs that you bring back next time and get a discount. And the condo management has expanded the driving range since you were here last. You really need to see it."

"That sounds great, Mom, but I already bought my ticket, and it's nonrefundable." One thing my mother can't abide, besides crooks who get away with their crimes, is wasted money.

"Oh. Well, maybe you can take a week around Easter and come down here."

"Maybe."

"I found a desk set made of seashells in green and turquoise. It will go great with your curtains and knick-knacks."

"Mom, about that. I'm thinking of changing things around a little."

"Oh."

And in that "Oh," my friends, was a message every guy who loves his mother understands. "We'll talk about it at Easter, Mom, when I come to visit."

ABOUT THE AUTHOR

Maggie Pill is also Peg Herring, but Maggie's much younger and cooler.
For more great stories visit
http://maggiepill.maggiepillmysteries.com
        OR
http://pegherring.com.

Books available in print, e-book, and audiobook from most major booksellers.

The Sleuth Sisters Series--follow sisters Barb, Faye, and Retta as they start a detective agency, hoping to overcome middle-aged stagnation. Each sister has talents and...eccentricities: Barb sneaks out at night and corrects mistakes on local signs; Faye would try to pet a wolverine (if Michigan had any); and Retta is used to getting her own way because she's just so cute.

Trailer Park Tales – Couples at the Beautiful Bird RV Park enjoy Florida's warmth all winter long, but they can't resist investigating crimes that disturb the peace of the park.

BOOKS BY PEG HERRING

***

The Loser Mysteries *(Contemporary Mystery/Suspense)*
Book #1- *Killing Silence*
Book #2 -*Killing Memories*
Book #3- *Killing Despair*

***

Clan Macbeth Historical Romance (*medieval Scotland*)
Book #1-*Macbeth's Niece*
Book #2- *Double Toil & Trouble*

***

Mercedes Mysteries *(Modern Suspense with Historical Elements)*
Book #1- *Shakespeare's Blood*
Book #2- *Charlie Dickens' Documents*

***

Kidnap Capers (*Thrillers with Cozy Tendencies*)
Book #1- *KIDNAP.org*
Book #2- *Pharma Con*
Book #3- *The Trouble with Dad*

***

Standalone Mysteries
Somebody Doesn't Like Sarah Leigh (*Contemporary Cozy Mystery*)
Her Ex-GI P.I. (*'60s-era mystery*)
Not Dead Yet... (*'60s-era paranormal mystery*)

***

Women's Fiction
Deceiving Elvera-Two women meet on Michigan's Mackinac Island and start a lifelong friendship, but they face danger and betrayal on the borders of Thailand